THE SPELTHO[

Spelthorpe
at War

BOOK TWO
ASHLEY CLARK

Copyright © 2025 Ashley Clark

The moral right of the author has been asserted.

Apart from any fair dealing for the purposes of research or private study,
or criticism or review, as permitted under the Copyright, Designs and Patents
Act 1988, this publication may only be reproduced, stored or transmitted, in
any form or by any means, with the prior permission in writing of the
publishers, or in the case of reprographic reproduction in accordance with
the terms of licences issued by the Copyright Licensing Agency. Enquiries
concerning reproduction outside those terms should be sent to the publishers.

The manufacturer's authorised representative in the EU for product safety is
Authorised Rep Compliance Ltd, 71 Lower Baggot Street, Dublin D02 P593
Ireland (www.arccompliance.com)

This is a work of fiction. Names, characters, businesses, places, events
and incidents are either the products of the author's imagination
or used in a fictitious manner. Any resemblance to actual persons,
living or dead, or actual events is purely coincidental.

Troubador Publishing Ltd
Unit E2 Airfield Business Park,
Harrison Road, Market Harborough,
Leicestershire. LE16 7UL
Tel: 0116 2792299
Email: books@troubador.co.uk
Web: www.troubador.co.uk

ISBN 978-1-83628-407-9

British Library Cataloguing in Publication Data.
A catalogue record for this book is available from the British Library.

Printed and bound in Great Britain by 4edge Limited
Typeset in 11pt Minion Pro by Troubador Publishing Ltd, Leicester, UK

This book is dedicated to the late Lawrence Lyle MBE and Mark Joplin of Simon Langton Grammar School, Canterbury, who inspired a love of history with the need to challenge and question, and to Colonel Alain Chissel with the original comrades at Anglia Tours who afforded me the opportunity to pass that wisdom and enthusiasm onto thousands of school pupils over many years.

Contents

Dramatis personae 1938

Earl Simon Spelthorpe MC (Twelfth Earl of Spelthorpe) b. 1890
Countess Helen Spelthorpe b.1893
Victoria b. 1920; Edward b. 1923; George b. 1924
Black Labrador: Zulu; Siamese cat Simba Jike

Julian Johnson (Estate Manager) b.1881
Julia Johnson b.1888
Joanna b. 1914 (wife of Jeremy de Lisle); Jennifer b. 1916

Ash Cromwell MC (Deputy Estate Manager) b. 1890
Lisette Cromwell b. 1892
Michael and Lucy (Twins) b. 1920
Red Fox Labradors: Trooper, Rafe; Hunter; Kipling; Nimrod and Shackleton.
Collie: Odette (Odi)
Siamese Cats: Duma and Chui

Major Rufus de Lisle (Estate Veterinary Surgeon) b. 1880
Anna de Lisle b. 1885

Jeremy de Lisle (Deputy Veterinary Surgeon) b. 1911
Joanna de Lisle (née Johnson) (Assistant Veterinary Surgeon) b. 1914
James de Lisle b. 1937

Red Fox Labrador: Boudicca

Boynton MM (Estate Head Keeper) b.1890 Agatha Featherstone
b.1893 (Live-in mistress)
Labradors: Black and Tan

Reverend Paddy Collins MC (Vicar of Spelthorpe) b. 1880
Ruth Collins b.1882
Irish wolfhound: Gelert.

Amrik Singh (Butler to the Spelthorpe household) b. 1883
Jasmir Singh (Estate Shop Manager) b. 1884

Dramatis personae 1945

Sir Ash Cromwell MC BEM b.1890
Helen Cromwell Countess of Spelthorpe b.1893 (former wife of
Earl Simon Spelthorpe Twelfth Earl of Spelthorpe)
Victoria b.1920 (wife of Michael Cromwell); Edward Spelthorpe
b.1923; George Spelthorpe b.1924

Michael Cromwell DSO and bar, DFC, BEM b.1920 (son of Ash
and Lisette Cromwell)
Victoria Cromwell b.1920 (née Spelthorpe)
Lisette Cromwell b1940; Simon Cromwell b 1941
Family Labradors: Nimrod, Kipling, Shackleton, Hardy, Zulu,
Mbwa and Siamese Cats: Simba Jike, Duma, Chui.

Dr Johann Muller b.1917
Lucy Muller GM née Cromwell b. 1920 (daughter of Ash and
Lisette Cromwell)
Matilda Muller b.1944

Julian Johnson (Estate Manager) b.1881.
Julia Johnson b.1888
Joanna de Lisle b.1914 (married to Jeremy de Lisle) Dr Jennifer
Roy b.1916 married to William Roy b. 1915 (Chief Estate
Engineer)
Jack b. 1942 Labrador: Nellie.

Major Rufus de Lisle (Estate Veterinary Surgeon) b. 1880.
Anna de Lisle b. 1885
Jeremy de Lisle (Deputy Veterinary Surgeon) b. 1911 married to
Joanna (née Johnson)
(Assistant Veterinary Surgeon)
James b.1937; Juliet b.1942. Labradors: Boudicca, Foxie

Gabriel Boynton MM, BEM (Estate Head Keeper) b.1890
Agatha (Aggie) Boynton (Headmistress of Spelthorpe School)
b.1893
Harry b.1934 (adopted). Beverley b.1932 (adopted)
Labradors: Black; Tan and Hund.

Reverend Paddy Collins MC (Vicar of Spelthorpe) b.1880. Ruth
Collins b.1882
Irish wolfhound: Methuselah

Amrik Singh (Butler to the Spelthorpe household) b. 1883
Jasmir Singh (Estate shop manager) b. 1884

Richard Chandler DSO DFC b.1918 (Flying School Manager)
Linda Chandler b.1918 (Teacher at Spelthorpe School)

Robert Roy b.1892 (Head Estate Shepherd)
Elsie Roy b.1894
William Roy b.1915 (Head Estate Engineer, married to Dr
Jennifer Roy (née Johnson)
Emma Roy b.1924
Emily Roy b.1931 (adopted)

Introduction

This book is the sequel to '*The Tale of the Merdogs*'. Having introduced the Spelthorpe Estate and the key characters in the first book, we now move on to see how they endured the tragedies, challenges and triumphs of the Second World War. In the first book we saw how the Great War had melded the community together. The 1930's were a time of rapid technological change. This had a profound effect on agriculture. It also brought about the start of diversification in farming to ensure its survival and profitability. Those who owned the land could have a profound effect on the quality of lives of the people who worked for them, and those who did that in a benevolent way held their communities together. Where it worked, it worked well, but this benevolence was not universal, particularly in urban areas and as the war ended, we started to see the state taking a more proactive role in providing a universal safety net.

Whilst this book, like its predecessor, remains a work of fiction many of the varied events and themes are fact-based and it is hoped that the book will act as a stimulus for readers to delve deeper into the matters covered. Whilst the first book was essentially history with mystery in respect of the adventures of the dog characters, readers will find that in this book there is a far greater emphasis on the human characters and some key wartime events in which they were involved. Some of the conversations in the book would have taken place in the French and German languages but for ease of reading it is all in English.

Above all I seek to make this roller coaster ride through a fascinating period as enjoyable as possible for the reader. As Kipling said, "*If history were told in the form of stories, it would never be forgotten.*"

Ashley Clark
Whitstable 2025.

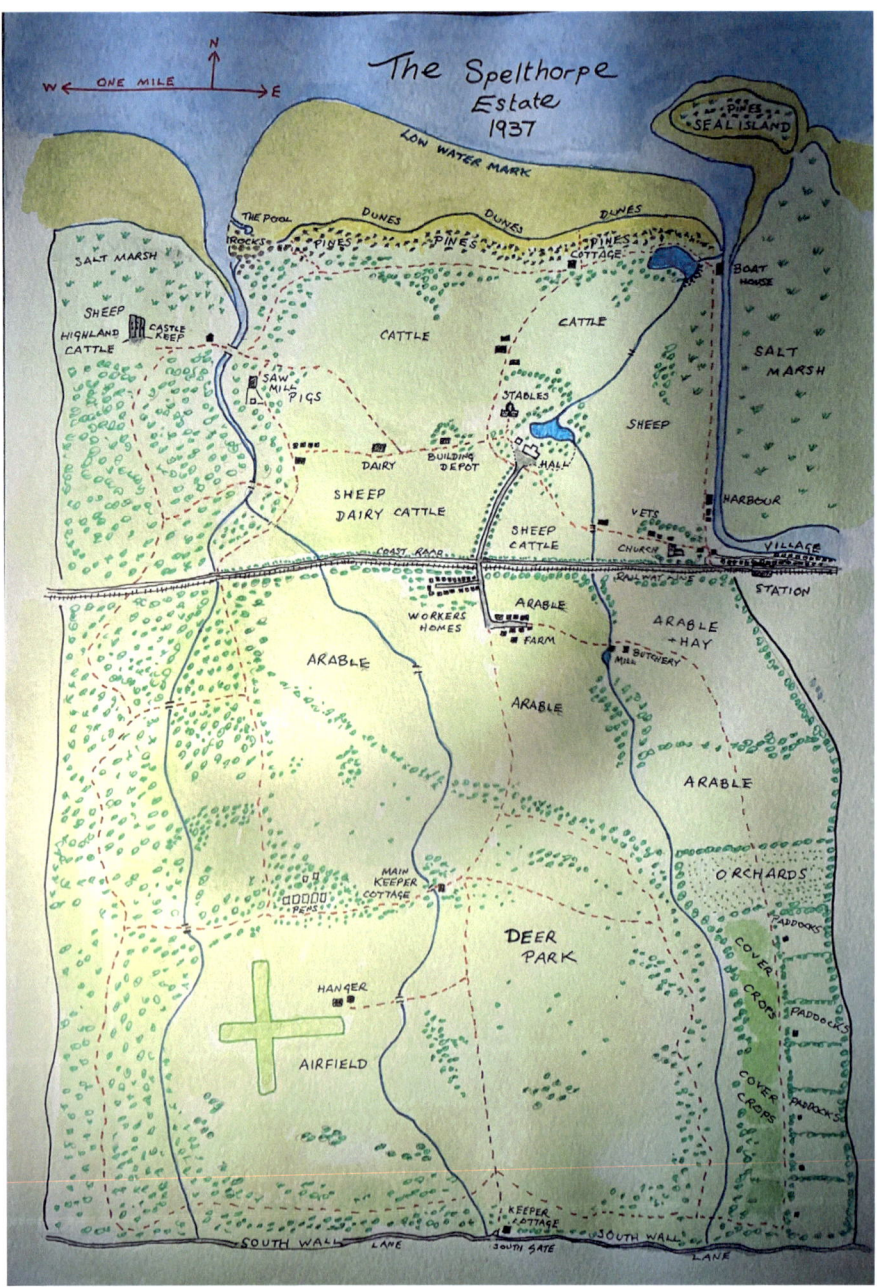

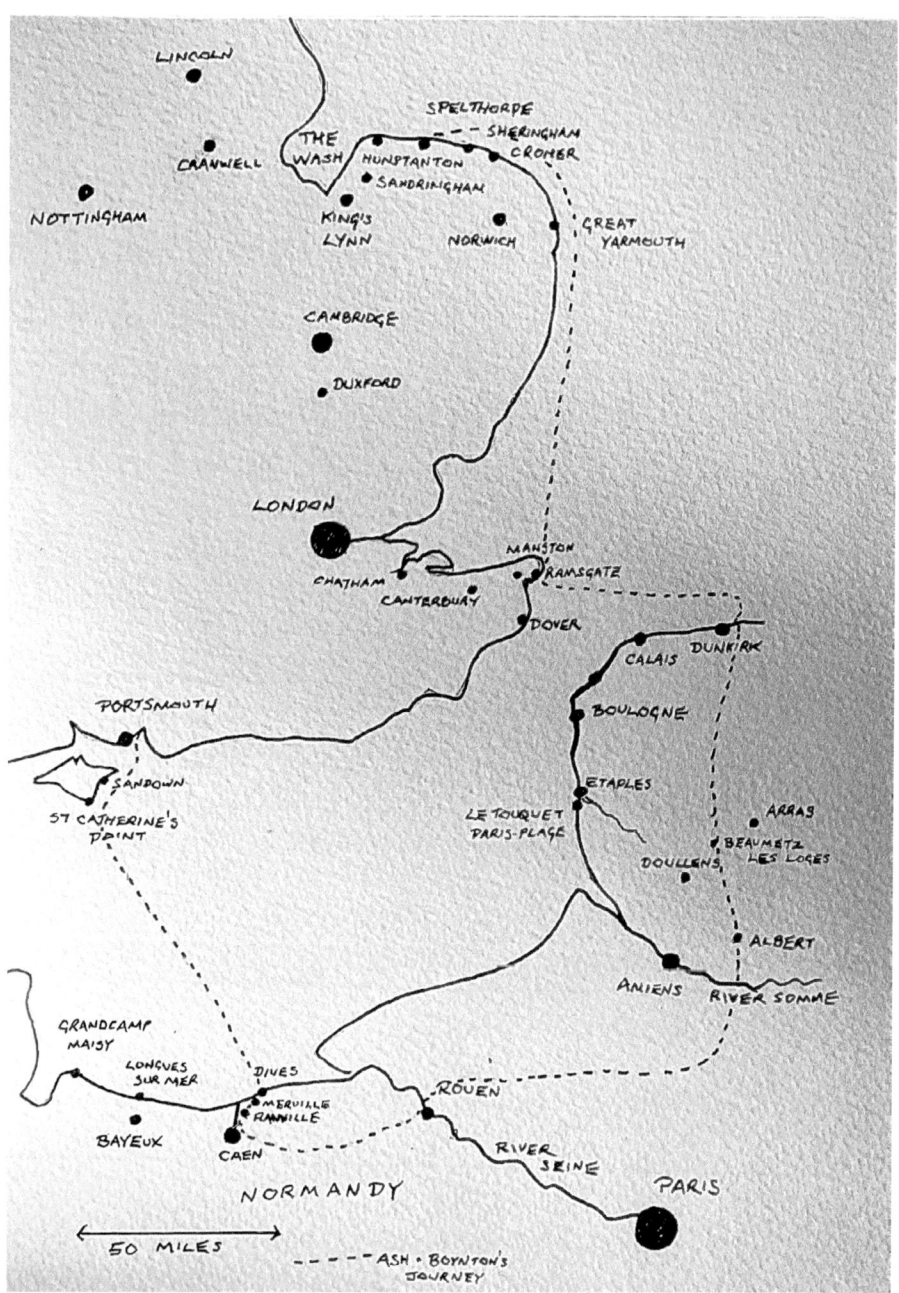

LINCOLN

SPELTHORPE

CRANWELL · THE WASH · SHERINGHAM
HUNSTANTON · CROMER
SANDRINGHAM

NOTTINGHAM

KING'S LYNN · NORWICH · GREAT YARMOUTH

CAMBRIDGE

DUXFORD

LONDON · MANSTON
· RAMSGATE
CHATHAM · CANTERBURY
DOVER · DUNKIRK
CALAIS
BOULOGNE

PORTSMOUTH

SANDOWN · ETAPLES · ARRAS
ST CATHERINE'S POINT · LE TOUQUET PARIS-PLAGE · BEAUMETZ LES LOGES
DOULLENS

ALBERT
AMIENS · RIVER SOMME

GRANDCAMP MAISY
LONGUES SUR MER · DIVES
MERVILLE · ROUEN
BAYEUX · RANVILLE
CAEN · RIVER SEINE · PARIS

NORMANDY

50 MILES

- - - - ASH · BOYNTON'S JOURNEY

xvii

"We sleep safely at night because rough men stand ready to visit violence on those who would harm us"
– a construct variously attributed to Churchill, Orwell, Kipling and others.

1

The new arrival

December 1937

Christmas 1937 had passed on the Spelthorpe Estate with the usual family gatherings that followed the Christmas Day service at the medieval church of St Michael and all the Angels that graced the eastern edge of the estate opposite the veterinary practice. This was quite a new venture. It was owned by the estate but managed by Major Rufus de Lisle formerly of the Royal Army Veterinary Corps. His wife, Anna, a trained nurse dealt with the paperwork. Their son Jeremy was the second veterinary surgeon along with his wife of four years Joanna also a qualified vet' who dealt principally with the smaller animal side of the practice. The business served the estate and the neighbouring farms and villages. Joanna was the elder daughter of Julian Johnson and his wife Julia. Julian had been the estate manager since the end of the Great War. Jeremy and Joanna had met back in 1932 shortly before the practice became established and the pair were married after what could only be described as a lightning romance.

At first light on Boxing Day Joanna rose and insisted that her husband visit the stables with her. Joanna had two other passions besides her husband and her work. One was the violin, which she excelled at, having formerly played for the king at Sandringham, and the other was the estate's horses, two of which had attended her wedding at the church directly opposite their cottage. Joanna had a special friendship with Princess Elizabeth who shared the same passion for horses. It was only a short walk to the stables. They were at the back of the Hall occupied by Earl Simon Spelthorpe and his wife Countess Helen, and near the annexe where her parents resided. It might have been a short walk, but it was a bit of a struggle for Joanna, who was expecting her first child at any moment. Joanna was as stubborn as a mule, and nothing was going to stop her doing what she wanted to do, although she did obey her husband in accordance with the vows taken at the wedding service conducted by the Reverend Paddy Collins, the local vicar.

When they got to the stables, they discovered that Ash Cromwell the estate's deputy manager was already there. Ash looked after the forest and coastal section of the estate along with the deer park. That comprised just over half of the total area of some 9,000 acres. Ash explained his presence.

"Hello, you two! I've just come down to check the horses and to let them out into the paddock. I gave the grooms the morning off as they both have young families. I don't suppose we will see you both later for the polar bear dip for obvious reasons, but you are both most welcome at the cottage. Of course, I wouldn't expect Jeremy to chicken out, but I suggest you come in the car. I wouldn't recommend riding unless you want to bump-start the delivery."

Jeremy responded. "We will both be there. We haven't missed it for the last five years and I expect another bar to be added to my polar bear badge."

The annual dip in the sea had been the tradition on Boxing Day for the three families who ran the estate. The Spelthorpes, the Johnsons (including the de Lisles) and the Cromwells were all very close. They had collectively forged themselves over the years into one mega family. This closeness had come about because the patriarchs of each family had fought and served together as brothers in arms and were united by a bond that only soldiers can deeply understand. Rufus de Lisle had also served but as a specialist and not in the same military company as the other three.

Joanna walked up and down the line. She stroked and talked to each horse in turn. They responded to her affection. Suddenly she stopped and clung to a stable door. Then she cried out.

"My waters have just broke. I've got to get back."

Ash and Jeremy supported her on both sides. Jeremy said "Don't worry darling. We've got lots of clean straw here. You'll be OK!"

Joanna didn't quite see the joke, "I know it's Christmas, and Jesus was born in a stable but I'm not going to repeat that here. Next, you'll be getting all the village kids out to watch the nativity play. As I told you before, if it's a boy it's James, not Jesus!"

The three walked slowly and went to the annexe. It was the closest building and Joanna's mother, and sister would be there. On arrival they took Joanna up to the large guest room that she and Jeremy had shared following their engagement. Jeremy said, "I'd like to stay with you. I know the tradition is that we all wait downstairs, but I want to be there."

Joanna was clearly experiencing pain.

"You are staying," she said. "I bloody well insist on it! It's you that got me like this, and no midwife or anyone else is going to chuck you out. And as well as that – I want you here because I love you!"

So, Jeremy remained along with her sister, Jennifer who

was two-thirds of her way through her medical degree and had undertaken her obstetrics training. Jennifer set about some checks.

Within forty minutes the midwife had arrived. Earl Simon had brought his Rolls around in case there was a need for a hospital dash. Downstairs Lisette (Ash's wife) had turned up along with Countess Helen, Rufus de Lisle and Anna. On hearing who was there Joanna felt confident as she was attended by two vets, a medical student, a nurse, a midwife, a volunteer ambulance driver in the form of Earl Simon, and Ash who had delivered most of the estate's lambs over the years. So, they waited. It was 9-am, and downstairs the coffee and cognac were circulating along with bacon sandwiches. An hour later a cry was heard. Master James de Lisle had become the latest addition to the Spelthorpe community. The kitchen scales were taken upstairs and recorded the figure of seven pounds and twelve ounces. All was well with both mother and baby. Jeremy beamed with delight, having been present all along. The unique and special bond between son and father who was there at the very outset, had been established.

Boxing Day in 1937 fell on a Sunday, and attendance at the church was expected for the greater family. Simon suggested that he go with the new granddad (Julian), Ash and Rufus and that the ladies and Jeremy stay at the annexe to deal with any family issues relating to the younger members and, of course the ever-faithful dogs who would be expecting a bit of breakfast. Lisette undertook to release the horses into the paddock on her way back to their cottage set in the pines and dunes near the sea. All agreed that the afternoon dip scheduled for high tide at 3-pm would go ahead, but Julia and Jennifer would stay with Joanna and the new arrival.

And so, at just before 11am the four patriarchs, along with Simon's black Labrador, Zulu turned up at church, not in their Sunday best, but Reverend Paddy would be the last one to worry about things like that. As he would often quote from the good book 'The life is more than meat, and the body is more than raiment.'

No one, not even the Archbishop of Canterbury, could beat Paddy when it came to his knowledge of the good book, and he had a text for every occasion. That was what made Paddy special. He was no political priest. He was a true priest and the whole community, even the atheists, loved him for the love that he exuded.

When they walked up the path to the church Paddy beamed.

"Boy or girl?" he asked, not that it would be difficult given that Joanna lived opposite, and the signs were more than obvious. Paddy was perceptive, and the delight in the faces that approached him gave the game away.

"It's a boy and the boy and Mum are doing well. His name is James," said Julian.

With that Paddy said, "Praise the Lord and thank you Lord!"

He hugged each one in turn including Zulu. Paddy was well known for his affection to all God's creatures, and they too were all welcome to attend his services.

"And what was the weight of Master James?" asked Paddy.

"Seven pounds twelve ounces," was the response.

"That's good." said Paddy. "When Jesus was born, they knew the weight straight away."

"How come?" asked Ash.

"They had 'A weigh in a manger,'" said Paddy as he grinned, and with that, he led them in and changed the first hymn to 'Away in a Manger'.

The service as expected for Boxing Day, was attended by less than normal, but Paddy's announcement and obvious joy at the birth were reflected in the smiles and congratulations that flowed from the congregation. There was little doubt that within the hour, all Spelthorpe would get the good news.

They assembled on the beach at 3pm and that included all the dogs. Reverend Paddy and his wife, Ruth, had been invited.

"No cheating Paddy," said Simon. "You are not allowed to walk on the water."

As with previous years, Ash's Webley revolver sounded and there was a headlong charge into the waves. Nobody stayed in for more than a couple of minutes apart from the merdogs (Ash's Labradors). Their thick fur provided good insulation. Only Trooper and Rafe came out before the others. They shook themselves and waited on the edge. Ash had noticed that they had been slowing down considerably over the shooting season. They were both keen and wagged their tails at the thought of going picking up. Rafe still chose the best place to watch and wait because he had the ability to sense the wind and scent with the noises from the pheasants. He was invariably right, but when it came to running and collecting the birds, it was Nimrod who moved at three times their speed. He was a strong dog and effectively was now leading the pack. The other dogs respected that. When Michael and Lucy came out on the shoots with Shackleton and his sister Boudicca (Joanna's dog) who were nearly a year old, Nimrod spent time showing them what to do, and they learnt by watching him perform. Trooper and Rafe were sixteen and fifteen respectively, and that was quite old for Labradors, so Ash was content to let them go at their own pace and, as long as their quality of life was maintained, things would carry on. Joanna had given them extra attention over the last few months and had applied medication to keep them going.

As the party retreated up the beach and started to walk back to the cottage Paddy noticed that all the dogs including his wolfhound Gelert and Simon's Labrador Zulu were in a semi-circle facing out to sea. It was as if they were getting a briefing.

Paddy said to Lisette "What's going on there? Gelert normally sticks with me!"

"Don't worry about that Paddy! It's Minerva the mermaid. The dogs will come back when she has finished. I'll explain it all back at the cottage."

The dogs all trotted back but left Trooper and Rafe listening to Minerva.

"I expect you two might have guessed what I wanted to tell you. We have been together now for the last six years, and you were already ten years old when we first met. I've noticed that you have slowed down a lot and your time will come but do not worry. When that time comes you will go somewhere that you will love, and you will be able to wait there knowing that at some stage the others will join you. I know you have been teamed up together, but I wanted to know if when the time comes, you will move on alone or together."

Rafe said "Together would be my choice. It will be better for those we leave so they know we will be together!"

"I agree with that," said Trooper. "It was good of you to bring that up because we both know that all good things must end. Nothing on earth lasts forever. We were thinking about that. Could we tell the others?"

"That will put them at ease when the time comes, but do not worry, I will deal with it for you." said Minerva.

Minerva turned and swam off as the two old comrades walked back to the cottage.

Back at the cottage after everyone was dry and changed, there was Lisette's warming French onion soup with cheese and croutons followed by the famous Spelthorpe sausages and other goodies. They raised their glasses and toasted Joanna and the new arrival. Ruth presented Jeremy with a teddy bear that she had made. It was a work of art that must have taken her a long time with fine stitching, glass eyes and artificial fur.

Lisette beckoned Paddy over and enlightened him with the story of the merdogs, how she, Ash and Helen had met them many years previously. She and Ash had met Hunter and Odi on the beach at Étaples in France in the war when both were working there at the military hospitals. Helen had met the mermaid and dogs on the Kenya coast as a child. It would seem that the dogs were able to go back in time with the help of mermaid who was only visible to young children and animals. Lisette mentioned the meeting on the beach with Princess Elizabeth who had told her the mermaid's name. There were anatomical changes on the front paws. She mentioned their underwater prowess and the miraculous fishing trip where the dogs had directed Ash to the place teeming with fish. Paddy was deeply interested and what made things more credible was the fact that the events had occurred at different time and places and with different people.

Paddy concluded. "You can rest assured that your secret is safe with me. The church hierarchy already thinks that I'm a heretic and if I were to repeat the story, they would cite that as evidence to confirm their viewpoint. It never ceases to surprise me that for an organisation that boasts of faith, so many of the leaders are disciples of Doubting Thomas. '*Oh, ye of little faith*!' says the good book and when I look up to the stars at night I marvel at the creation and all those things that we will never fully understand. You know that I stick with simple faith. I weep inside when I think of all those over the ages who have died because of religious dogma. It's a way bad men try to control others, and I won't have it here!"

Lisette gave him a hug and said, "I knew you would understand. Thank you, Paddy."

Given the circumstances Julian and the de Lisles retired after an hour but not before Lisette handed out their 1937 bars to their polar bear badges. Paddy and his wife Ruth gained their badge for the first time. Simon and Helen stayed on with the boys and Victoria. As ever, Victoria and Michael remained close but, on this occasion, displayed their obvious affection in a more open manner. Michael had turned eighteen in November and Victoria's birthday was only two weeks away.

In just over six months they would be leaving school. Career or further education choices had to be made. For Michael the choice had been made already. Since his first solo flight at mid-summer, he had gained his pilot's licence, and at weekends was now going up on a regular basis. He had taken Ash and Simon on flights initially along the coastline to Cromer and in November he flew up to Lincoln for views of the splendid cathedral on the hill. On one occasion he took Victoria up and along to Great Yarmouth and then back over the Broads and Norwich. Also, in November he had spent five days at the RAF Officer and Aircrew Selection Centre and had been accepted for officer and pilot training from September.

Ash asked Victoria. "Have you decided what you would like to do when you leave school?"

Victoria simply said. "We haven't decided yet, but we have some ideas."

Helen looked a little shocked at the mention of 'We' because although she had always been happy with Victoria and Michael's school friend relationship, this was the first time she was aware that it was more than just that. Lisette was more perceptive and thought that an in-depth probe into their relationship at this juncture would be inappropriate.

She said, "Well, there's a few months yet and I'm sure you will work out what is best but for now, I think it is time for mince pies and the warmed mulled wine will be ready."

Paddy looked knowingly at Lisette. He missed nothing. With that, the party continued.

Simon, Ash and Paddy walked outside and partook in a Christmas cigar. None of them smoked by habit, but they would take the occasional cigar at social events. It was very much a convention, a vestige of the days of Edward VII when gentlemen were expected to retire for brandy and cigars and the ladies engaged in talk those full-blooded males found incomprehensible.

Simon asked, "Are you a little worried about Michael's career choice with war imminent? They are all talking that way in London at the moment. I've heard that they are now making gas masks for the whole population. That Bohemian corporal has brainwashed the entire German population and some of ours as well including our former playboy prince and his American wife. This country won't take it. I know that the 'Bright Young People' like the Mitford girls, have all gone along with it. They might have money, and they think they have influence but all they want to do is get drunk and take horizontal refreshment with each other's husbands and wives. The British people just won't stand for that, as they proved with Moseley's black shirts in that Cable Street battle a year back. I know in this country the government seems to bumble along from one crisis to the next but at least we have a system where the ordinary people do have a say and the opportunity to kick out a poorly performing government even if it is replaced by another."

"You have a short memory Simon," said Ash. "Just remember what we were up to back in 1912 when your father set up the

Spelthorpe Company and we all volunteered en masse to the king's colours. Most of us got through it, and I can understand, and I can't see all this white feather nonsense like the last time happening again, but deep down, boys will be boys and girls will be mothers, and real boys will always fight to defend this country. I know we get it wrong most of the time with our party-political bumblers but it's still the best country in the world and I have a plan for Michael".

"Yes, I can see that, and you are right on that score but what is your plan?" asked Simon.

"Our flying instructor Squadron Leader Peregrine Smith, or 'Stooper' as they used to call him," said Ash.

"Why 'Stooper?'" asked Paddy.

"He lived up to his Christian name," said Ash. "The peregrine is the fastest bird on the planet. I'm sure you must have seen them at the castle keep. Their dive is called a stoop and when they stoop, that's a certain end for a wood pigeon. Peregrine had twenty-five kills in the war, and you don't get a score like that without a sixth sense of survival and flying tactics. There were so many young pilots in the last that ended up as Fokker fodder because they didn't have the experience and the cunning. They would teach them to take off, and land and fly in formation but hardly anything else. So, they went like lambs to the slaughter and half were killed in training. Michael is a good pilot, but Peregrine will improve on that, and he will teach him the things you do not see in a textbook. I know planes are more powerful, but the principles are the same, so I've arranged for Peregrine to give him the edge. I'm also going to ask Boynton to tip him off about survival on the ground. There's no better tutor than Boynton. I could teach Michael, but he respects Boynton, and it will be better coming from him."

Shortly afterwards they returned to the ladies. At 10 pm, the guests took their leave and walked home.

2

Choices and matches

December 1937 – January 1938

The holiday continued onwards towards the new year, although, as with any farm there was never a day off because the stock had to be cared for and in good weather, opportunities to get things done had to be taken. There was one shoot day on Wednesday twenty-ninth of December. This was a commercial day with guns coming via the agency. There were eight guns. Ash discreetly checked them out as to their shooting ability. All appeared sound. Julian ran the day. Ash ran the pickers-up and Boynton the head keeper managed the beating side having selected the drives in consultation with Julian.

As it was in the school holiday, it was an opportunity for the children of the estate to provide most of the beaters and to get a bit of pocket money. They were joined by Simon's sons Edward and George who were fourteen and thirteen. Neither had shown any great interest in country sports or farm activities unlike their elder sister Victoria. Edward was a brilliant mathematician who showed talent well in advance of his years. George seemed a little lost in the shadow of his elder brother and sister. Ash was of the view that, given interest and time, things might develop, so he was lined up for some of the shoots and to get involved in the lambing in the months that lay ahead. Joanna and Jeremy had undertaken to give him some riding coaching.

Although Ash was nominally in charge, it was Nimrod who had learnt from Trooper and Rafe, who was effectively running the pickers-up. He was assisted by Hunter, Kipling and Odi (Odette) the border collie who were with Lucy and Ash. Victoria managed Zulu, her father's black Labrador. Michael was looking after Shackleton and Boudicca who were ten months old and were there to get a gentle introduction. Two of the regular team from the village were also present. As Lisette and Helen were engaged on the hospitality side, Trooper and Rafe – in semi-retirement, were on guard duty at the cottage. The day went well, and the numbers shot matched what the guns had paid for. They left fully satisfied and intimated they would be back. This was a valuable source of income that supported the shooting side of the farm business.

On the following day Michael and Victoria went out pigeon shooting on the edge of the woodland. They took the truck and went to an area on the edge of the wood in a clearing where Boynton had spotted pigeons feeding on the acorns. They put out a dozen decoys made from thin pressed sheets of aluminium that had been painted to look like pigeons. Michael had made another in wood with levers and springs that would flap like a live pigeon when a string attached was pulled. As the volume of shots would be much lower, they took Trooper and Rafe as a consolation for the previous day. Their joy at the opportunity was palpable.

Michael and Victoria were both good shots and had

mastered the requirement for a mental calculation as to the amount of 'lead' required. A fast pigeon would need more 'lead' than a slow one and the distance was important too. Just firing directly at a pigeon unless it was coming straight at you or going away would mean a miss because in the split second it took for the shot to travel, the bird would be outside of the shot pattern. The general technique was to remain absolutely motionless until the bird was in range and then to aim with both eyes open going with the bird and overtaking it before firing. The distance of the overtake was the critical factor and this was only learnt by experience and practice. They had made two hides from some fishing nets with brown and green patches like leaves and they had cut some of the low-lying branches and scrub. They wore old Barbour coats covered with lots of mud and had darkened their faces with charcoal. They put a bit of spit and tissue in each ear to mitigate the worst of the bangs. The pigeon was a difficult bird to bring down, because with acute eyesight it would veer, twist and turn at the slightest threat. It was a tough bird and to be sure of a clean kill, it was best shot at under thirty-five yards.

They put the hides sixty yards apart but facing the same way so any birds that veered might be shot by the other. Trooper went with Victoria and Rafe with Michael. For the first hour, however, they sat together in the same hide looking out over the clearing. The winter sun was low, producing long shadows. Most of the trees had lost their leaves but the stubborn oaks held onto theirs. They were mid-brown. Then suddenly the leaves started dropping like a mass of confetti. They had both witnessed this before. It was as if the trees were talking to one another. In the golden winter light, it was a scene of total beauty and serenity which they both appreciated.

"I'd love to be able to talk to these trees," said Victoria.

"Some are over 400 years old, some older still. They must have seen so much. I love this place, and we are part of it. I wonder if they are talking about us. I'm sure Paddy would agree with that. He always says there is so much we don't know, and we should just accept that. We don't know how old these trees are but that doesn't matter until some bright spark comes along and cuts it down to count the rings so they can say that the tree is 464 years old. There's nothing clever in that. They might have the knowledge, but they killed the tree to get it."

Suddenly the pigeons started coming. Victoria got one but missed the other. Michael got that and another. After ten birds they split up and used the dead birds as decoys propped up with twigs. By 4pm it was getting dark, but they had managed sixty-five birds between them with several left and rights. That was the idea with two barrels, to take two birds rather than two shots at the same bird. It was a lot easier with slow flying pheasants in a straight line, but not with fast pigeons.

They packed up but before returning they had a kiss and cuddle together.

Michael said, "This charcoal make-up seems to make you even more passionate."

"And you too," said Victoria. "I feel like I am in the back woods as a squaw having found my Red Indian brave who loves me. I've been thinking. After school I'll do that one-year agricultural diploma at Nottingham. That will set me up to help run this place and it's not far from Cranwell where you will be doing your officer training. That should work out well for us. I'm going to have to tell my mother sooner or later but leave that to me. She seems to want to play the countess sometimes, but I wish she would be herself. It's not as if she were born into the aristocracy. Your mother knows how we feel. I'm sure of it so we won't have any problems there, but I'd rather knock any silly notions from my mother now rather than later. I'd rather you not be there for that part, but I'll let you know straight away."

Michael responded. "It's worried me a bit. I don't think I will upset your father. He's down to earth really and he's been good to me. I will ask him, although once you have tackled your mother it will have to happen. We've been together for almost six years and properly together for the last two. I think they were content to keep their heads in the sand. That was good for us, but reality must be faced. We love each other deeply and we love doing the same things together and that counts for a lot." Then he kissed her again passionately. They got in the truck with the dogs in the back and drove down to the Hall.

Michael dropped Victoria off at the Hall. She took her shotgun and ten pigeons for her mother's cat Simba Jike and Zulu.

When Victoria entered the Hall, she went to the downstairs gun room where she cleaned the gun and deposited it back in the rack. As she came up the stairs she encountered her mother in the central lobby. Helen gasped in horror thinking it was a burglar with the camouflage and charcoal face.

"Victoria, I'm glad you are back I wanted to talk with you," said her mother.

"Can I clean up first. I've got ten pigeons for Zulu and the cat, but I've got to take the breasts off," said Victoria.

"Leave that. I'll get Amrik to sort that out. I'll see you in the library in half an hour," responded Helen.

After a shower and a clothing change Victoria met her mother in the library. She had an inkling of what it was about.

"I wanted to talk to you about your coming out and attendance at Queen Charlotte's ball that is scheduled for the summer in London," said her mother.

"I'm not doing that!" said Victoria.

"But you must. Remember who you are. You are Lady

Victoria Spelthorpe, the daughter of the Earl of Spelthorpe. It's expected. That's what we do".

"Who is 'We'"? asked Victoria. "Did you go? No, of course not, because you were not an aristocrat. You were the daughter of a coffee and tea plantation owner and from what you told me you married Daddy to get away from all that society stuff. It's not a ball. It's a cattle market where we parade up and down like prize cows, just for some aristocratic stud to turn up who we marry. Then they service us to make an heir, after which they toddle off and get drunk and go to bed with every woman they encounter. I know that for a fact. I've spoken with some of the other girls at school and they told me how miserable they were because their parents were always at it. That's the only reason they sent them to the school in the first place. It's in all the scandal papers about the Mitfords and all the others and I don't want to be like that and if you want to do that to me, then you are not fit to be my mother. I thought you loved me."

Helen was shocked by this outburst and even more so because it was true.

"We both love you and we want to give you the best, and we didn't think you would want to miss out on what is seen as such a prestigious event."

Victoria responded, "Well, you have my answer. I'm not going. Hell would freeze over before I went to anything like that. I suppose I had better come out with it. I love Michael, and Michael loves me and yes, we are intimate and have been for some time. I'm not some vestal virgin off to a lifetime of imprisonment in something I would hate. We will marry and if we have to wait, we will wait until we are twenty-one but if you refuse, we will be off to Gretna Green. You can't stop us. We'd like to do it with your agreement. You are my mother and Michael's godmother and we both love you and we want it to stay that way."

"What do you mean by intimate?" asked Helen.

"I would have thought it was obvious from what I said, but if you need it spelt out, it's called sexual intercourse and before you ask, it was always lawful, and we have been taking precautions. After I leave school in the summer I will take the agricultural diploma at Sutton Bonington Agricultural College. That's near Nottingham, and that's a stone's throw from Cranwell where Michael will be training. We have worked it out and it makes sense. Edward and George have shown no real interest in this place, but I love everything about it, and I want it to work. I'll get a year's theory and the rest I can learn on the job here and this is where I am staying because the alternative is RAF married quarters after Gretna Green, but if it comes to that, so be it, because I love him, and nothing will stand in our way!"

Helen was speechless as it rapidly dawned on her that Victoria was no longer a little girl but a grown woman. She had cast aside fripperies in favour of what was really important. What she had planned with Michael was good sense and good sense for the future of Spelthorpe. It was clear that she was totally loyal to the estate. In that she was showing loyalty to her parents. That was important. However, Helen needed to save face because Victoria's forthright approach had shocked her.

"I'll have to discuss this with your father. He should be back from London later this evening. We will talk about it tomorrow," said Helen.

"Alright Mummy," said Victoria. "I'll take Zulu out for a walk. He hasn't been out all day. Don't worry about food. I'll see Cook later or help myself."

Zulu was in the Hall. Victoria said the word 'walk', and he reacted with instant pleasure.

As she walked out, Helen asked, "Where are you going?"

"That should be obvious," said Victoria. She needed to get out and fast.

Fifteen minutes later she was at the cottage. She saw a light in the barn and walked in. Michael was inside with Nimrod looking on as he finished the last of the pigeons. He was surprised to see her.

"What's up?" he asked.

"It's in the open now," said Victoria." I told my mother. She tried to push on me some notion of going to a debutante ball. It's a high society cattle market for young ladies searching for a husband. So, I gave her the lot with both barrels, and I told her that she can take it or leave it but if they say no, we will be on the first train to Gretna Green in Scotland where you can marry at sixteen without parents' permission. I think I might have been a bit strong, but I felt it was the only way of yanking her head out of the sand. She knows about my plans for agricultural college too."

"Well, it's certainly a bit quicker than I thought and I know that there are a few on the estate who might know. I didn't tell you at the time that Boynton got me those first French letters (*condoms*) and told me where to get more because he said he cared about you, and he didn't want me putting you in the Spelthorpe Pudding Club so he must have noticed our visits to the castle keep. I know my dad is quite close to Boynton. He's a good chap, a bit rough on occasions. He's got something going with your housemistress. He sees himself as our guardian angel and he doesn't miss a trick. But as it's out, we had better let my parents know. I think we'll get an easy ride from them. I don't think they will be too surprised, but we shall see."

Michael gathered the pigeon breasts on a tray and tossed one filet each to Nimrod, Zulu and to the two cats who had been rubbing up against him for the last half hour. All the debris went in a corn sack for incineration.

They went in together.

"Surprise, surprise I hear you had a good day," said Lisette. "What brings you and Zulu down here in the dark?"

"It's something you might have suspected," said Michael, "but it's in the open now at least as far as Victoria's mother is concerned."

Ash got up from his armchair, and they sat around the kitchen table. Michael and Victoria then outlined their plans and started by saying that they had been intent on keeping things low key, but Helen's plans for this debutante ball had bought matters to a head. They explained how deeply they felt, and this was no flash-in-the-pan romance. They hinted at their intimacy avoiding any graphic detail.

It was obvious from the outset that Ash and Lisette were on the same wavelength by the way they smiled in a bemused manner. This gave Lisette the signal to speak out.

"Without going on I can say you have our blessing. I've detected for some time how close you have been, from years back and how happy you are when you are together."

Ash said, "Yes, I was aware of your visits to the castle keep and it's a credit to you that you were very discreet, but this place is all eyes, and you can only keep a secret for so long. What impresses me most of all is that you have not just thought about each other but about this place too. That will impress Simon because at the end of the day, he has to keep the estate going. It's not just about the land but the community that goes with it and that has come down through the generations. Victoria, you are our goddaughter. We welcome you as a future daughter. Your happiness has brought about our happiness and both of you remember this. We will always be here for you. There is a clear precedent for this at Spelthorpe. You must remember how Joanna and Jeremy got together after just four days. She was the same age as you, but they kept things quiet as far as the school went, and I'm sure you will do the same. It's only six months."

Ash reminded Victoria that it was getting late. Michael said that he would take her back in the truck. In the morning Ash and Lisette would go and see Simon and Helen. They both hugged Victoria. She left with Michael who dropped her off at the Hall. Victoria went straight to bed. She was tired out from the shooting and the nervous energy she had used up over the confrontation.

On the following morning the phone at the Hall rang. Ten minutes later Ash turned up with Lisette and Michael. Victoria went downstairs and met them in the lobby.

Ash said, "We parents have some talking to do. I think the best thing the pair of you can do is to take Zulu out for an hour. We will all see you when you come back."

Michael and Victoria took a walk to the church and the harbour. On the way down they called on Joanna who was now at home with the baby. After inspecting the new arrival, they told her what had transpired. Joanna said, "I wouldn't worry. Most of us know how close you are. Remember what happened to Jeremy and me five years back. The two important things for them are avoiding scandal and keeping the greater family together and they won't risk jeopardising that. Your plan is a good one and they have to go along with it."

They walked around the churchyard and then on to the port and got back to the Hall where the parents were waiting. They all went into the library.

Simon kicked the conversation off. "I'm not going to beat about the bush, and personally I am not surprised. It's been obvious to me that the pair of you are very close and were trying to keep things low key until you had left school. It was only this debutante nonsense that brought things to a head. Essentially, we are country people tied to the land and the local folk. Your loyalty to Spelthorpe is impressive. When I go to London to the Lords, as I sometimes have to do, I see what is going on and the last thing I want for you Victoria, is to expose you to Sodom on Thames and all that goes with it. We know you are passionate and determined but we don't want you dashing off to Gretna. We know we couldn't stop you unless we imprisoned you in the castle keep dungeon, but the castle keep is used for other things as you well know! If only those walls could talk!"

Victoria blushed.

Simon continued. "We know you have feelings, and you have been sensible in that area, but the castle keep is not appropriate for that, so this is the plan upon which the four of us are agreed. You will both have a room at the cottage where you can be together. You spend most of your free time down there anyway. That would not be appropriate in the Hall because, although we trust Amrik and Jasmir the same cannot be said of the younger members who like to talk. We expect you, Victoria, to stay here overnight on some occasions and we trust you to be sensible in that area. There will be no announcement of your engagement until the day you leave school so any ring can wait or not be worn openly. Victoria, we like your plan to do a year at agricultural college to deal with the theory, but any more would be a waste with all the experience here, but at least you will have a qualification that sets you on a professional footing. As far as we are concerned your engagement starts today. Lucy will be told but as far as the boys are concerned it will simply be the case that Victoria will be staying at the cottage from time to time with Lisette and Lucy to improve her French. We love you both and you have our full support. Congratulations."

"Thank you, Daddy, thank you so much," said Victoria.

"I was going to ask you, sir, at the end of school," said Michael, "but we were overtaken by events. Thank you for your understanding."

"You can leave out the 'sir' from now on. My name is Simon, and your future mother-in-law is Helen. She would like a hug from you. Can we expect a wedding at the end of August? I'm not trying to rush you but if minds are made up there's no point in delaying things." said Simon.

"We'd both like that," said Victoria. "It worked well for Joanna."

At that point Simon rang the bell and Amrik appeared with champagne and glasses.

There was a bit of hugging and relief all-round that common sense had prevailed.

As it was only 10 am Michael managed to borrow his father's Morris. He took off with Victoria. Half an hour later they were in Sheringham where Michael went to his bank. He had £550 in the account (£32,000 at current values). This was money he had accumulated over the years by work and from family gifts. Living on the farm all he ever wanted was always there, so he never spent much money. He drew out thirty pounds. They went on to Cromer and stopped outside the fish shop and purchased sixteen cooked crabs for fifteen shillings. They were all a good size. It was something his mother had asked him to get before they left. Michael said, "I assume you like crab. The Cromer ones are the best in the country."

"I have had it once or twice and it was nice, but I get confused about the dead man's fingers that you are not supposed to eat!" said Victoria.

"Don't worry about that. I'll give you an anatomy lesson. You can't beat a whole crab with a freshly baked baguette like you had in France with butter and a nice white wine when we stayed with Lucy at my grandparents back in the summer. I'll pick up four bottles in Norwich. That will be our rent!" and Michael smiled.

They went on to Norwich and straight to the main jewellers in the city near the cathedral where he invited Victoria to select an engagement ring. She found one she liked at ten pounds.

Michael said firmly. "You are worth more than that. There's a sapphire and diamond one here for twenty-four pounds. What do you think about that? Is it better than the other one?"

"I love it," she said," but it's too expensive."

Michael insisted she try it on. It was a little tight. "We can adjust that quite easily," said the jeweller. "It's no extra and it will take less than an hour."

"I should think not!" said Michael.

They measured her finger, and a half-size increase would be adequate. Michael handed over one of the large £5 notes as a deposit. He was handed a receipt, and he told them they would be back at 2 pm.

Both were hungry as they had not had any breakfast, so they opted for a restaurant nearby that did fish and chips. On the way back they passed a barber shop.

"Wait here," Michael said. "I have to get something for the weekend." When he returned, Victoria asked. "What was that about?" He explained the procedure that Boynton had taught him, and she laughed. At 2pm they returned and collected the ring that now fitted to perfection. Victoria insisted on wearing it and said she would put her gloves on when they got back.

"We did it then!" she said as she kissed him.

"After your ultimatum I never had any doubt. I'm proud of you. I think your mother realised her mistake and regrets it. She just wants to put it behind her and that is what we will allow her to do. And on New Year's Day I just want to wake up with you beside me. I'm sure my mother will sort a few things out. My bed is a double anyway, as you know, but I expect when you get back you will want to pick a few things up."

They picked up four bottles of Chablis in Norwich, and by 4 pm they were at the Hall. Victoria couldn't wait to show off the ring as she took off the glove. Helen was impressed. Lisette and Helen had been planning. New Year's Eve was never a big thing at Spelthorpe. November the fifth was the highlight of every year for the whole village community with the torchlit parade, fireworks, bonfire and Guy competition. On this year for the first time there were no Kaiser Guys but there were no less than five Adolf Hitlers, which was symptomatic of the mood, not just in Spelthorpe, but across the nation.

Helen and Lisette had decided on a quiet family dinner for the full Spelthorpe Company of which Rufus, Anna, Jeremy, Joanna and Jennifer were now considered full members. It would take place in the main dining room at the Hall. Amrik and his staff would be cooking and serving. It would be black tie, but Michael need not worry as he was the same size as Simon and a spare had been found. This being the case Michael handed over the crabs and Helen confirmed they had been waiting for them. He also handed over the four bottles of Chablis as a present from 'The two of us'.

In order to put matters right Helen said to Victoria "You will be sleeping at the cottage tonight. I'm sorry about yesterday. Had I been paying a bit more attention I would have worked it out like the others."

"Forget it Mummy," said Victoria. "That's ancient history now and it's forgotten already. I will sleep here on a couple of days next week. Michael is doing some ploughing work and that is tiring. I might spend part of the day with him and the horses so he can teach me. I will need to be able to do everything on the estate because that is what leadership is about. When they see me in the muck, I will gain their respect and that has to be earnt."

Victoria went upstairs to sort an overnight bag whilst Helen chatted with Michael. "I'm glad this has happened," she said. "I see you have all the best qualities of an officer and a gentleman. You will look after Victoria as you have for many years. I can't be happier for Simon and me, and both of you, all at the same time."

The dinner was a lavish affair in the best traditions of Spelthorpe. Apart from Edward and George, all were in on the secret, and that was a cause for a discreet double celebration. In fact, Edward and George both decided to go to bed at 10 pm so that afforded Victoria one last chance to display her ring before it was consigned to the safe. For Lucy it was the first time that she had to congratulate her brother. As twins they were close and had a natural telepathy. To her Victoria had always been like a sister and there were no real secrets between the three of them. She said to Michael, "It looks like things are well mapped out for you two. I'm so happy that you have both got over this hurdle together". Michael responded, "Have you thought any more about what you want?"

Lucy said. "I'm not looking for a husband if that is what you are thinking and there's no way I'm putting myself up for offers. That will come in time and when I meet the right person I will know, but in the meantime, I am looking at following in Grandpa's footsteps and that is why I have been working on my French. I'm fine with the colloquial stuff, as we both are, but I have been studying diplomatic texts and how they are put together. Mummy has written to Grandpa to see if he can get me an interview with the diplomatic service. Grandpa has got a first-class reputation with them, and I'm sure that he will stress that it's not the usual nepotism they must encounter but having a good candidate who will be an asset. I think I can show them that if I get the opportunity. Doing a degree in French would be a waste because I'm way above that level in linguistic terms, and most of the time they seem to just waffle on about French literature when a deep knowledge of the French psyche is far more valuable. Although on the literature side I like Voltaire because what he says makes a lot of good sense. My favourite is, *'God is not on the side of the big battalions but those who shoot the best,'* and that's probably a good one for you too. I think I'm well on the way with all the background knowledge. From what Mummy said I think Grandpa and Grandma may be both coming over for a week at Easter and that will be good because it's been a few years since they were last here."

Just before midnight, all the domestic staff were invited up for a New Year drink, thanks and celebration.

But the best thing of all came later because when Michael and Victoria woke on Saturday the first of January 1938, they were truly together with nothing to hide, at least for now, within the Spelthorpe Company.

3

Metamorphosis

January 1938

Michael and Victoria lay together until 8.30am. That was a bit of a luxury because normally they would both be up an hour before that, but they still couldn't believe their luck and how their lives had been totally transformed in the previous thirty-six hours. As far as the senior members of the Spelthorpe Company were concerned, matters had been settled in a workable harmonious manner, and swiftly too. That was the Spelthorpe modus operandi and something that all three of the original Spelthorpe Company patriarchs would say, "I don't want your problems, just your solutions," and that was a maxim that they applied just as harshly, if not more so, to themselves.

Going back to school in just over a week would be hard, not in the educational sense, but in having to put on their school uniforms and that would seem awkward given their newfound status, but at least there would be weekends, half-term exeats and the three-week Easter break. They had both decided that they would let Paddy in on the secret as it would be no different to telling God and he would know about it anyway. From an earthly perspective, Paddy held the absolute trust of the entire community.

They went downstairs to be greeted by Ash and Lisette who were having a simple breakfast of porridge with eggs and bacon. Lucy was still in bed making the most of things.

Lisette simply said. "A happy New Year to you both and I suppose this will be the one you will always remember."

Victoria responded. "And we can't thank you enough for making it happen. It has meant so much to us."

"On that note," asked Michael, "is there anything you would like us to do around here today?"

Ash replied. "If you could dig over the six raised beds at the far end outside, then put up the temporary chicken wire and put the hens in so they can rake it all over and dig up all the bugs. They will love that. There are some logs in the barn that need splitting and stacking, and as Joanna will be out of it for a while, can you give all the horses a run along the beach and take the dogs with you two at a time. Just keep it gentle for Trooper and Rafe because they can't be overworked anymore. I've got to go and see Boynton, and I suspect he feels that the time has come to open up about his special relationship with Miss Featherstone. She must spend all her free time up with him. I know he's been discrete, but he's not the only one around here who knows what is really going on, but we shall see. By the way, I think you should be aware that I'm asking Boynton to give you a few practical lessons on survival and evasion behind enemy lines. It will be the sort of stuff they probably won't teach you in the RAF. It might come in handy and when he's had a few sessions with you, I'll get him to do the same with Lucy too, and indeed Victoria, but I warn you now, it won't be very ladylike, so not the sort of thing that debutantes get up to, but we all know your feelings on that!"

"Consider it done," said Michael. "We will do the beds and

chickens first. That won't take long, then the horses and dogs, and the wood after that. You are aware that on Thursday and Friday I will be ploughing."

Ash nodded.

"And yes, I would appreciate some lessons with Boynton too," said Victoria, "seeing as I'm not going to be a debutante anymore." She gave out the broadest of grins.

Ash took off in the truck with a bottle of Spelthorpe Sloe Gin which he knew Boynton would appreciate. He drew up and noticed an aging Austin 7 outside. As he parked up Black and Tan – Boynton's two Labradors, rushed up to be petted. Any outsider would have got different treatment. As he walked up to the door, a lady emerged from the front of the cottage. She looked familiar but unfamiliar in the sense that she wore no glasses, and her hair was down and flowing. She wore a hint of make-up and appeared of similar age to Lisette. She looked radiant with happiness – in all a very attractive lady, and the total opposite of the frumpy school housemistress that he had expected.

"Miss Featherstone, I presume," said Ash.

"Indeed, it is," she said. "I'll go and put the kettle on. He's in the barn."

Ash walked the fifty yards across to the barn at the edge of the tree line. Boynton was inside, repairing some pheasant egg incubators.

"It won't be long now," he said, "and we will be rounding up all the remaining hen pheasants. A happy New Year to you, Ash."

"And to you too, in fact, to you both should I say. My word! I hardly recognised the lady. What a transformation," said Ash.

"She's transformed me too. She has worked wonders. Have you noticed. I have been totally cured of my swearing all the time and not just when ladies are present. I am allowed the occasional 'bugger' or 'bastard' if something really gets up my nose but that's it. And she's been teaching me German. In the house, on our own, we speak German all the time. I've even given up smoking. I expect you were aware of my nocturnal welfare visits to the war widows. I can't deny it. While it lasted, it was good, but after ten years of that sort of thing people move on, and they are mainly now in proper relationships or have gone to pastures new. Going to Joanna's wedding was the best thing that ever happened to me. I half felt that it was Joanna's little joke on her frumpy house mistress, but it has worked out the best for both of us. We just got closer and closer and realised that we couldn't be apart any longer, and all the secrecy is not good, so we have decided to go public, but I wanted you to be the first to know, so that is why I asked you to come. We will be getting married as soon as I have asked Paddy," said Boynton.

Ash responded. "All I can offer is my most sincere congratulations. You absolutely deserve true happiness because not only do I see you as a friend, but you have been a true pillar of this community. Simon knows that too. We know you care a great deal about this place and the way you have watched over our children over the years is something we genuinely appreciate. With your consent I would like to mention this to Simon. I know he and Helen will feel the same. I know you won't want a big show because it's not your way, but the estate needs to voice its approval of your loyalty and service and for that matter, your lady. She played a good part as a house mistress, and she has steered and looked after all our kids over the years and that's important too. I know I can say this to you, and it won't go any further, but yours will not be the only wedding this year. Michael and Victoria will be tying the knot in August, but it must remain under wraps until the end of the summer term for obvious reasons."

"That's absolutely marvellous," said Boynton. "They've been

inseparable for years – so well matched. It did occur to me that he needed a bit of advice on a certain issue so you can probably work out why his hair was so short a couple of summers back with all those trips to the barbers. Anyway, come and meet Aggie, as she likes me to call her. Sounds better than Agatha but I'm staying as plain Boynton, and everyone knows that."

They walked into Boynton's cottage. It had been transformed by the addition of running water and gas for cooking and water heating but transformed even more by Aggie's touch.

Ash broke the ice by saying, "Aggie, I am absolutely delighted for you and Boynton, and I speak for the rest of the estate by stating without any fear of contradiction that we are all extremely pleased at what you have decided. Never forget that we are here for you both. Your total loyalty is recognised. I have to say that I have rarely seen such a transformation in a lady such as yours. I had a certain impression of you when I saw you at school and I suppose that we are all actors in that we act up to a role that people expect us to be. As a housemistress and teacher, you perform splendidly, but to see the real you, is absolutely splendid. It is obvious that you are good for each other and have found true happiness. You both deserve it. I said to Boynton that the estate will do something for your wedding, of your choosing, of course, but don't sell yourselves short. If you want a simple reception as we did for Joanna, I'm sure that will be sorted. Just let me know."

Aggie responded. "I feel a little embarrassed at your words that were so kind but perhaps I didn't realise how high was the esteem in which you held us. We don't want anything lavish but a simple reception with friends would be nice. Neither of us have any close living relatives because my family has been the school over the years and Boynton, – the estate."

"With your permission, I'll speak to Earl Simon and get

back to you both. Anyway, I think that coffee would be nice and perhaps a tot of that sloe gin I brought up for you. That is one of Lisette and Helen's creations but after that if I'm not taking up too much of your time, I'm intrigued as to how you ended up as a German speaker, but not in German for me, please. I'm just French and English like the rest of my little tribe, as you well know," said Ash. They took coffee and some homemade biscuits and a large tot of sloe gin and toasted the new year.

Aggie outlined her story. "I was born back in 1893 in Cape Town. My father was a mining engineer. When I was five, we moved to a place in German Southwest Africa called Swakopmund, which was quite a nice place, although the name means stinking hole. My father was extremely well paid. They had found masses of diamonds. It was on the coast. We could swim in the sea, but it was cold despite being in the tropics because of the Benguela Current that comes up from the Antarctic. It was all very German. They had a Hotel Kaiser, that I remember. The coast was a mass of huge sand dunes but with mists because of the contrast between the sea and land temperature. There were shipwrecks all along the shoreline and huge colonies of fur seals with hyenas and the odd lion coming down to the beach. They called it the Skeleton Coast because of all the shipwrecks. It was quite beautiful really. I went to school and by the time I was ten I was totally fluent in German as well as English. My father travelled all over in his work and was mainly south of us at a place called Luderitz. I felt safe there. The native people dressed in Western dress and were kind.

Anyway, that all changed, and my father kept coming home with horror stories. They started forced labour camps for the local people, where they worked them to death. They took their land and destroyed burial grounds. Then they started killing them, hunting them down and shooting and hanging them.

They even took photos of the hangings and made postcards. We heard about medical experiments on the people. Finally, they started driving whole tribes out into the desert to starve them to death. They tried to wipe out all the Herero and Nama people. It was just evil what they did and not many knew what was going on, but my father saw it because he was travelling all over the place. In the end after five years, we got out. My father had made his money, and I feel a little guilty because of that.

We came back to England. I went to a good school and then university, where I studied history and German. That came to an end in 1916 but when I finished someone from the military came to the university. They wanted fluent German speakers. They gave me some sort of military grade in a unit that was experimental because there was still nothing for women then, as you know, other than as a FANY or a Voluntary Aid Detachment, but they were not really appropriate. I never wore a military uniform because I was undercover. I was posted to a large country house that was in fact a prison for German Officers. I had to act as a domestic who spoke no German, and my role was to eavesdrop and report back on anything that might be useful.

Anyway, in just over a year, the war came to an end, so I went into teaching. In 1920 I gained a job at the school and five years later they made me a housemistress and the rest you know."

"I find that fascinating," said Ash. "From what you are saying all this Nazi business started back in that German colony – a whole generation before Hitler came to power."

"There's no doubt and I could tell you a lot more. That's why I'm so worried because I've seen it all before, and I have mentioned it to some of the high-powered visitors and parents that visit the school but if I went on about it all the time, they would think I was a crackpot. That would have jeopardised my position. I did write a long account and sent it to Winston Churchill. I met up with him in Kent a few years back. I spent a day at Chartwell with him. He said he would respect my situation, but he was in the wilderness then and he still is. All the others just want to feather their nests, keep their jobs and stick their heads in the sand," said Aggie.

"That's politicians for you I'm afraid. We get one or two up here for the shooting and in our coastal lodges. It's all about retaining power and I can't see that ever changing. As soon as they get their seat, with the odd exception, any integrity they might once have had gets cast aside. The ones with integrity get ground down by the political establishment. They can't make any headway, and they eventually give up. Will marriage change things at the school for you?" asked Ash.

"We are thinking about that one," she said. "I'm very happy here with Boynton, and I don't like driving on dangerous narrow country lanes even though there's not a lot of traffic. He does take me and pick me up a lot of the time, but I have to be there for the whole week, and one of the senior staff has to stay the weekend for the few that don't go home, so I'm thinking that I will be putting my notice in to leave at the end of the summer term."

"That's interesting," said Ash. "We need a new head for the village school from September. It's small, just sixty children from five to fifteen with three teachers, one head and a caretaker. The head takes some classes. Lisette and Helen are two of the governors, along with Reverend Paddy. Could I send Lisette up to see you? I'm sure she would want to get to know you better as you transform into one of us Spelthorpians. She was a FANY in the war. You probably have quite a lot in common. Boynton's a good chap but you ladies do need some lady time too."

"I'd like that very much. She would be welcome at any time and as soon as is convenient," said Aggie.

"Excellent," said Ash. "I shall now leave you two lovebirds to enjoy the rest of the day, and can I take it you have no objection to me explaining things to Earl Simon and Julian?"

"Not at all," said Boynton. "We have both decided that the time for secrecy is over. We will pop down and see Paddy to fix a date, and I will get back to you with that as soon as I can."

Ash shook hands firmly with Boynton and gave Aggie a little hug. He walked out and Boynton walked with him to the truck.

Boynton said. "If you can pull off the post at the school that would be brilliant not just for her, but for the kids around here. They deserve better, and she would do that. Aggie wants very much to be a part of what we have here. I have just one favour to ask. Will you be my best man?"

Ash replied. "No question of it. I thought you'd never ask, and I have a favour to ask of you. Will you teach my kids to survive? You know what I mean. For Michael it will be unarmed combat, proper shooting and escape and evasion, the sort of stuff they should teach officers, but they never do. We both know that sometimes you have to play dirty to win. He needs some insight. For Lucy and Victoria whom I now regard as my daughter, the same thing but possibly a bit less on the escape and evasion. They are all sensible, but you know those with the edge survive and you never know when you will need it. They will take it from you because they respect you. I am too familiar for them to take it as seriously as they should."

Boynton answered. "I'll gladly do that, and I agree with you. In less than two years, my bet is that we will be at war again, and it will be every bit as bad as the trenches, but everyone will be getting it, not just the military. I'll do anything I can to give us all the edge. Send Michael up here at 8-am on Monday morning. I'll start with weapon familiarisation. I have quite a collection, but that is between the three of us."

"Thank you, my friend," said Ash, and he patted Boynton on the shoulder then jumped in the truck and headed back via the Hall.

Simon was delighted when he heard the news about Boynton and Aggie and even more so when he learnt that Aggie might go for the school job. "That would inject some real quality and excellence, and I'm sure if a bit of extra funding is needed, the estate will find it. Most of the kids end up working here anyway. We need to help them realise their true potential. We can lay on a reception if that's what they would like. We did it for Joanna, and as there is no commercial element, it will not be costly to us, but it will mean a lot to them. She has tamed Boynton, but I hope it hasn't taken his edge because we still need that."

"You won't take his edge," said Ash. "I've known him well for a long time. Aggie has brought out his softer side, but when it comes to protecting you and yours and this place, he's a hard, ruthless bastard, and we need people like that even if publicly we might not admit to it. We can hardly judge given what we got up to when we were trench-raiding just over twenty years back. That quality might be dormant but we both still have it."

Ash explained that Boynton had agreed to deliver some personal safety training to Michael and the girls. Simon fully approved of that, particularly given the possibility of war.

When Ash got home, he noted that all the work had been done. Lisette explained that Lucy had joined in, and all three were out riding with Jeremy and Rufus exercising the horses. Rufus was riding his Arab gelding, which was a new addition to the stable. All the ponies had been out and now they were exercising the Suffolk Punches for a more sedate ride. They were also going along to the sawmill to give the other two Suffolk Punches a run in the forest. Nimrod, Kipling and Zulu were out with them. The other dogs were resting under the oak in front of the cottage.

With the garden and domestic work taken care of and the others all out, Ash opted for a relaxing break with Lisette on the sofa in the lounge. They sat cuddled up in front of the open fire to the sound of Vaughan Williams on the gramophone, a piece of Christmas cake and a glass of Calvados that had come from Lisette's parents in Normandy. Ash had a rare opportunity to read a newspaper that he had picked up in the village. Lisette was thrilled at the news of Aggie and Boynton's wedding plans and said she would visit her on Sunday after church. She telephoned to congratulate them and arranged to pop up for an hour to see Aggie.

The trio got back with the dogs on foot just after 6pm. They had stabled the horses then called to see Helen who had been pleased to note that Victoria would be spending Thursday and Friday nights at the Hall after two days on the plough. All three were worn out from their exertions so it was showers, supper and bed. Bathing hillbilly style in the lake was now something of the past, at least in the winter months. Secretly they were all pleased with the extensive improvements and structural additions that the cottage had gained over the last few years. It wasn't quite up to the Hall or the annexe standards, but with five bedrooms, a full-size study and an extra bathroom and toilet facilities, they could no longer be accused of living in the stone age.

Sunday was largely uneventful, a day of rest. Lisette made a firm and friendly connection with Aggie and the village school headmistress idea was looking positive, although a formal interview would need to take place following a governors' meeting.

Ash would be tree planting with his foresters on Monday. They had some red oaks and pin oaks to go in around the eastern entrance and along part of the upgraded track. These were North American varieties that had been in England for the last 300 years. They were popular for their spectacular autumn colour and often planted near entrances to estates. These were homegrown on the estate, and now was the perfect season to dig them up and get them in. He had discussed with Paddy the planting of a ginkgo tree close to the war memorial. The ginkgo was an ancient species, sometimes described as a living fossil with again a spectacular autumn display in yellow. Close to the Aubers Ridge battlefield site in France was the Le Touret Memorial with the names of over 13,000 soldiers with no known grave including many of the men of Spelthorpe who had fallen. Next to the edifice was a ginkgo tree that graced the memorial. It had looked splendid in November a year ago when he had flown there a year ago in a Dragon Rapide along with Paddy, Simon, Boynton, Rufus and Julian on an old comrades' day out. They had driven there in a hired car from Lille airport, took lunch in Lille then flew back to Norfolk. The tree would link the two sites together. Paddy was pleased. They selected had the best spot.

Le Touret Memorial and ginkgo tree.

Boynton and Aggie attended church together now their secret was out. Aggie was wearing an engagement ring. For the wedding, they had settled for St George's day. It fell on a Saturday in the April holiday.

4

Just deserts

January 1938

Monday morning was always busy in the village shop after the Sunday closure. It was owned by the estate and managed by Jasmir Singh, the wife of Amrik Singh, the butler to the Spelthorpe household. The Singhs had come across from Kenya at the request of Countess Helen when she married Simon in 1912, and since that time by hard work and loyalty, they had worked their way up to the top positions amongst the household staff who respected them greatly.

Jasmir's management of the shop was legendary. The variety of stock was huge and not just the produce from the farm. It was rare not to be able to get any of the essentials. She had two full-time and four part-time staff who worked with her. She rapidly gained a reputation for her kindness coupled with determination to satisfy customer needs. As a result, she had become a valued and respected member of the greater Spelthorpe community. The shop was placed at the western end of the village on the main street between the station and the upgraded track that led to the harbour and the west side entrance to the estate. It was close to the church and the veterinary practice on the estate as well as the pub, the memorial hall and vicarage on the village side.

About 9.30am a car pulled up directly outside the shop, which was quite crowded – mainly with women who had just dropped their children off by the village school that was about 150 yards to the east along the main road. The school was close to the police house. Two men got out of the car. Both wore hoods with what appeared to be black stockings over their heads with slits cut for the eyes. One held a sawn-off shotgun and the other a revolver. They entered the shop. The one with the shotgun fired into the ceiling. Screaming ensued as the debris fell from the ceiling and a voice shouted. "We want the money, or you are dead!"

Instinctively, Jasmir and the shop staff cowered as the men went behind the counter.

Ash and his team were working 100 yards away planting trees on the eastern entrance to the estate. Ash heard the shot and ran the short distance towards the shop with the others. He had his shotgun and half a dozen cartridges in the truck. They had two other trucks with them. Instinct and military training turned to orders. He shouted. "They are robbing the shop. We can't risk a fire fight here!"

To one of the drivers, he ordered.

"Block their escape going back the way they came. Park the truck in the middle of the road behind them then run to the police house."

The under-keeper had come out from the gate house. Ash shouted. "Get your gun and come with me."

And to the others he said. "Ring Boynton. I'm going to block the main road further up, so we force them up through the estate. We will chase them up to Boynton's crossroads, where we should be able to stop them without anyone else getting hurt. Is that clear?"

"Yes, Boss!" came the response.

"And block the road here to stop them going up to the port or this side of the estate!"

The team were used to working together and this stemmed from the appreciation of danger and rapid movement needed when felling large trees. They sprang into action.

In the shop the robbers were confident they had time on their side. It would be ages before the police got there in rural Norfolk and in any case, they wouldn't have guns. They smashed open the till and emptied it. Then they stripped the shelves of cigarettes and as many bottles of spirits as they could get in their bags.

In the meantime, one of Ash's team got through to Aggie. She told them Boynton was out with Michael on the edge of the wood. She calmly took the message then ran out of the cottage to Boynton and Michael who were examining several of his weapons.

"Someone is robbing the shop. They are armed. Ash is blocking the main road at the bottom to force them up here. You have about five minutes maximum." Boynton took his Mauser rifle loaded with five rounds. He gave Michael the Lee-Enfield with ten in the magazine.

"Are you OK with that? These are the legal ones for culling the deer!"

"I'll be fine," said Michael. "I've used it enough times!"

Boynton shouted. "Aggie! Get a blanket and some leaves and cover this lot. I'll deal with it later, then go inside and hide. You won't see anything, if you know what I mean, and be quick!".

Boynton dashed in the barn and seconds later came out with a hessian sack.

They got in his truck and parked it just below the crossroads.

"Get in your position, behind the engine block. That will stop a bullet. You shoot over the top! I've got something here that will stop their car. I will be behind that log pile just to the side. And if you shoot, you shoot to stop. Shoot to kill! Dead men tell no lies. Got it?" said Boynton.

With that he scattered the fifty or so caltrops across the track, then took his position.

Meanwhile Ash drove through the estate with the underkeeper, Jack. They had shotguns with enough bird shot to start a war. They came out through the main entrance onto the main coast road which they blocked with the truck, leaving the main track onto the south side of the estate as the only escape route. Jack positioned himself in the road behind the truck. Ash was by the main gate onto the Hall access road which he pulled shut then took shelter behind an ornamental pillar. They had grabbed a stockman on the way and sent him up a hundred yards behind Jack to wave down and stop any traffic. They were in the nick of time.

"Just pepper them. We don't want a blood bath here. We just want to get them up to Boynton where we can stop them properly out of the public's way." shouted Ash.

A car came rapidly up and slowed when they saw the truck blocking the road. Ash saw the black hoods of the occupants. They were fifty yards out when he emerged and blasted the front of the vehicle. The windscreen shattered and the driver almost instantly turned south and into the estate and up the slope. Ash and Jack jumped in the truck and gave chase keeping 200 yards back so as not to compromise whatever Boynton had planned.

Boynton and Michael heard the shot and then saw the car heading up towards them with the truck at a safe distance. They could see that the windscreen had been shot out. The vehicle came on at speed towards the truck and started to slow. Then the caltrops took over as both front tyres burst and shredded. The vehicle slewed, and the other caltrops burst the rear tyres. The vehicle came to a halt. The figure on the driver's side burst out brandishing the sawn-off, and the passenger side opened too but Boynton had no clear view. There was a shot from Boynton, and the man with the sawn-off dropped as his brains exited the back of his head. A split second later there was another shot from behind the truck and the second figure dropped as the shot hit him in the middle of the sternum and bloody debris came out the back of his chest.

Boynton walked over. He pulled off the mask. The shot had hit the robber between the eyes. He walked to the second robber. Michael had him covered. There was no movement. Boynton looked at the point of impact in the centre of the chest. The pistol was still in his hand in a death grip.

"Well done lad. Good kill," he said. "We touch nothing and wait for the police. Our guns can rest in the back of the truck. Stay here. I have a little clearing up to do. You are certainly a chip off the old block. I remember back in 1915 when your dad saved the Earl's life when he was caught on the wire. I was there. Three Germans ran up to him and he did all three with his Webley. Three shots, three dead Huns. He's a brave man your dad!"

Boynton went back to the pile of weaponry under the blanket, collecting it all together. He secreted it in the rack under the trap door in the barn, reapplying the straw and debris. He went back to the cottage. Aggie was in the kitchen. She rushed over and hugged and kissed him.

"I'm so glad it worked out alright."

"You saw it then, you naughty girl! Do you still want to marry me then?" asked Boynton.

"All the more I do because you proved beyond all doubt that you will look after me. I love you. But I know where you are coming from so when the police arrive, I will say. I hid in the house because I was too frightened to look. I heard the tyres burst, then shouting, 'Stop. Drop your guns. We are armed!' And then two shots and I waited until you got me and that's it," said Aggie.

"You have been trained well. I'm impressed. Now, I think we all want a nice cup of tea. It will be at least an hour before the police get here. Where's Black and Tan?" asked Boynton.

"They are in the lounge. Couldn't be bothered. They are so used to bangs, and they know instinctively when you want them," said Aggie.

"Best keep them in," said Boynton. "Can't have them peeing on the evidence."

Boynton made a quick phone call to the shop. Jasmir answered. She was calm and told Boynton that nobody was hurt. Amrik was there with Earl Simon and Helen. PC Carter was there, too. Boynton asked to speak to Simon. "We got them, Sir. Both dead. Nobody hurt. They won't do that again."

"Who shot them?" asked Simon.

"I got the one with the sawn-off, and Michael shot the one with the pistol. Good clean kills. Just two shots fired. We will have to stay here for a bit until the police have done whatever. I'd better go and wait outside. Aggie can take any messages."

Simon thought to himself and remembered the conversation earlier with Ash. Boynton had clearly kept his edge, and his future son-in-law had one as well. He was reassured and knew that Victoria was in good hands.

Boynton went out and saw Ash with Michael. He updated them that all was well at the shop then suggested Michael go in with Aggie for tea.

"Well, that is the first day's tuition done! The boy's got balls. He doesn't get flustered. You should be proud of him, and he certainly has that vital killer instinct. And in case you wondered I didn't arrange the robbery just to prove the point!" said Boynton

"Thanks, mate," said Ash. "The first is always the hardest, but we have got him over the hurdle, not that I expect him to be a homicidal maniac, but I'm stunned at his calm attitude. He told me that as far as he is concerned, a gun is just a tool to do a specific job, in fact no different from a saw or an axe and the job for today was to take out two evil bastards who would end up killing somebody sooner or later. They made no offer to surrender. They came out to fight us with guns, and they got their just deserts- simple as that, and now we just move on."

Boynton and Ash elected to wait on for the police. Ash thanked Jack for his help and asked if he could walk back and pass on the news, but only to those who needed to know like the foresters who had helped so efficiently at the early stage. He would see them later.

The police were slow as ever. Boynton said that the crows would get first pickings if they didn't get up there fast enough. He got a couple of hessian sandbags and placed them over the exposed wounds after he first replaced the hood on the figure that he had shot. He noted the positions of the ejected cartridges and left them in situ.

Michael walked in on Aggie. On the previous day he had seen her at church and had been taken totally aback by her new look. She had told him there and then in no uncertain terms that it was Aggie at Spelthorpe and ma'am only at school. She went on to offer her warmest congratulations and said that his and Victoria's secret would be safe with her and Boynton.

"I know it will seem awkward for the two of you, but I've learnt that Spelthorpe precedent is not to hang around once a decision has been made. Joanna did the same five years ago, but it was a little easier for her because her husband was not at the school," said Aggie.

"I'm not worried," said Michael. "It's just basic discipline. You can imagine how the school would be regarded if all the next crop of debutantes were bed-hopping in the boys' dormitories."

Aggie laughed. "Yes, I saw your mother yesterday and we had quite an amusing chat about Victoria's views on debutantes. I'm very proud of the pair of you."

Aggie explained that she would be keeping her new appearance for school and that the time for overacting had ended. She confided in him on her wish to be a positive part of this special community and he enlightened her on some of the activities over the year, like the polar bear dip, the Guy Fawkes parade, the riding, the sea and lake swimming, the castle keep, and he offered to take her up for a ten-minute sight-seeing flight when it was a bit warmer at Easter. He spoke about flying and Victoria's ambitions for agricultural and estate management and all the reasons why they both loved the place.

It was an hour before the police finally turned up in a convoy of three vehicles that came up the incline. There were a couple of plain-clothes officers in the first, and Ash instantly recognised one of them. There was a photographic scenes-of-crime vehicle with an officer and the doctor to go through the motions of officially pronouncing life extinct. Ash remembered one police doctor who would routinely take out his stethoscope even for a skeleton. In the last vehicle, a standard patrol car, were two constables, one of whom was PC Carter from the village, together with a sergeant.

"Long time no see, John," said Ash to one of the plain clothes officers. "Still working your way up the ladder?"

John Skingle had been the village copper here back in the late 20s. Ash had worked with him, and they had successfully dealt with several cases. It was obvious from the start he was going places.

John replied.

"Detective Chief Inspector now running the CID for the entire King's Lynn and north Norfolk Division. Sorry about the delay but we went to the shop first and learnt there that you had it all under control up here, so we took all the statements and photos down there first. We've been after these bastards for weeks. They've hit about twenty shops and post offices in rural Essex, Suffolk and more recently five in Norfolk. We've had four people shot, but miraculously nobody was killed. Bloody marvellous! You've saved the nation a fortune. No trial, no prison and people can sleep easy now."

Ash outlined the events and indicated that nothing had been touched. The guns were available for inspection.

"Well as far as I am concerned this is just a coroner's job with a justifiable homicide result, but I need to make absolutely sure that it runs that way so I will take the witness statements myself. That might take a little time. Where are Michael and Boynton?" asked the DCI.

"They are in the cottage. We need the guns back straight away because they are doing a deer cull, and the stock and cash back from the robbers' vehicle as soon as your man has taken the photos," said Ash. "And if you could get rid of their vehicle too, that would help a lot."

"We will sort that. I just need Boynton and Michael out here to point out to me which gun they had, where they shot from and which one they shot. I'll get the photos and searches done and the doc' to do his bit and then you will get it all back and we can get rid of all this rubbish, and the corpses can go off to the morgue at King's Lynn. It might take a while to identify them especially the one with the headshot, but what I need to do most of all is to tie them in with all the other robberies, so we get them cleared up. We also have to get all that the coroner needs. I presume there is a phone in the cottage because I need to offer him the opportunity of coming out and having a look for himself. With a double homicide that's a strong possibility. He's a good guy and very thorough."

Ash went back to the cottage and explained. Boynton and Michael came out and did what was required, then the DCI issued his orders. The police officers went about their business. Boynton explained about the calthrops. They took a couple of photos, then Boynton collected the lot to stop anyone treading on one. The whole process took another three hours.

The coroner did turn up. Aggie provided tea all around. He seemed very happy and said to Ash, "Your quick thinking and organisation in getting them out of the way up here saved a bloodbath. All that plus these courageous fellows puts us all in your debt so I expect I'll see you in about a month's time when I can put a line under this. There's nothing to worry about here. I wish all my cases were as clear cut."

Before he left, he shook hands with all three of them.

John Skingle was conscientious in the way he crafted the statements, and he made sure that it was Ash Cromwell MC and Boynton MM at the head of the first page on each. Ash asked if names could be kept out of any police press release. They agreed on 'estate manager and other estate staff'.

As they were clearing up the recovery vehicle turned up for

the car, along with the undertakers. Paddy suddenly appeared. DCI Skingle asked if he wanted to do anything with respect to the bodies before they were taken away.

Paddy said, "Most certainly not. Those who live by the sword die by the sword. If they want forgiveness, they can seek it in the next world not in this but I'm sure they are in the depths of hell already and that's where they belong. I'm here to make sure that the Almighty is looking after my flock as I am sure he will. I bless you all for the unpleasant nature of what you have to do from time to time. Yours is a noble profession."

With that Paddy went into the cottage to see Michael, Boynton and Aggie. John Skingle commented to Ash. "That's one hell of a good priest you have here. I wish the rest of them were a bit more like that!"

"They all love him. He helps hold the place together," said Ash.

By 4 pm the site was clear, and the police were gone. Ash and Michael loaded the stolen items on the truck. It was just cigarettes, spirits and seven pounds in one pound and ten-shilling notes and a few half crowns and florins. The guns had been returned. Aggie dished out some Christmas cake and sloe gin. They unwound together for half an hour then Ash and Michael drove down to the Hall to update Simon on the day's events. Paddy stayed for a bit longer.

Back at the Hall Simon, Helen, Lisette and Victoria were all waiting. As soon as Ash and Michael were inside Victoria grabbed Michael and hung to him and kissed him out of sheer relief. Simon brought Amrik and Jasmir up. She had been reassured by so many, including Paddy and seemed happy with that, but it was important that both were aware that the evil men were no longer a threat to anyone.

The goods and cash were put to one side for return to the shop in the morning. The maintenance team had been into the shop and the ceiling had been repaired already, yet another example of the Spelthorpe way – the rapid resumption of normality. All were aware, not least of all Amrik, that his wife would need some discrete attention in the days ahead as the shock came out. All were impressed by the cool way in which Michael had handled things. Most of that was down to controlled exposure to risk and what he had absorbed from a set of well-disciplined parents over the years. It was so often observed that sons and daughters follow in the footsteps of their parents because of the attitudes and skills they had absorbed over the years. All Michael wanted to do now was to go home for a bath and a snack and most of all to curl up in bed with Victoria, and that is what he did.

At the crack of dawn Michael and Victoria were up. They took all the dogs onto the beach for a run and play, then headed back. They breakfasted with Ash and Lisette. Ash agreed to lend them the Morris. Helen, secretly relieved of the heavy financial burden of a formal coming out for the debutante farce, decided that her son in law and daughter would still need to 'come out' but together in a few months' time and that would require a little more in terms of clothing than school uniform and the moleskins, jodhpurs, Barbours and wellies that they had in abundance. So, she handed over £70 (£4,010 at current values) to her daughter with instructions to get themselves fitted out for the purpose. The sales were on in Norwich, although Helen had signalled that it would be wise to opt for durable quality rather than silly fashions or the rubbish that was going cheap because nobody wanted to wear it. They had invited Lucy to go too, but she indicated she was going riding with Jennifer as they were trying to initiate George into the equine arts. Lucy remained aware that she too, might need to upgrade her wardrobe if her plans for the diplomatic service worked out, but it was a case of one bridge at a time.

Michael and his lady took off at 9am, and an hour later were in the centre of Norwich.

Meanwhile, Ash went off in the truck with Kipling and Nimrod to update and thank the foresters who were finishing off the tree planting. It was going well but taking time because the holes needed were a good size. The trees were not huge but considerably larger than the three-foot whips that were normally planted. Good root capture was essential with trees of that size plus lots of water in the first year to get them established. Paddy had turned up and was digging out a hole at the agreed spot in the churchyard for the ginkgo. Nimrod and Kipling had a mooch around with Gelert.

At 11 am, Simon appeared. He wanted to thank the foresters too. "You all did a splendid job yesterday and it might seem incredible, but I've just taken a call from the king. He was most impressed by what you all did. He had been worried because they were making their way all over north Norfolk, and he didn't want Sandringham village to be hit next. As you all know keeping this place safe for all of you is my top priority and the word will get about to all the criminals out there that we will not be messed with. Unfortunately, the police find it difficult to deal with travelling criminals especially in isolated rural communities like ours. Constable Carter does what he can, but there are limits for just a single policeman with only a truncheon to fight with, so we have to do things ourselves, as we have done for centuries. Police are alright for towns, but I don't think they will ever get their act together in the countryside. We are on our own, but not really because we have each other and we need to remember that, so well done to you all!"

He walked off to the side and spoke to Ash. "You know I'm off to Sandringham tomorrow as Bertie's guest. It was just me, but there's been a change of plan. We don't have a shoot here tomorrow, so you are coming as the King's guest too with Michael as your loader and Boynton as mine. All three of you will be taking lunch with the king. He wants to thank you all personally. He was that impressed by your swift implementation of a plan and brilliant execution – if you forgive the pun! You can turn down all sorts of things but never a personal invite from the king. He even had the coroner ring him and both were highly impressed. And to cap it all I've invited him, Elizabeth and the girls to Michael and Victoria's wedding on the twentieth of August. Given the times we have visited them and they here on a personal family basis, if he found out that they hadn't been asked that would have been a snub and that would be very unwise particularly as Michael will hold the King's Commission. Can you let Boynton know? And the etiquette will be 'sir' and 'ma'am' from Michael and Boynton and first names for us as usual. Best shooting tweeds, and if Michael needs anything I'm the same size."

"Any dogs?" asked Ash.

"Bit difficult with the Rolls, and if they are fussing with them it might mess with the king's focus on the three of you. I think when this is done and dusted, he's looking at British Empire Medals all round. He seemed quite strong on that. Perhaps he's putting out a subtle message to the powers that be, that we need a greater level of policing in the countryside and a new open season on criminals all year round. He complained that there is no real equivalent for civilians for the military medal or military cross and he intends to change all that because he feels that there will be a lot more civilian involvement in the next conflict, and we both agreed on that. I know in the last war there was a lot that went unrecognised but with hundreds getting killed every day, the system just couldn't cope with the paperwork. It's wrong but no amount of courage will change it, and we just have to have the serenity to accept matters."

Ash responded. "I feel quite taken aback at this level of gratitude from the king, but I know how passionate he is about Norfolk and I'm sure Michael and Boynton will feel the same. While you are here Simon, you will remember our trip to Le Touret two years back. The ginkgo goes in today. No leaves at the movement but good buds and good form. It's ten feet tall."

Ash stayed until all the trees were in, then headed off up to Boynton's place. Aggie came to the door and invited him in. Boynton was drafting his end-of-season report and costings as the season would be over in less than a month. Ash simply said. "I come as the king's messenger," and then went on to explain that the three of them would be going with Simon to Sandringham as the personal guests of the king to dine with royalty. Aggie was impressed and indicated that they would have to delay a visit to the solicitor in Sheringham about a name change.

"What's that then?" asked Ash.

"Well, we can't have the reverend use Boynton's real name, and we can't have. 'Do you Boynton Boynton take this woman and so on,' so by the end of the week he will be Gabriel Boynton. I discovered a well-thumbed copy of Thomas Hardy's '*Far from the Madding Crowd*'. Boynton told me that Gabriel Oak was the character he liked the most. He opted for that, so we will change his name by deed poll. I did find another well-thumbed book by DH Lawrence published abroad called '*Lady Chatterley's Lover*', but I went back into school mode and told him that there was no way I would accept John Thomas Mellors as an alternative because the road up here just wouldn't take the traffic when the ladies of Norfolk found out about it, especially as he is the keeper as well."

Gabriel seemed very pleasantly surprised by the invitation as Ash related his conversation with Simon.

In the meantime, Victoria and Michael were busy. He noticed that once in the car she was wearing the engagement ring again, which she must have got out of the safe on the previous evening. She had dressed in a business-like manner, and Michael too was smartly dressed, with a good pair of tan brogues. Footwear was always the giveaway. Michael's friends at school had told him that shopkeepers always look at the feet. The poorer classes would be ostentatious in their dress, but footwear was invariably cheap, but those of standing always wore good shoes because foot comfort was important. He had always remembered that and was of the view that those of standing usually get better service in the hope of further custom.

Michael got a three-piece Irish tweed winter suit and after a good deal of searching a summer wool suit in a navy pinstripe with a couple of matching shirts and ties. He also got a dinner jacket with collars, a matching evening coat and scarf, an appropriate shirt with cuff links and a pair of dress shoes. From her own funds and separately, Victoria bought him a slim turnip pocket watch and chain which she had engraved on the inside cover with the words:

Semper Unum (Always one)
Michael and Victoria
1938

This was her equivalent of an engagement ring. For Victoria, things took a little longer, but she bought two pairs of shoes with heels, a pair of women's country shoes, a winter and summer dress, a tweed two-piece suit, three elegant evening gowns, three jumpers and a classic ladies tweed skirt and appropriate hosiery. In fact, she now had the full kit for a country lady, and she instinctively knew that her mother would approve.

Victoria then dragged Michael into the lingerie department. He displayed an inevitable degree of embarrassment, but she said, "If I'm going to wear it and take it off while you are watching me, then it had better do the trick, so you make sure you like it or else we are going to the local marquee company like some of the larger ladies from the village and you won't like that!"

Once he had come to terms with his embarrassment, he actually became quite interested, but only selected items that increased his pulse rate. He felt the store would draw the line at allowing him into the changing cubicle area, but his imagination worked well for him and a good selection was made including two very revealing night dresses. It became apparent that Victoria was awakening a dormant part of Michael's masculinity and that quite appealed to her.

Much of this came as something of a shock to a couple who had spent most of their summers in bare feet, wearing little more than forest rags. Both remained of the view that when things warmed up, they would return to that for much of the time. However, they both realised that Countess Helen of Spelthorpe wanted Lady Victoria and her husband to look the part when the situation demanded it, and she could not be blamed for that. Deep down they were appreciative. They had a sandwich in a pub then returned home via Cromer where they purchased five cooked crabs and a bottle of white wine. They filled the tank with petrol. As the sun set, they got back to the cottage.

The crabs and wine were well received along with some French-style bread that Lisette had freshly baked. Michael was pleased to display his engagement gift from Victoria. At least there would be no need to keep that locked in the safe although in the privacy of the cottage Victoria was pleased to still wear her ring. Michael's wardrobe indicated that he could now play the quintessential English gentleman if the need arose, but he reassured all that he was happiest in his summer shorts and canvas shirt riding bareback in the surf. That activity would resume as soon as the weather allowed it. Victoria was similarly minded. Ash broke the news of the king's invitation for the following day and that in all probability he would be attending the wedding. Although both had wanted a quiet affair, they recognised that the wedding had to fulfill a greater social and family need. Snubbing the king was simply just not on. In any event, the protocol was that the bride's parents sent out the invitations. An appearance by the king would not go amiss for the estate and village, but the king too, craved family privacy, and with Elizabeth and the girls would want to come along as long term personal and private friends of the Spelthorpe Company. It would be no state occasion so secrecy until the appearance at the church would remain absolute. As Duke of York things had been much easier, but early notification was essential. Bertie had told Simon that he would instruct that no other business other than a declaration of war would stop them from coming.

Lisette summed up for all. "Let's all be sensible. You two were married effectively on New Year's Eve with full parental consent. Yes, there are a few constraints mainly due to the estate's relationship with the school but that is all. Because we are what we are, certain expectations will always apply but the advantages we have are beyond the dreams of the majority out there. In all my life, the things that happened spontaneously were the events we treasured the most. Daddy and I met in the war where there were huge constraints. Our real honeymoon was three days in Paris whilst the war was raging, but it was over a year before we could make it official with the actual wedding. Planned events create huge expectations that often fail to materialise, so raise your glasses with me with three words, spontaneity, love and responsibility."

Nobody could have put it better, but diplomacy was always Lisette's strong point and probably a quality that she had absorbed from her diplomat father over the course of her childhood.

On the following day just before 8 am Ash and Michael met Simon and Boynton at the Hall. They immediately took off to Sandringham. Lisette telephoned Helen and invited her to the cottage for lunch. Julia, Joanna and Jennifer would be coming along with the new arrival James. She also telephoned Boynton's cottage and asked Aggie if she would like to come and meet the others. Victoria would collect her in the truck at 11.30 am. Boudicca and Zulu would come along too for the Labrador party in the barn although Black and Tan had been assigned guard duty. She sent Victoria and Lucy up to the village shop for a few extras.

The day at Sandringham was a relaxed affair and that was the way the king liked it. His stammer had virtually disappeared thanks to the services of a maverick Australian speech therapist called Lionel Logue. On the drives, both Simon and Ash were happy to take turns with their loaders.

At lunch, Elizabeth made a point of speaking to Michael and congratulating him and Victoria and asked him to pass on congratulations to Joanna and Jeremy on their new arrival. She gave him a special phone number so that any of them could come up and go riding with Lilibet as she was missing them with fewer visits since the coronation because of the pressure on the king. She was keen to maintain the private family relationship that went back a long way. Lilibet was now coming up for her twelfth birthday. Her riding ability and confidence had improved considerably.

Once the other guests had departed, the king had a private audience with Simon, Ash, Boynton and Michael. He temporarily forgot his regal role and spoke to them as a fellow member of the north Norfolk community that meant so much to him. Sandringham was his favourite part of the kingdom, and he tried to spend as much time as he could there, but the political necessity of the role required more time than he would have liked to be spent at Windsor and Buckingham Palace. He went overboard in his praise for the way they had protected the Norfolk community of which he counted himself and his family as fully paid-up members. Whilst his private views on dealing with the criminal element who threatened his people were fully supported by this audience it was not something that would be appropriate for the press. Prior to departure he made it clear that he wanted to see as much as possible of his true Norfolk friends and henceforth Michael and Gabriel Boynton would be included on Christian name terms in private. To him, it was so important to have real trusted friends in whose company he could relax. He and Elizabeth shook hands with each of them in turn with a firmness that underlined the point he had made.

They left at 6pm and got back to the Hall an hour later. On the way back Boynton commented that he had been taken aback by all the fuss. As far as he was concerned it was a simple ambush and the type of thing he had carried out dozens of times in the desert and Ireland. Ash and Simon could understand that. They said that in wartime acts of courage often go by without any recognition, but in peacetime, the reverse is true. It was all a question of relativity, but nobody was going to change that, and, in any event, it was never wise to look a gift horse in the mouth. Boynton also mentioned that the Sandringham gamekeeper had tried to recruit him.

"What did you say?" asked Simon.

"I told him to stick it where the sun doesn't shine. Born

in Spelthorpe, die in Spelthorpe. That's my life mapped out although I'm not inviting the final chapter quite yet and nor is Aggie."

When they arrived at the Hall Amrik came out with the message that all the ladies including Aggie were awaiting them at the cottage.

On arrival, it was apparent that much alcohol had been consumed, and the only sober ones amongst them were baby James and the Labradors. Countess Helen piped up with slightly slurred speech. "You boys are not the only ones who were going to have some fun today. We did too and it's been bloody marvellous!"

It was surprising because nobody had ever quite seen her like that before. The boys took it well and joined in the spontaneous event that had lightened up the post-Christmas doldrums. They understood from wartime the pressures on those who wait. The events of the past two days had inevitably had an effect that was not readily visible from the outside, particularly to those who had gone into a disciplined mode to deal with the situation. The girls had welcomed Aggie into their inner circle along with the soon-to-be newly baptised Gabriel.

It was too good a bonding opportunity to miss out on, so they all remained for a couple of hours.

In a few days with the start of Lent term, the normal routine would resume. To some those last few days of holiday were precious indeed.

5

Lent term

January – April 1938

On the following two days Michael and Victoria were up early to carry out the ploughing. They had a team of two Suffolk punch horses and on the first day Michael managed a full acre which was good for a novice. It was reckoned that a single horse in experienced hands could manage one acre in a day, but that meant days when light levels were longer and not mid-winter.

As promised Victoria went back to the Hall to stay the night only to be met by her mother. Clearly the party had affected Helen who simply said, "Why have you come back here? Get back to your future husband because that is where you belong!"

They spent an hour together. Helen had been impressed with the wardrobe selection as modelled at the ladies' event of the previous day, but Victoria had remained sufficiently sober not to model the alluring underwear and nightwear. Helen was pleased that Victoria was fully prepared to honour her agreement but as far as she was concerned a new and more mature relationship was evolving between them. That was what she aspired to in the long term. She told Victoria that she had been pleased that young George had taken to Lucy's riding tuition, so things were looking brighter in that area. Edward's isolation might be problematic, but time would tell.

Victoria unexpectedly returned to the cottage at 7 pm. She explained her mother's welcome change of mindset and thanked Lisette because she had no doubt that Lisette's initiative had brought about the new direction. She took supper with them all, then showered and went to bed. As an experiment she tried on the alluring nightwear. Despite Michael's apparent tiredness from the ploughing, the effect of the nightwear reversed the exhaustion and markedly so. After further nocturnal exercise, they both slept soundly. On the following day they took two extra horses for the ploughing. With double the horsepower, they managed almost three acres between them.

Both were determined to make the most of the final Saturday and Sunday. On Saturday morning they exercised the ponies and dogs along the beach and in the afternoon the wind picked up, so they went flight shooting the pigeons for the last two hours of daylight on the edge of the woodland where the flight lines came in from across the fields. Lucy came too, along with all the dogs apart from Trooper and Rafe who needed a rest after the morning. They took up positions about a hundred yards apart along well-established lines that the birds would always take. A lot of ladies would only use the lighter twenty bore gun but not these two. They had learnt from the very start that the heavier twelve bore put more shot into the air and the more shot, the cleaner the kill, and that was the object of the exercise. The higher wind brought the birds lower down. It made them faster but well within range, and if the shooter gave the right amount of 'lead', then the results would be good. All three had mastered this, so they concentrated on the shooting, and the dogs did the rest.

The whole thing was a glorious experience. Shooting was the only effective way of control. Nothing would go to waste. Being in the open air with the wind and the bare silhouettes of the trees against the winter sunset was something that can only be appreciated by those who have experienced it. To go home to a log fire and a glass of sloe gin put the icing on the cake. It was good just to be alive and to be able to do that. Between them they got forty pigeons, and those stewed up with vegetables and mixed with Winalot would feed all the dogs and cats for several days.

Early on Monday morning it was back on with the school uniforms, but all three knew there were only eighteen weeks of this before their lives would change forever.

Within days the normal routine had re-established itself. At Spelthorpe just one shoot day remained, and that was a commercial day. It went well, and although the birds on the estate were more spread-out Boynton and his team had managed to round up 250 pheasant hens, and they had been enclosed to prevent them getting shot. They would provide the eggs for the next season. He had also managed to concentrate most of the cock birds in areas where they would be driven over the guns to create an impression of bountiful numbers overall. Just before the end of the season, more hens would be rounded up for egg laying duty along with up to fifty cock birds needed for fertilisation. The same applied to the partridges. Fifty deer had been selected and culled. Most had been butchered and sent to market, but a few carcasses had been retained for domestic consumption. Ash had a large haunch that would serve several family meals along with two forelegs for sausages and some lesser cuts that would be stripped off the bone for dog consumption.

Michael and Victoria did find it difficult being back at school as they were both boarded on site, but the school grounds were extensive. A limited degree of intimacy was achieved, but both were sensible in that area. They maintained their studies with diligence as final examinations would take place in a few months. Weekends provided what they yearned for.

Aggie's new looks came as a shock. She openly wore her engagement ring and made no secret of the forthcoming wedding. In mid-January she made a formal application for the post at Spelthorpe School. A rapidly convened governors' meeting determined that an interview should take place, and the panel would consist of Countess Helen as Chair of Governors, Lisette, Paddy and one of the two parent governors.

On Saturday the fifth of February, at the Hall, the formal interview took place. They went through a series of background questions and ideas that she put forward. Aggie intimated that she would have liked to have visited the school, but that had been difficult because of her current role, and she did not wish to be seen as meddling whilst another head was in charge. She said that there is more to a school than the building. The school will always be the pupils and staff and with that in mind she had discreetly talked to children and parents as she walked around the estate and village, but this had been done in a way so as not to give any inkling as to what was afoot.

Helen asked what she felt the school needed most. Aggie felt that the school needed an outside sports field with some permanent courts for a variety of sports and she had identified two acres of land to the west of the churchyard that would fulfil this requirement. It was a five-minute walk from the school. Sport was important for developing self-discipline, healthy competition and team building. Aggie felt that in a coastal village all the children should be able to swim. Reading, writing and arithmetic were vital but as passports to all the other areas of education. She intimated that by speaking with parents, they too could be encouraged to help, and ideally, they should be working towards a situation where all children could read before they got to school. That way, they would hit the ground running when they started.

Lisette asked one final question: "If you had to answer in one simple sentence what your attitude to education is, what would that be?"

Aggie answered, "Education is not about filling buckets; it is about lighting fires!"

With such a response, the panel was spellbound. After a short break the panel reconvened.

Helen simply said, "The job is yours and the sooner you start lighting fires, the better!"

Two days later, she received the official letter of acceptance. On receipt of that, she wrote her letter of resignation from her current post to take effect from the end of the summer term. The three teachers at the school were informed that an individual had been selected as head teacher and that would be formally announced one month before the end of the summer term.

At the end of February, the King's Lynn coroner presided over the inquest on the two armed robbers. The coroner asked for Ash, Boynton, Michael and Jasmir to be present as witnesses. Simon came along in support, and as a precaution he had appointed a King's Counsel to act for him and Spelthorpe in case of any issues because, given the nature of the case, the coroner was required to have a jury to decide on a verdict as to the circumstances relating to the deaths. The press was present and there was no way of preventing that.

As it turned out, there was little need for concern. The full circumstances of the case were outlined by DCI Skingle. He had done a thorough job, and the coroner intimated that he would be happy for statements to be read rather than direct evidence. The DCI stated that both offenders had been identified by fingerprints. Both were known to the police, and he outlined a long list of previous convictions for serious violence. For the last twenty years they had spent most of their time as guests of His Majesty and on each release, they carried out more violent crimes. He was able to link them to over twenty offences of armed robbery and four shootings that had taken place over the month before the Spelthorpe case. Statements were read out. The coroner summarised the evidence and in conclusion said. "Members of the jury. These two men had a long history of violence and carried out a string of robberies in which four innocent members of the public were shot, and it was only due to the skill of the doctors that there were no fatalities. Numerous members of the public were terrorised in the raids. When they were finally confronted and presented with an option to surrender, they came out fighting with guns in their hands. With full justification they were shot dead. In the circumstances, there is only one verdict that you can properly return, and that is one of justifiable homicide. Will you now retire and consider this?"

The jury retired and came back in less than ten minutes with a verdict of justifiable homicide. They asked if they could add a rider thanking Ash, Boynton and Michael for their quick thinking and courage. The coroner commended the three for the splendid service they had rendered the people of Norfolk and their care in keeping them safe. He also commended the Detective Chief Inspector for the thoroughness of his investigation and ordered that the costs of the King's Counsel be met from public funds. This was of both local and national importance. The case was fully reported under the headline:

'Justifiable homicide verdict on armed robbers. Veteran war heroes and a schoolboy commended by Coroner for their service to the public'.

Ash thanked the DCI and invited him to pop in at any time he was passing.

Although the school was not identified it was immediately obvious to all at the school that they had a hero in their midst. The headmaster dealt with the issue with a full disclosure and his own commendation but instructed that there be no further discussion within the school as the matter was now closed and to prolong things would be unfair.

So, the affair was finally over, although in four months' time an announcement was made in the London Gazette that the king had seen fit to award Ash Cromwell, Michael Cromwell and Gabriel Boynton with the British Empire Medal for service to the Norfolk community.

Two days later at 2 pm on the Saturday Michael, Lucy, Victoria and her brothers were dropped off at the Hall for the rest of the weekend. Michael and Victoria dashed back to the cottage to change. Lucy had gone to the village shop and would get back later. The dogs welcomed them. Ash and Lisette were out. They flew up the stairs and as the uniforms came off their feelings overtook them. What followed was brief, noisy and passionate – an understandable reaction to the frustration of the school regime where at times, they were so close yet so far away. Furthermore, although there was never any doubt in respect of the inquest, the fact that it was going to take place had overshadowed their relationship. Victoria had turned eighteen half-way through the first week back at school but other than a cake and candles at the school there had been little else to mark the occasion. With the compass reset, normality could resume. An intimate family gathering had been planned for Sunday afternoon at the Hall to make up for it, now that the grey cloud had finally passed over.

As soon as they had changed into their Spelthorpe rags, they were off to the stables with Hunter and Odi. They picked up two ponies and went on to Boynton's. As had been arranged, Victoria took Aggie out for a ride along the woodland trails with the dogs. Aggie had picked up the basics over the last few weeks and was gaining confidence.

In the meantime, Boynton and Michael set to work on starting to gather eggs from the penned pheasants and to place them in the incubators in the barn. The penned pheasants had ribbons tied onto one wing side creating an imbalance that stopped them from flying and a few male pheasants had been placed in each pen to fertilise the hens. This was time-consuming, but a lot cheaper than buying in pheasants from elsewhere. Whilst they did this Boynton continued with his survival tuition. On previous weeks they had dealt with weaponry, car stealing, housebreaking, improvised explosives, incendiaries, booby trap setting, techniques for a quick clean kill and dealing with personal attacks. Not all of this was about the killing side. Getting away and avoiding contact was probably more important because all contact increased risk. Boynton kept drumming it in.

"Trust nobody, keep at least an arm's length away from any opponent and watch him, watch his eyes, his hands and any movement and always prepare for what might happen. Stand slightly sideways on so you give him less of a target and with your feet perpendicular for a stable platform. Always have or think about an escape route! If you see a chance to strike, do it, but do it quickly and with extreme violence. Never hesitate, because when you hesitate, they get the advantage."

He talked about reading the landscape and using it to avoid trouble and to become invisible. There were good times to travel. Moonlight was good but never in pitch darkness because you could injure yourself in a fall. Tread quietly and watch the ground so as not to make twigs snap and look for trip wires. Hug hedgerows so as not to be silhouetted. It was important to stop and listen at regular intervals and to sniff the air. You could detect cigarette smoke from hundreds of yards away. All soldiers smoke and some even wear aftershave so you could smell them at a distance. Importantly you must not smell yourself, so no smoking and if you see a dung heap, roll in it so you smell like the countryside. And so, his lessons went on with constant challenges and questions and new material that gave Michael an insight that few others would get. Michael always remembered Boynton's opening remark. "It's never your job to die for your country. Your job is to make the other bastard die for his."

Just as it was getting dark Victoria and Aggie returned. They had been right around the southern end of the estate and met up with the other underkeeper, Brian, who was engaged with the eggs and incubators in the same way as Boynton. Brian was with his wife and three children, and they were all helping out. He was pleased to see them as his cottage was the most isolated on the entire estate, but he had a phone. They seemed happy there. The children went to the village school. Aggie asked him what they wanted from the school. What Brian wanted was more help on what and how to teach them himself and books to help them read at home, especially in the long holidays when the children forgot things. Aggie said that there were opportunities all the time. Counting eggs and dividing them was a maths lesson. All that was needed was the spark to set things off, and she felt that would be coming soon. Michael and Victoria had tea with the Boyntons then took off back to the stables.

The following day went as expected. They walked to the church and took Odi with them. They inspected the new red oak trees but had to imagine what they would be like once in leaf. In the mid afternoon there a was family gathering and late lunch at the Hall to belatedly mark Victoria's eighteenth birthday with just the Cromwells and Spelthorpes in attendance. Victoria opened presents but when Edward and George were out of the room, she said that the biggest present that she could have, was the arrangement that had been made for her and Michael. At this moment Michael produced a little box which he handed to Victoria. Inside was a diamond and sapphire pendant and earrings that matched the engagement ring.

It was perfect and she cried with the happiness and commitment that these gifts represented.

She asked Michael, "How did you manage this because we have always been together?"

"But not at the inquest," said Michael. "Whilst the others were in the pub beforehand talking to the King's Counsel, I popped out for half an hour and sorted it."

She held him firmly and kissed him in front of them all.

On the following day, reality kicked in. School resumed, and the first of the new lambs had started to arrive. Lisette's father had been in touch to say that he had secured an interview for Lucy at the foreign office in London on Tuesday the twenty-sixth of April, but as they would be over before that he would be able to brief her as to what to expect.

Michael and Victoria continued their Saturday afternoon visits to the Boyntons and became quite close. Aggie was taking on the mantle of a country lady and keeper's wife. Her ideas for the school had fallen on fertile ground. Helen had agreed to finance the playing field works from her Kenya funds, and after talking through the issue with Aggie, work started almost straight away. Helen was determined to create a lasting legacy for the school and the people of Spelthorpe, so they settled on a total of four acres with a grass area to support a football pitch, a netball court, two all-weather tennis courts and an area for safe archery. There would be a pavilion with changing rooms and covered decking and a brick garage for storage of a tractor, mower and other equipment. In addition, there would be a play park with swings, a slide and other apparatus. The whole area would be fenced in a way to exclude dogs. Over a hundred trees of differing varieties would be planted in stands to create shade and interest around parts of the perimeter. In fact, they would have, in a reduced form, all the facilities that were available at Aggie's current school. In due course it would be opened as Countess Helen's Recreation Field.

At school, work was well underway for the final exams. Michael was majoring in history, geography, French and maths, Victoria in French, economics, history and geography and Lucy in French, English, history and Latin.

6

The return of Biggles

U p on the airfield over the last year, there had been many significant changes and these were paying off. It was now run as a limited company, but the direction and shareholding remained with the estate. It was in operating profit but that was largely because the capital cost had been met by Helen from her Kenya funds, and that meant there were no interest repayments and no land charges, unlike other enterprises. The actual runways were grass and could be harvested and grazed when there was no flying taking place. The company now owned a de Havilland Dragon Rapide, a Tiger Moth and two Gipsy Moth aircraft and was effectively running as a flying school and charter business. All the aircraft could be safely housed in the main hangar, and a secondary hangar had been built for maintenance purposes. In addition, there was a conference and dining facility with training rooms and a restaurant and bar with overnight accommodation of ten rooms. Three houses were provided nearby: a detached house for the chief executive and instructor and two semis for the deputy instructor and the head mechanic. It was fortunate that the three wives ran the office and hotel side of the business, and this included the chalets between the boathouse and the lake. Ladies from the village carried out cleaning, cooking, serving and laundry services on an ad hoc basis, but for larger events, the Hall's domestic staff would come up.

Half a mile away from the airfield on the edge of the woodland at the top end of the valley, a shooting school had been set up. This operated by pre-booking on days when there was no game shooting. Boynton and the underkeepers were the instructors and liked the set up because the tips from rich clients could be quite generous. Some of the retired workers from the estate would operate the clay pigeon traps and do the scoring. It gave them a few hours out and a bit of pocket money. This had gone down well with some of the parties staying in the lakeside chalets who would often come up in the chartered Dagon Rapide. There was a small brick-built lodge for storage and light refreshment. Ash was pleased because it meant that novice shooters had the opportunity to get some practice and that might mean more birds cleanly shot.

Squadron Leader Peregrine Smith MC or 'Stooper' as he was known – a veteran of the Great War with twenty-five victories, was in overall charge. Like so many others, he had come up in the ranks, starting as mere mechanic, then progressing to observer and finally a pilot where his success in the sky resulted in rapid promotion. His deputy, Jim Barker, had joined slightly later after the Royal Air Force had been created from the Royal Flying Corps (part of the army) in 1918 and despite only three months flying in the war he had gained twelve victories. He remained in the RAF for ten more years serving mainly in the Middle East until he finally left the service in 1930 as a flight lieutenant. Both were experienced instructors and national examiners. Most of those who flew in the Royal Flying Corps were public-schoolboys and had joined the army at a time when it was felt that only public-schoolboys had the right leadership qualities. They sometimes mocked those who had come up the hard way. However, it soon became apparent that many of those with humble beginnings were better pilots and with so many losses the RAF was forced not only to accept them, but to promote them too. Britain's top two aces in the war were initially maligned because they had been 'born in the barracks', and that simply was 'just not on' for an officer. The army, too, was afflicted with snobbery, more so in some regiments than others, but the winds of change were afoot. Prior to that, it had only been in the navy that a truer form of meritocracy existed, but even there, family wealth, social rank and position carried a degree of weight which meant that bumblers might unfairly rise to levels and roles which they were unfit to carry out.

On the afternoon of Saturday the second of April, as usual, Michael and Victoria went up to the Boyntons with the horses, but Michael walked on the short distance to the hangar where Peregrine 'Stooper' Smith was waiting for him. It was good flying weather with a few cumulus clouds at 2,000 feet.

"Hello, Biggles," said Peregrine. "Nice to see you back!"

With the winter weather and school commitments, there had been fewer opportunities since Michael had qualified back in the autumn. Michael shook hands with his instructor.

"Today we have a couple of things. Firstly, I want to check you out in the Tiger Moth and if that is OK, you can show me what you can do, then I have something special. So, it's over to you. Pretend I'm not here."

Michael walked over to the plane and carried out a full visual inspection. Then he got in the cockpit and checked out the control lines, the instrument panel and for any loose articles in both cockpits. When he was satisfied, he bid Stooper into the plane and checked his straps. He did the same for himself. Stooper had asked him to do a couple of take-offs and landings and a few circuits.

Michael took off and performed the first task with ease. It was then that Stooper said,

"Right, Biggles. You show me what you can do. I won't hit the controls myself unless we start to go wrong."

Michael took off and climbed to 2,000 feet. Then, he did a series of loops, rolls and stall turns. He took the plane up another thousand feet, then put it into a spin, pulling out cleanly at 1,000 feet.

He had seen Aggie and Victoria riding on the ridge above the valley going towards the castle keep, so he put the plane in a dive then pulled out and flew at maximum speed winding down the valley just above the tree line and lower still as the trees met the salt marsh beyond the castle. He took the plane up to 3,000 feet and went parallel to the coast above the lake, where he took the plane into a loop gaining height but at the top rolled over and came back on himself having turned with the half loop and roll. He dropped down to 500 feet, at which point Stooper signalled for him to return to base. Three minutes later they were on the ground. Michael taxied back close to the hangar, and they alighted.

"Well, Biggles," said Stooper. "I'm not one for lavish praise but that was impressive, and what do you call the last manoeuvre?"

Michael replied, "That was my Immelmann turn. I read about it, so I thought I would give it a go."

Stooper came back, "For a first attempt that was quite good, so you are into fighter tactics now. I will go over that in the summer when I teach you how to survive in the sky, but from now until then we will concentrate on air navigation and your first lesson is not in this kite. We are going to up in the Dragon, but no aerobatics in that please. I want you to take her up because next Saturday, weather permitting, you are taking her to France to pick up your grandparents. Simon is going with you, and he has flown it dozens of times, but now it's your turn."

They spent half an hour going over the aircraft, then they jumped in. This was very different with an enclosed cockpit and a great deal more comfort. They sat side by side with Michael at the controls.

"I want you to take me to Lincoln and back. Given the fuel level, I want you to give me a flight plan and timings. We will cruise at 130 mph." said Stooper.

Michael looked at the map. "Sixty-five miles in each direction on an outward bearing of 285 degrees and return on 115 degrees. We have a headwind of twenty mph, but that is countered by a tail wind for the return which makes outbound slower and the return faster, so approximately one hour plus another ten minutes for climbing and a turn. The tank is half full, so we return with enough for another 130 miles."

"Take us there then," said Stooper. "When we get back you can have a twenty-minute play to build your confidence. We fly at 1,500 feet."

And so, Michael took off. He was impressed by the increased power of the two engines. All went according to plan. They flew around the cathedral and came straight back across the wash, and then Michael spent the next twenty minutes getting the feel of the aircraft. It lacked the manoeuvrability of the Tiger Moth, but he didn't want to push matters. Michael made three landings and take offs. By 5-pm the lesson was done.

"By the way," said Stooper. "That was your qualification test. We took a few shortcuts, but I am happy, so you are now qualified to fly twin-engine aircraft. I'll get a certificate to you. Between now and the summer, we will do some night flights and low cloud flying, and we will get you qualified on that too, and after that, it's tactics, so when you land at Cranwell, you should hit the ground running, but you may have to bite your lip for a bit. I'll come to that later."

Michael walked the fifteen minutes back to the keeper's cottage. "Did you have a good ride?" he asked Aggie and Victoria.

"It was OK until some maniac came flying down the valley. He was lower down than we were!" said a grinning Aggie.

"That wasn't me. That was Biggles!" he said.

Michael and Victoria rode back, leaving the horses at the stables. On returning to the cottage, they took all the dogs out for a quiet walk on the beach. Whilst the dogs played in the surf, they watched the sun go down over the castle keep and held each other close. In less than a week, the term would be over, and they would have almost a month without restriction in a place they never wanted to leave.

7

Oh, to be in England!

April 1938

The Easter holiday came, and with it joy for Michael and Victoria that for almost a whole month the new regime was back. All around, spring was fully evident with the horse chestnuts and hawthorn in full leaf, and the race was on between oak and ash as to who would be the first for the buds to burst. In the woods and on grassy banks, primroses abounded, and the first bluebells were showing through. The meadows were a mass of dandelions. With lambing over, the lambs frolicked in small groups but dashed back to their mothers when they had the urge to feed. The sun could be quite powerful but every now and again there would be a shower, but this was April, and it was uplifting that after the winter darkness, at last, there was a new beginning.

School had ended early at 2 pm on Friday the eighth of April. By 3pm, the children were back on the estate. Michael had already worked out his flight plan for the following day. At 7.30pm whilst supper was being cooked Michael, Victoria and Lucy walked the dogs down to the lake. The sun had been on it all day and there was nobody else around.

Michael said, "It's no good. I can't resist it,"

With that he tore off all his clothes and jumped in off the springboard. All the dogs apart from Trooper and Rafe ran along the board and took the plunge, too.

Victoria said, "Oh, why not?"

Spontaneously the two girls stripped naked and ran into the water.

It was a little cold, but it was a wonderful celebration of total freedom. Trooper and Rafe, now showing their age, sat together on the bank, surveying the scene in the sunset glow.

After a quarter of an hour, the three emerged. There was not the slightest hint of embarrassment as they shook themselves dry before putting their clothes back on.

When they got back to the cottage, Lisette had made a venison pie.

Lucy piped up, "No need for showers tonight, Mummy. We all went in the lake."

"You had no towels or costumes," said Lisette, pretending to be shocked but sporting a broad grin.

"There was no one about, so we just did it and it was great. Not too cold, so we can start up again, but we will wear our costumes for Grandma and Grandad when they get here," said Michael.

"And your mother and I will make sure there's nothing under the water while you are picking them up tomorrow," said Ash.

The following day Michael was up early. He shared a quick breakfast with Victoria, then grabbed his passport, his flight plans, and a wad of French francs and they were off to the Hall.

Victoria had elected to spend the morning with her mother. Simon came out with George and the three of them went up to the airfield. Michael handed his flight plan to Simon, then did all the checks on the Dragon Rapide. At a pinch they might be able to get back without refuelling with a capacity of seventy-six gallons, but Michael had reckoned on a top up of thirty gallons in France to be on the safe side.

Stooper was up with Jim and waiting for their first two clients for pilot training. They would normally give them an hour in the classroom followed by up to an hour in the air. Saturday was normally quite busy and even more so as the weather improved. There was an increased demand as people had been inspired by the likes of Amy Johnson and others. Several ladies were on the books. Today, they had a total of eight trainees.

As planned Michael took off on a direct route taking the plane slightly east of Greenwich, then over Surrey and Sussex to Beachy Head and thence across a hundred miles of Channel. It was 270 miles on the map so considering a slight cross wind they should touch down at Carpiquet airport on the western side of Caen in two hours and ten minutes. Visibility was good with some cumulostratus cloud at 6,000 feet but that should clear with the morning sun. Simon was impressed by Michael's disciplined approach. It was obvious that Stooper was doing a good job. For George, it was his first time up and he seemed to be enjoying every minute of it. His brother Edward had shown no interest whatsoever.

They crossed the French coast at Luc-sur-Mer. On the left Michael could make out the village of Ranville where his grandparents lived. It was five miles to the east of their flight path. Michael spoke to the tower in French and was given permission to land and told where to go after landing.

Overall, it could not have been better. Michael knew the

whole coastline well from his summer visits. From home to Normandy, it would normally take at least fifteen hours of travelling plus an overnight stop at Folkestone or Boulogne, so effectively, they had cut a twenty-five-hour journey down to a mere two hours. They were on half a tank on arrival, so they put in another thirty gallons. After Michael had greeted the airport officials warmly in French, nothing was too much trouble for them. They dispensed with any passport formalities altogether. That was so often the way with the French. The simple trouble to speak to them in their own language demonstrated respect and an appreciation of France and its people. They invariably reacted in a very positive way. So many other British people made no effort whatsoever and then they wondered why the French ignored them. Simon was aware of this from the war where a simple "Voulez-vous promenez avec moi madame," could sometimes get far beyond what the average Tommy had expected.

Michael walked into the waiting room and greeted his grandparents with enthusiasm. He saw there was a small shop, so he went in and purchased a premium bottle of Calvados, which he presented to Simon.

"You'll like this. Just a little token of appreciation for making this possible, but don't tell Dad because he'll help you polish off the lot."

They boarded the plane. Michael quickly checked all around, and when he sat in the pilot's seat his grandparents looked at each other in surprise and even more so when he spoke to the tower and promptly took off. He flew west for twelve miles and gave them views of the Bayeux Cathedral then he flew northeast for 5 miles to the coast and along the shore to the Caen canal and river and around Ranville barely a mile away. That provided an aerial view of their home. He dropped down to 1,000 feet and did a couple of circuits so his grandfather could take some pictures.

He then headed back across the Channel and forty minutes later they were back over Beachy Head.

"How do you navigate this?" asked his grandfather.

Michael handed back a Shell roadmap. "This is quite handy," he said. "And sometimes they let me use a compass."

He took them along the coast at 1,500 feet over Eastbourne Pier, then northeast to Canterbury for a couple of quick circuits around the cathedral, then over the small fishing port of Whitstable. They flew across the Thames Estuary, then directly north to Spelthorpe where they landed one hour later.

To say the least Michael's confidence was impressive, and his grandparents had no idea that he was now a fully qualified pilot although they did know that he was heading into the RAF in the autumn. He now appeared to them in a totally different light to the adventurous schoolboy who had spent his summers with them for the last few years.

Michael topped up the fuel to full, then parked the aircraft on its allocated spot and filled in the flight logs. In the meantime, Ash, Lisette, Lucy, Helen and Victoria had come up to the airstrip in the Morris to welcome the guests and witness the landing. They had been talking to Stooper about Michael's prowess although he constantly referred to him as Biggles and somehow the name had stuck. Victoria walked up to Biggles and kissed him. There would be some explaining to do as the grandparents were not in on the secret yet. Michael thought that was best done by his parents so he carried the bags to the Morris and said that he and Victoria would walk back to the cottage.

Michael and Victoria walked back via the Boyntons who were working with the newly hatched chicks. They took tea with them, then walked back to the cottage via the woodland thinking that Ash and Lisette would need at least a couple of hours to settle the grandparents in and update them about the secret engagement and wedding scheduled for August. They returned to the cottage at 5 pm. The grandparents were sitting outside taking tea beside the large oak at the front of the cottage. The dogs were sitting with them and Grandma was nursing one of the cats. They appeared very relaxed. With the spare guest bedroom at the cottage and improved facilities, there had been no need to move anyone around. When they spotted the pair, they both stood up and walked towards them.

Michael's grandfather said, "Warmest congratulations to you both. Your mother has explained everything to us, and we heartily approve. Life is about seizing the moment, and you have certainly done that."

His grandmother added, "We did wonder back last summer when all three of you turned up. You two seemed so very close and now it all makes sense. You are good for each other, and that's so important."

Michael and Victoria sat with them for an hour and explained their plans and aspirations. It sounded good. Dinner was scheduled for 7pm so they asked if they wanted to come to the lake to see them swimming. The offer was taken up. Ash and Lucy came too, with all the dogs, but on this occasion, the only ones permitted not to wear costumes were the dogs.

Over the next week the grandparents had a splendid time. Lucy spent several hours with her grandfather talking about current issues and the role of embassy personnel, so she knew what to expect at her interview. On the Monday, Lisette went with Helen, Victoria and Grandma to Norwich to select and order dresses for the bride and her attendants while Ash and Michael took Grandpa up to the shooting school. Lucy and George went too.

They met Boynton who introduced Grandpa and George to clay shooting. Over the last few weeks, it was noticeable that George was finally coming out of his shell. Simon was pleased with the efforts that members of the greater Spelthorpe Company were putting in to get him to do that. On the other hand, Edward stubbornly resisted anything that would take him away from his world of mathematics. He had a few friends at school who displayed a similar mindset.

Later that week, Michael took his grandfather up for thirty minutes in the Tiger Moth and after ensuring he was fully willing and properly strapped in, he did a couple of loops and rolls. His grandmother declined the offer but was delighted that her husband still had it in him.

Ash and Lisette took them to Cromer, where after a walk on the pier, they took them for a slap-up lunch at the Hotel de Paris. Lisette's parents intimated that they were looking forward to the wedding. It was fortunate that it fitted in superbly with other arrangements they had made as they had planned to come across at that time for a three-week tour looking up old friends from Lisette's father's days in the diplomatic service. For the rest of the time, they just enjoyed being at Spelthorpe and all it had to offer in April.

On the Saturday, Michael flew them back in the Dragon Rapide and this time Lisette and Victoria went along for the ride. The weather was good, although they experienced a couple of showers as they crossed the French coast. On the way back, they flew around the Isle of Wight and over Windsor Castle and Cambridge.

The following day was Easter Sunday, and this meant a full attendance at church. Arrangements were made for a spot of riding for Victoria and Lucy with Joanna and Jennifer. Since leaving school, the regular contact had been lost, and all the girls were keen to maintain their close relationship. Jennifer was nearly five years into her medical training and increasingly she was undergoing hospital placements. Currently she was at King's Lynn, but she did manage two days off most weeks, and her holidays matched school holidays, albeit a little shorter. Her finals were scheduled for a year hence. Joanna's clientele at the small animal side of the veterinary practice was showing a marked increase. Her mother, Julia, was always pleased to take young James, who was now in his fourth month.

In the meantime, Michael was doing two sessions every week in the air with Stooper and, for part of the holiday was undertaking farm work of all sorts to maintain his savings as Julian always insisted that any of the youngsters be paid at the standard rate. Victoria never minded because she was doing the same, and every night was spent where they wanted to be. That more than made up for things. The horses and dogs still got plenty of exercise and use of the lake increased as they got back to their old ways.

St George's Day was the occasion for the Boynton wedding. The two previous days had been wet but, on this day, they were bathed in glorious sunshine. There was a huge turnout at the church, and even some of Boynton's old flames had turned up to wish him well. Many of the teaching staff from Aggie's school turned out. In the front row, in the care of Lucy, were Boynton's dogs, Black and Tan. Reverend Paddy was more than happy with that. There were no bridesmaids, but Joanna and Jennifer played Vaughan Williams' '*Prelude on Rosymedre*' on violin and cello as Aggie walked up the aisle. It was not the conventional wedding tune, but it suited the setting of a country church and estate with beauty all around. It was simply sublime. There was hardly a dry eye anywhere in the building. Both bride and groom looked stunning. With both parents deceased, Aggie had asked the headmaster of her school to give her away. This had a profound, deeper meaning as, given her recent resignation, the school's loss was the village school's gain. Ash was the best man. A reception for sixty guests was held in the Hall. That, along with a return flight to their honeymoon destination, was the wedding gift from the estate.

At the reception, Ash praised their dedication to their respective roles. Hitherto those constraints had held them back from true fulfilment, but they had got there in the end. Above all, they were good for each other, and they were doing all sorts of things that their previous lives had denied them. Both were blissfully happy.

The victors for the day were the happy couple and the Spelthorpe community, as news had now leaked out as to Aggie's forthcoming role. People had eventually guessed, and nobody had issued a denial. The work on the land next to the church was an indication of what was to come.

Spelthorpe now had two named angels: St Michael (the name of the church) and now Gabriel. Both had a reputation for protecting all that was good. On behalf of the whole community, he wished them, health and true happiness, and that was seconded with a huge cheer.

Gabriel and Aggie mingled with their guests. Aggie's colleagues confirmed that she had made the right choice, and some of her female friends hid a secret envy for what she had achieved. There was something deeply appealing to them in her union with somebody who came across to them as a real man. The headmaster discretely mooted that he would like to see Aggie as a governor of the school she was about to leave. He was acutely aware of the advantages available to the privileged few and recognised that children of humble beginnings often displayed a flair and determination that was lacking in some born with silver spoons in their mouths. Consequently, he felt that there was much to be gained from the school having a close relationship with the village school. Kindred philanthropic motives had existed with their Victorian forefathers, and there was a good reason to maintain them. Since, and partially due to the war, it was more frequently seen that those on the bottom rung with a sense of purpose could reach the top. A guiding hand could make all the difference.

On the following morning Michael and Ash flew them down to the Lea Farm airport on the Isle of Wight near Sandown, where a taxi was waiting to take them to their Ventnor hotel for the next three nights.

As the Easter holiday came to the last full week it was time for Lucy to head to London for her interview at the foreign office. Lisette went on the train with her as it presented a rare opportunity to purchase a few odd items that were not normally available in rural Norfolk.

To get her in the mood, they spoke French to one another for the whole journey. The interview was scheduled for twelve noon, and on arrival, it was apparent that several other contenders had gone through the same ordeal. Having taken her grandfather's advice, she was dressed smartly and in a way that embassy staff were expected to dress, with nothing ostentatious. There were three people carrying out the interview. Two appeared quite senior, and there was a younger woman in her mid-thirties with a slight French accent that gave away the reason she was there. Lucy was asked the usual questions as to her background and education and why she was applying now rather than by going to university first. She explained that rather than spending three years away, she had done a lot of research already and that she felt that her French was at a level where she could cope, and importantly, be of service. In her view, three years of work with real experts in their field would equip her better than any degree, and she wanted to start now rather than later. Working on the coal face in the embassy with the people who knew the reality, would in her view be better than a purely academic foray into the issues. She outlined her analysis of the current political situation and felt that she could be of use. Importantly she felt that with her background she had a greater understanding of the way the French think, and that would help her.

At that point the interview changed into the French language, and Lucy was able to impress with her vocabulary of diplomatic terms and language that would not be available to others without a great deal of research. They bombarded her with searching questions and really put her through the mill, but she could see that she was making headway in this area and hoped it would single her out from the others. With each question she demonstrated that she recognised both sides of the argument and came to a conclusion based on the evidence.

The interview concluded with a question: "Where would you like to serve if we were to take you on?"

Lucy replied, "Naturally I would like Tahiti or Martinique, but in all seriousness, I would serve anywhere you wish to send me because with an open mind, I realise that wherever I go, there is always something new to learn. It is those challenges that would make the work even more interesting. I seek to learn and to serve."

The panel seemed to like the touch of humour at the end. Before Lucy left, she made a point of thanking them all for the opportunity and offered her hand which they all accepted. They asked if she would wait outside whilst they deliberated. The fifteen-minute wait seemed an eternity. Lucy could feel her heart beating.

In the discussion that followed behind closed doors, it was clear they had a candidate with a maturity well in advance of her years. The two elder members knew her grandfather. She had demonstrated her knowledge and thorough preparation. In their collective view here was a candidate who could almost hit the ground running. Her French was perfect.

They invited her back in after fifteen minutes.

The chairman said, "Miss Cromwell. You have impressed us all and because of your knowledge and command of the language, we are prepared to offer you a post as a trainee foreign service officer. That would normally be open only to graduates, but you have demonstrated that you have the skills we require and as we do not want to miss out on an opportunity, we are making this exception. We know you have to finish your schooling so we would like you to start here for a two-week induction into the service on the fifth of September. After that you will be posted to Paris. Congratulations! We will confirm this in writing within the week and forward your joining instructions."

Lucy gave them a beaming smile and thanked them. "I look forward very much to joining the team. I will not let you down".

The whole process had taken just over an hour and a half. By arrangement Lucy walked up Whitehall and met her mother in Trafalgar Square at 3pm.

Her mother was delighted at the news and simply said, "Well done my darling. That's you and Michael settled. Daddy and I can have some fun of our own from September."

Lisette asked if she wanted a meal, but Lucy replied, "I'm just too tense still. Can we have a bite on the train? I don't really like London, but I love Paris. I feel so relaxed there compared to here and I will get plenty of it. But for now, I just want to get home for a swim in the lake."

And that is what they did. They were home at just after 7pm so shortly afterwards the whole clan descended on the lake with all the dogs. All the tensions of the day were washed away.

Back at the cottage, it was Spelthorpe sausages from the Aga with freshly baked rolls and vegetable soup. Ash gave his daughter a congratulatory hug then broke out a bottle of Calvados that the grandparents had brought over with them. They all took a good-sized tot and toasted the next ambassador. It had been a good day.

The following week school started up again. Michael, Lucy and Victoria had examinations that started at the end of the month, and this concentrated minds but at least with the future mapped out they felt that they were now on the home straight. Up at the airfield, they took delivery of a North American Harvard trainer. The flying business was doing well. From friends who were still serving Stooper had got wind that the RAF was going to order many of these aircraft. With an increased number of faster monoplanes being developed, he was determined to stay ahead of the game. The Harvard would fly at twice the speed of the Tiger Moth aircraft, and this was something more challenging for existing clients who wanted to progress to the next stage. When it arrived Simon and Stooper took it up. They thought the investment worthwhile. With the profits over the last year, the purchase had been covered.

8

Doldrums

May – June 1938

Early in the morning on a mid-May day Ash had gone out in the truck on his rounds. He had just gone past the dairy and looked over into the 300-acre sheep grazing field on his right. Some 200 yards south of the track, he saw four sheepdogs standing over a mound. Ash alighted and walked over with Hunter, who had been sitting in the cab. The dogs were watching over a figure lying on his back. As soon as he saw the large white beard he knew it was Amos – the head shepherd who had held that post for nearly sixty years. Ash leaned over. Amos was not breathing. There was no pulse, and he was cold. It appeared that he had been there overnight. He looked quite peaceful, gazing up with his eyes open. It was only the presence of the dogs that had kept the crows away, but Ash took off his jacket, closed Amos's eyes and covered the shepherd's head.

Ash drove the short distance to the Hall to call for the police, who had to attend for any sudden death. He also summoned the village doctor, and he put the local undertakers on notice. He put a quick call in to Paddy and then Julian, who said they would come straight away. He then went back to wait with Simon and a few minutes later Julian turned up with the Reverend Paddy. Ash was aware that Amos had angina, but steadfastly he refused to retire. Ash knew that Amos was coming up for his eightieth birthday, but he always said that he wanted to die along with his sheep and his dogs, and he had done just that. To make sure Ash checked the body. There were no signs of violence, and his purse with a few coins was still in his pocket.

Constable Carter turned up an hour later with Doctor John Bowen from the village. John Bowen was somewhat red-faced, but that was probably due to his liking for strong liquor. He had served the village for some thirty-five years and was due for retirement himself, but like Amos he too had no desire to pack up. He was a first-rate diagnostician and served the village well. How he got around in his dented car without any serious harm remained a mystery because on the majority of calls he would top up his alcohol levels, as it was custom for his patients to offer a small dram to keep him happy and they felt it might help to keep his charges at an affordable level.

Dr Bowen had been treating the angina for several years. He examined Amos on the spot and promptly wrote out a death certificate with heart failure as the cause of death. That concluded matters as far as the police were concerned. There would be no need for an inquest. Reverend Paddy gave a short prayer. He knew Amos well as he regularly encountered him in the churchyard. Amos's wife had died from the Spanish influenza back in 1919. Amos would visit her grave weekly. He would spend half an hour talking and reminding her that one day he and she would be back together again. Amos lived with his dogs in the shepherd's house. He had two married daughters who lived further along the coast at Cromer and Sheringham. They would visit him on alternate weeks.

Two hours later, the Sheringham undertakers arrived. As they lifted the body onto the stretcher, the dogs followed all the way and attempted to go with him when they loaded Amos into their vehicle. Ash took charge of the dogs and delivered them to the under-shepherd who agreed to look after them. Trained dogs were an asset to the estate and there was no question that they would go elsewhere.

Later that day, the two daughters turned up. Julian helped and reassured them. Amos was a minimalist in terms of possessions. Julian admitted them into the house and left them with a key to sort what they wanted. The estate would deal with the final clearance after the funeral. Julian told them that the estate would meet those costs.

Two weeks later, Paddy conducted the service. Amos was well respected and there was a huge turnout from the estate and village. After nineteen years, he was finally reunited with his wife.

The loss of Amos meant that a new head shepherd would have to be found. Ash had spoken to the under-shepherd and the other shepherd who looked after the Romney marsh flock on the salt marsh. Things were easier now that the lambing had taken place, but both were happy in their current roles, and neither wanted the overall responsibility that the job entailed, despite any increase in pay. It was then he remembered Robert Roy.

Every year, an Australian shearer would come to the farm to shear all the sheep. On his previous visit in April, he had told Ash that he was getting tired of all the travelling and was looking to settle down somewhere. Robert Roy was currently living with his wife in a rented house in Lowestoft, Suffolk along with his son, William and daughter Emma.

Robert's parents had emigrated to Australia back in 1902 when he was just ten years old. They had worked and lived on a large 50,000-acre sheep station in Western Australia a few miles inland from Albany. Robert learnt sheep farming inside out and became a very efficient shearer. He married a local girl in 1912, and they both lived on the sheep station. It was a nice place to live with a slightly cooler climate due to the Southern Ocean. There was plenty of work, so earnings were good. Albany had a huge sheltered natural harbour called King George's Sound named after King George III. It also had a busy whaling station, which attracted large numbers of great white sharks. Sea bathing was not popular.

It was also the place where, in 1914, huge numbers of Australian and New Zealand volunteers were loaded into troop ships to be escorted in convoys across to Egypt. For many, it was a great adventure as they posed for photos en masse against the Sphinx and the pyramids. Like so many others, Robert found himself swept along after volunteering to defend the Empire. In April of the following year reality dawned as he found himself in the blood sacrifice of Gallipoli on the Turkish coast. After that fiasco, in 1916, Robert, who had gained the rank of sergeant, found himself at Pozieres on the Somme for yet another bloodbath and all for barely five miles of French territory. There was no home leave for most of the Australian troops, just letters, and one received in Gallipoli months earlier, told of the birth of his son. Robert spent six weeks in England on local leave and found his way to Suffolk, where he engaged in some sheep shearing for pocket money and a reminder of home.

In April 1918 he was back in France at Villiers Bretoneaux holding the line against the massive German Michael offensive. As always, the Australians did what was asked of them. They held the line and because of their fighting prowess, these shock troops of the Empire led the August attack at Amiens that culminated in the armistice a hundred days later.

Robert went home, arriving in 1919, only to learn that his wife had died after being bitten by a brown snake that got in the house. Brown snakes are some of the most venomous snakes in the world. Most of their victims in Australia were sheep and cattle dogs. The Australians would kill them on sight, but they couldn't kill them all. His son, William, was four years old. Robert's wife had been buried before his return. Robert stayed for another year, but the death of his wife played on his mind, and he had a fixation that his son would be next, so in 1920 he took his son back to Suffolk in England and looked up a war widow, Elsie, who had been kind to him three years earlier. She agreed to look after William while he went shearing. He earned a lot of money during that time but was away a lot.

William went to school in Lowestoft. In 1922, Robert and Elsie were married. A daughter, Emma, was born two years later. They continued to live in Suffolk. Robert carried out lucrative sheep shearing in the late spring and summer across East Anglia. In the quieter months, he carried out lambing and other farm work closer to home.

After a discussion with Simon and Julian, Ash drove across to Lowestoft and found Robert between shearing jobs. Ash had been given carte blanche to negotiate a deal.

On meeting Robert again, he outlined the role in full and told him about the two shepherds who would work for him and that one was also looking after a small herd of Tamworth pigs and a dozen Highland cattle. He put forward the offer of a detached tied cottage and truck, a regular income with two weeks paid leave annually, which might be taken at the height of the shearing time if he wanted to make an annual boost to his salary. Unpaid leave could be taken by mutual agreement, but Spelthorpe had to come first in respect of all such matters. A contract of employment would be drafted to settle matters.

Robert agreed but insisted on two conditions – that his family come too, and that his son, William, would be offered employment on the estate. William was now twenty-three years of age and had qualified as a mechanical and agricultural engineer. He often worked with his father and carried out such work on farms whilst his father was shearing. Ash couldn't believe his luck. With Spelthorpe taking on more agricultural machinery, this was needed and would prove to be a bonus.

Ash waited for William to come home. He interviewed him there and then. Ash was shown all the relevant certificates, and one was of particular interest. He had extra skills on a lathe and could machine spare parts. With periodic supply issues for spares, his ability would be a real bonus. William was offered employment at the standard mechanics' rate of pay with a review after a month. All was agreed with a start date of Monday the eighteenth of July. Spelthorpe would pay for the removal from their rented accommodation to the three-bedroomed detached cottage on the farm, which the estate would redecorate prior to the move.

Ash spent another hour with them, talking generally. He related how he had met many Australians whilst he was at Étaples in the Royal Army Medical Corps. Robert had been extremely lucky to get through it unscathed. For Australians things were always more difficult because of the distance, but the British rarely took that into account when dealing with disciplinary issues. The Australians had a different way of doing things that didn't go down well with starchy imposed rules. It resulted in a disproportionate number of Australians clashing with the British military authorities. William said that he liked riding and often exercised horses on farms where he worked. Ash explained that there would be plenty of opportunities for that at Spelthorpe. Elsie was working on a part time basis as a teaching assistant at the same school their daughter attended, and she would have to resign from that position. Ash said that while he could make no promises, but he would enquire about taking Elsie on at the Spelthorpe village school, where the estate exercised a controlling interest.

Ash got back at 6 pm and outlined the good news to Simon and Julian. Things were looking up again. An hour later, he was back with Lisette. It was like old times again as they rushed along to the lake where they swam naked in the sunset glow and talked over the success of the day.

One week later, on Tuesday the seventh of June, Ash was up with Lisette at 6am. They swam in the sea with the dogs, but Trooper and Rafe had failed to appear. They had been getting quite slow. Joanna was visiting on a regular basis. Ash walked into the barn and saw the pair curled up together in the straw. The other dogs came in and sat looking up knowingly. Ash went back inside the cottage and returned to the barn with Lisette. She was in tears. She stroked the curled-up pair. They were cold. They had passed in the night. She looked up at Ash and said, "Nothing ever lasts forever. All good things come to an end, and we have had sixteen wonderful years with these two boys. They were the first. They led the way."

Ash said, "We will miss them, but they are together. It's

almost like a greater hand took control and made it like that so they would never be alone, and we should take comfort from that. We can't tell the kids yet. It's their exam week so we say nothing until they get back on Saturday."

They hugged the other dogs then Ash got a large wheelbarrow. He wrapped the dogs in old blankets, lifted them into the barrow and pushed them into a little clearing in the pines where the dogs would often sit amongst the purple foxgloves in the dappled shade of the trees. Together for the next hour, they dug a deep hole and placed the dogs in the blankets side by side as they had found them. The other dogs and the two cats sat silently in a line and watched. They filled the hole and Ash shed a tear as he patted the soil down.

"Goodbye, you two. You did us proud."

And with that they walked slowly back to the cottage.

The resting place of the merdogs

Later that day, Ash called in at the maintenance depot and spoke to the stone mason, where he arranged for a stone with a metal plaque for the grave. He called on Simon and Julian to let them know the sad news. The dogs and horses were companions and fellow workers on the estate. Whilst deaths were accepted as inevitable, just as night follows day, it didn't diminish the loss that was felt by those who knew them. Ash also called on Paddy, who agreed to attend at the spot in the pines on Saturday afternoon.

When Michael, Victoria and Lucy returned on the Saturday, Ash and Lisette met them at the Hall and broke the news. They took it hard because the twins had been with the dogs since their earliest memories. They were always there, always pleased to see them and an endless source of comfort as they grew up. They walked to the cottage and waited for a few minutes as others were expected. The Spelthorpes, the Johnsons and the de Lisles all turned out along with Gabriel and Aggie and their canine companions. Then, Paddy and Ruth arrived with Gelert. They walked to the clearing in the pines. The grave was marked by a single stone. It bore the words on a plaque:

Trooper and Rafe 1922-1938
At this Spot
are deposited the Remains of two Friends
who possessed Beauty without Vanity,
Strength without Insolence,
Courage without Ferocity,
and all the virtues of Man without his Vices.

There was little else to say. Ash had found the words in a book about the poet Byron and considered it a fitting tribute. Paddy gave a short prayer, and flowers were laid.

9

New horizons

July – August 1938

School finally came to an end on the eighth of July. For Michael and Victoria, it was a total liberation. Along with Lucy, they had achieved full success in their examinations, and all had secured places for the next stage in their lives. At the final assembly, Aggie gave her farewell to the school after eighteen years. She had been a popular member of staff, not because she sought popularity but because of her disciplined approach. Her loyalty and the way in which she brought the best out in her pupils had created an act that would be difficult to follow.

Her transformed appearance over the last two terms had gone down so well that other staff members had done the same and this had created a greater atmosphere of approachability in the school.

The headmaster had pulled some strings which resulted in her being offered a post as one of the school governors – an offer she willingly accepted. The school presented her with an Underwood typewriter and the latest Leica camera. Aggie subscribed to the doctrine that possessions must be either beautiful or useful, and these fitted that principle. Gabriel agreed fully and whilst he was never of the view that Aggie was a possession, he would often tell her that she fulfilled both conditions admirably, and on that basis, he had married her.

After the assembly, there was a farewell reception for leavers and parents. Victoria had changed out of uniform into a dress and was proudly wearing her engagement ring and the matching jewellery. Her closest friends were aware of a relationship, but the engagement secret had been well kept, and she put them on notice for the August wedding. The headmaster joked that in view of the history of romance at Spelthorpe starting with Joanna, then Aggie and now with the latest revelation, he felt there was something in the water supply there. It might be worthwhile bottling it and selling it as a love potion.

The return to the estate was a time to work hard and play hard. The three from the cottage along with Joanna and Jennifer rode as much as time would allow, and it was often bareback along the shoreline. Swimming in the lake and the sea cut down on bath water, and they all developed light tans with exposure to the sunshine. Ash and Lisette would often join them, along with the dogs.

Boudicca was about to undergo her second heat. Joanna wanted her to have at least one litter, and she had selected Hunter to perform, given his kind and gentle nature. Nimrod was clearly put out, but incest was definitely not on anybody's agenda. Michael, Victoria and Lucy did at least three full days' work on the farm every week. This was mainly hay making and harvesting. Victoria and Lucy underwent several sessions with Boynton for their safety and self-defence training. Michael was having two lessons a week with Squadron Leader 'Stooper'.

In the meantime, the dogs met up periodically with Minerva. Their relationship had matured and lacked the intensity of the earlier years. They didn't feel the need to go with her on journeys. She was aware of the demise of Trooper and Rafe, but the dogs were happy that they were together. The dogs knew they would be there waiting for them when their time came.

Minerva simply explained. "Where would you be if the sun shone all the time?"

She answered the question herself. "You would be in a desert, so we all have bad times because that way we appreciate the good. That is the way it is with all life."

The dogs accepted that.

Shackleton had made the grade as a merdog. Minerva took him on a couple of trips back in time which he seemed to appreciate. On one trip, they went up the coast to Staithes, where he met up with a young Captain Cook.

Michael was impressed by the new Harvard and its power compared to the Gipsy Moth and the Dragon Rapide. Flying this solo after a couple of flights with Stooper gave him a new confidence as he now felt that he would be able to master the new Hurricane eight-gun fighter that everyone was talking about. Michael had undertaken training in navigation, night flying and in poor visibility at basic levels but that was as far as Stooper intended to go because he would pick all that up anyway during his officer cadet training. What Stooper wanted to teach was the stuff they wouldn't give him at officer training, and that was how to survive, and how best to tackle the enemy.

Stooper said, "When your do your training, you will have to bite your lip. They will teach you how to fly in perfect formation, how to display yourself at an air show and how to engage in drills like some dance routine, and that is because since the last war the RAF has become an exclusive flying club, and all the combat experience has gone. Most of those teaching you will never have flown against an angry man. When you get into real combat, all that fancy stuff will have to go out the window unless you want to be another name on a memorial."

"What should I do? asked Michael. "I can't refuse to do things because they will chuck me out."

"Like I said, Biggles, just bite your lip and put up with it. When you get into combat apply the common sense that I want to pass on to you. What is the most vital part of any aeroplane?" asked the squadron leader.

"The fuel tank? The engine?" queried Michael.

"No, it's the bloody pilot," said Stooper. "You take the pilot out, and they are finished, so you have to think about the design of the aircraft and the defensive armament of what you are attacking and how best to attack. If you go in without thinking they will get you. Look at those latest German bombers. They are like a flying greenhouse at the front. That's good for their visibility but if you hit them head-on with 150 rounds a second of concentrated fire, you will smash up their glass house. You will probably kill the pilot and the navigator, and at the very least they will end up with a 250-mph wind in their face, making them blind to what is happening."

And so, the talk went on and it would be repeated time and time again. There were a few simple rules: "Beware the Hun in the sun. They will be up there waiting for you, so keep checking and try to get as much height as possible because you will be a greater threat to them. Never fly in a straight line. That's what our poor bastards had to do back in April in 1917 at Arras to take photos of the ground, and the Germans shot us out of the sky, not because they were better, but because we were easy targets for them. That's why they called it 'Bloody April'".

"Never get close to the ground. They will all be shooting at you – even our own because they can't tell the difference. We are all a bunch of Fokkers to them. You are there to kill the enemy and you do that high up and when they go down do not be tempted to follow them. Look what happened to the Red Baron – their top ace. He broke his own rule and chased one down until an Aussie machine gunner on the ground saw him coming and shot him up the arse. That's what did him, not that Canadian because those guys claim everything. They say with most pilots you have to half what they claim, but with Canadians you have to divide by ten or more."

Michael was impressed at the reality and good sense that came across from the squadron leader.

"Always get close before you fire. A hundred yards or less. It's no good spraying them from 400 yards away. Most will miss and go behind, and you will have no concentration or maximum firepower from your guns. You are not up there to spray them. You need to smash them up and kill them. You need to think about 'lead'. You know about that because I've seen you shooting, but these birds are flying at 300 mph not sixty, so plenty of 'lead' if they are crossing. Obviously, you don't need it directly on the tail, but if you stay on the tail for too long, they will be shooting back. Most of the other cadets won't have a clue about 'lead', but you know from the pigeons you shoot. For you, it will be simply adapting that knowledge."

"How can we best work that out?" asked Michael.

"Don't worry about that." said Stooper. "When we next go up in the Harvard, I will get Jim to fly the Dragon Rapide, and we can act out shooting him down from different angles. That will give you some idea. The most important thing is to avoid mass dogfights. No matter how good you are, you can't see everywhere, and if you get in the middle and stay there someone will get you. It's no good being a gung-ho hero because you won't last five minutes. If a dogfight is coming off, get out. He who fights and runs away lives to fight another day. Don't be greedy. Don't use up all your ammunition because you might need it on the way back. Spot your target. Look for danger, then go in fast and close and give him a full burst then get out as quickly as possible. Then, look for another and do the same. If you get just one or two every time you go on a sortie you will end up as a top scorer. By surviving, you are there to kill more of the enemy and that's your job. Reckless heroics will get you killed, and if you are dead, you can't shoot anyone down.

And finally, always be nice to your ground crew. Talk to them, tell them what you did, take tea with them, give them a Christmas card and listen to them talking about their families. Do that and they will look after you, and importantly they will look after your plane. Learn from them, too, about your aeroplane. Make them feel they are part of your team."

So, over the next few weeks, they went up in the Harvard and Jim took up the Dragon Rapide. They had a radio channel to talk to one another, and they carried out mock attacks. From the ground it looked impressive, and Simon kept his fingers crossed as Michael turned and twisted and attacked from every angle, but he saw the vital importance of giving his future son-in-law the edge.

In England they were now handing out gas masks to the civilian population and the latest Wills cigarette cards featured Air Raid Precautions. Prime Minister Chamberlain and his cabinet spouted hope, but it was a forlorn hope because anyone with real political or military acumen could see the writing on the wall.

The new head shepherd settled in quickly. The other two shepherds knew him from the days when he would visit to shear the sheep at record speed, and they warmed to his characteristic down-to-earth, no-nonsense, Australian manner. Robert was pleased to take on the dogs that had come from Amos. They knew the ground and swiftly adapted to his kindly manner. The Boyntons had taken it upon themselves to welcome them. Gabriel had something in common. Whilst serving in the Middle East in 1917 he had encountered Australians from their legendary Light Horse – mounted infantry who had probably made the last cavalry charge ever, in order to capture Beersheba. They used bayonets because they had no swords.

When the subject came up, and Elsie talked about her previous role as a teaching assistant, Aggie hinted that she might be able to find a position in the school for her when she took on the headship in September.

William, for the time being had based himself in the maintenance hangar at the airfield. They had a lathe, and he impressed them with his ability. It was a convenient location to fix farm machinery when it had to be done undercover, but the rest of the time he was out and about. He had gone to the stables where he met up with the grooms and Julian Johnson and after they saw his riding ability and totally natural way with the horses, they gave him carte blanche to ride any of them apart from Major de Lisle's horse that was reserved just for him and his daughter-in-law Joanna. William was a personable lad. He was attractive to the ladies with his fair wavy hair. He was physically very strong but gentle with it, and he knew his subject matter extremely well. William was a hard worker and by sheer determination he had engaged in several courses with examinations to qualify in an expanding area. He rapidly made inroads with the air mechanic, and they were soon learning from each other.

Victoria and Michael's wedding preparations were well underway. Lisette and Aggie had taken charge of the church decorations. The wedding was set for 3pm. Helen had sent out the invitations in the week after the engagement had been announced. An announcement had been placed in the Times heralding the engagement and marriage day of Lady Victoria Spelthorpe and Mr Michael Cromwell.

There would be just the one bridesmaid – Lucy. Joanna and Jennifer would be playing the violin and cello again because that is what Michael and Victoria wanted. They had been so impressed by their performance at the Boynton wedding, and they wanted the same – after all, one could not improve on perfection. Importantly they all remembered back in Sandringham in 1933 when the two girls had captivated the king when he was the Duke of York by a performance of '*The Lark Ascending*'. The king had confirmed that he would be attending with the queen and the princesses but only those who needed to know were told and they were sworn to secrecy.

Michael had asked Gabriel Boynton to be his best man. They had grown close over the years and since the robbery incident, they had become brothers in arms.

The reception would take place in the Hall with a hundred guests to include fifty from the estate and relatives. About twenty were allocated for school friends and the remainder for long-established contacts and friends of the parents of the bride and groom. Helen, Lisette, Victoria, Lucy, Joanna and Jennifer were attended by the outfitters from Norwich to finalise the dresses. Both Michael and Victoria had expressed a desire for a low-key but affectionate affair on the country estate that had moulded them over the years. They insisted that Hunter, Odi and Zulu attend to represent the dogs of the estate and that two of the Suffolk Punch horses be tethered outside the church for the duration of the ceremony.

Whilst the ladies were dealing with the wedding plans, Ash and Simon got together for a Jameson's in the library at the Hall. With the wedding, followed by the departures of Victoria, Michael and Lucy on their chosen career paths they both felt that they had come to the end of an era. Matters had been overshadowed by the deaths of Amos and the dogs, and both felt the need for a celebration to uplift spirits in advance of the wedding. Simon mentioned that Helen had been asking if they could all go for a day trip in the Dragon Rapide and she wanted to see where they had fought together in the war as she had never been there. Ash had read about the memorials, how the cemeteries had been created and how they were being lovingly looked after but at the same time, it would be nice to take the families on an adventure together and suggested a route down the front line then across to the coast along the line of the Somme and up to the fashionable resort of Le Touquet – Paris Plage. This was on the south side of the Canche River and Étaples, where he and Lisette had fallen in love back in 1917. There was a new airport at Le Touquet, so they could fuel up there, take a leisurely lunch and look around before heading back home. It seemed like a good idea, so Simon said that he would get together with Michael to plan the route. On a clear day, the navigation would be simple. The weather looked perfect for the next few days, and they settled on the Friday in three days' time – just over a week before the wedding.

Simon said that he had spoken to the king who would fly in for the wedding in an Airspeed Envoy of the King's Flight. He would arrive at 1pm. Simon would meet them. Bertie had agreed to unveil a plaque at the new recreation field that was now complete, given that Helen had agreed on naming it the 'King George VI Field' rather than what had been initially proposed. That would take place at 2pm and would present no difficulty as it was right next to the church. All interested parties would be attending the wedding anyway. Simon had drafted a short speech with the agreement of the king.

And now came the surprise. As a wedding present from the king and queen, after the reception, Michael and Victoria would fly back with them to Balmoral for a four-day stay on the Balmoral Estate. Simon would fly up to Aberdeen on the Thursday morning to bring them home. It had been fortunate that neither Michael nor Victoria had planned anything for a honeymoon. Being together was all they wanted but now they would have a once-in-a-lifetime experience.

On the Friday, the families met at 6am at the airfield. Lisette had booked a table in Le Touquet at a prime restaurant by telegram. A landing slot and refuelling at Le Touquet had been booked in a similar way. The only absentee was Edward who insisted on staying behind because two of his mathematical mates were coming to see him for the day. Simon thought it best to leave him rather than all having to suffer his morosity.

Michael took off and flew on a course of 145 degrees flying over Norwich and crossing the Belgian coast at Nieuwpoort in just over an hour. This was the start of the trench line that had stretched all the way to Switzerland. Although the land was now back in agriculture, from the air, they could make out the trench lines and shell holes from the deep disturbance to the land where the subsoil and chalk had come to the surface.

At Ypres in Belgium, they flew around the massive Menin Gate that had been opened just over ten years earlier inscribed with the names of 55,000 soldiers with no known grave. Twenty minutes later they were over the front line near Neuve Chappelle where Ash had saved Simon and where many from Spelthorpe had fallen in the disastrous Aubers Ridge battle. They passed over the massive memorial to the Canadians who fell at Vimy Ridge in 1917, then they carried on south until they met the meandering Somme River.

On seeing the massive basilica in Albert or 'Bert' as the troops called it, they knew they were in the middle of the Somme battlefield. The statue of the Golden Virgin shone out from the top of the basilica. In the war, the Germans had shelled all around and the superstition was that if the statue fell the war would come to an end. It was hit and left hanging at the top, but the Royal Engineers bolted the statue on perpendicular to the vertical. But the legend was right, because in 1918, it was hit again by a shell and fell to the ground, and the war did end. They flew around the massive crater at La Boiselle, created by a mine right under the German front line that blew with twenty-seven tons of explosive a few minutes before the British went over the top on 1st July 1916. Twenty thousand men on the British side died that day.

They flew on further towards Amiens with its massive gothic cathedral and over the spot where the Red Baron had met his end. Ash and Lisette knew this area well from their efforts to evacuate the wounded. It was the first time they had been back. From Amiens they flew on another forty miles northwest to the mouth of the Somme River and then northwards along the coast for another twenty miles to land at Le Touquet at 10am. Michael refuelled the plane, and after greeting the French officials in their own language, all were admitted without the formalities. That was what Simon and Ash loved about the French. If you looked a decent sort and treated them with courtesy, they would rarely bother with the paperwork, unlike their starchy British counterparts who applied the letter of the law.

A couple of taxis took them over the bridge and into Étaples. It looked very different from the last time. The camp and all the railway trucks had gone. All that remained was the massive Imperial War Grave Cemetery with over 10,000 graves. They all walked in silence. The sheer numbers had such a profound effect on the younger members of the party. Lisette found the grave of William Clark, the gas victim she remembered. She had written to his wife in Peterborough. They saw the graves of the nurses killed in the air raids and walked on the beach where they had encountered Jackie, the South African baboon and mascot. It was also the place where they had met Hunter and Odi on the beach. That remained a mystery that they could not understand. It all came back to them as a mixture of both happy memories of the start of their relationship and the agony of what they had witnessed.

They went back to the seafront at Le Touquet. It was chic and fashionable. There were wide boulevards with pines and hardy palm trees. There was a massive sandy beach that went on for miles. It reminded Lisette of Biarritz where she had spent part of her childhood. They wandered in and out of the fashion shops. It was a delight to Helen and Lisette and a marked contrast to Norfolk.

The restaurant was splendid and afforded an opportunity for all to indulge in their food fantasies. George turned his nose up at the escargots but gorged on the crepes. Ash had a liking for gésiers on a salad. For the others there was fish soup, turkey steaks in sauce, juicy beef steaks cooked quite rare, plates of charcuterie and frites done in the French style – a marked contrast to the greasy lumpy chips served up on the Norfolk seafront. For dessert there was crème brûlée, iles flottantes, glaces and the geography of France on the cheeseboard.

Conservative habits endured to an extent. Bitter experience advised avoiding shellfish in months lacking the letter 'R' in the spelling. Projectile vomit at 5,000 feet is not pretty.

Coffees and cognac came at the end with just the simple pleasure of sitting there and watching the world go by with a background of French café music on the accordion. France tasted different, it smelt different, and it sounded different, but they were nice tastes, smells and sounds. It was in France where cuisine was a profession. It had to be done right and presented properly, to be enjoyed and not rushed. The change did them all good. George had enjoyed his flight along with his father's explanations. He enjoyed his food too, but was pleasantly reassured that frogs' legs and snails would not be on the menu for the forthcoming wedding.

Simon took his turn and flew them back to arrive a few minutes before the sun set in the western sky. It had been a good day.

Back home the day had not passed without incident. Jennifer had just over two weeks' leave from the hospital placement for the wedding. She had risen early and got to the stables just after 6 am. Unbeknown to her, and just after she left the stables, William had turned up to grab a ride before he started his work. His start and finish times were flexible, providing he put the time in, which he did and more, so he could never be described as a clock watcher. He had been working till 8pm the previous day, fixing an issue with a tractor, and that was now working well.

He rode down to the shoreline to see Jennifer cantering along the edge of the surf. Suddenly, her horse stumbled. It must have hit a hole from bait-digging. Jennifer fell. William rushed over and gently helped her up. She was wet all over, and now so was he. She was slightly concussed but otherwise fine and looked up at her rescuer who was holding her and smiling reassuringly. He checked her over. It was a role reversal, but she was compliant. He held her hand. It was a shock, but deep-down, Jennifer was enjoying the moment and the careful attention. William introduced himself to her as he walked to the dry sands. He sat her down while he went back for the horses, and she watched as he checked her horse over too. He then tethered the two horses together against a wooden groyne post. He walked back and helped her up. She clung to him. She was shivering slightly from the shock and the wet, and he was warm against her. He held her like that for a few minutes. He talked and explained where he had come from, and she did the same. They walked back to the shelter of the pines. He took the horse leads in his left hand and held her hand with his right.

After twenty minutes, he said, "Your horse is alright. I've been watching. Let's get you back up. It's always best to get back up as soon as possible so as not to lose confidence."

He helped her re-mount, and they returned to the stables at a walk. Back at the stables he put a blanket around her and put both horses back after taking off the tack and putting it away. He made sure the horses were settled.

Jennifer said, "That's kind William but the grooms will be here soon, and they will sort things along with all the others. I'll come back later to check the horse. I suppose you have to go to work now."

"I will do that but not until I have got you home. I insist, it's the least I can do. There's just one thing."

"What's that?" she asked.

"You will probably think I am being cheeky, but could I see you again?"

Jennifer was pleased at that because it meant she didn't have to ask the same question.

"I'd like that very much. If you could meet me here at seven this evening, we could go for a walk. That would be nice."

William walked her back to the annexe then took off for work. Jennifer felt happy and looked forward to the evening.

Like her sister she had black raven hair. She was equally

attractive, but with a slightly fuller figure. During her medical studies, she had been asked out but had declined or had gone out for a short date, but that was it. She never followed up partly because she was so focussed on her studies but also because she found other medical students quite boring. In William there was something different that she couldn't explain but he had an inner spark that did something for her. She knew not why, but it must have been something in her genes because her sister, Joanna, had behaved in the same way when she met up with husband who was now one of the Spelthorpe Veterinary Practice surgeons.

They met at seven and walked and talked. They walked to the boathouse and sat on the bank. He reached out and took her hand and she wanted that. William offered to take her for a drink, but she explained that would only set off the village gossips, so they walked back via the pines and around the lake as it was starting to get dark. He put an arm around her, and they looked into each other's eyes, and then he kissed her. She put both arms up and pulled him down, and they kissed again. They walked back to the annexe. They agreed to meet on the following day when both had a free afternoon. It went well, and they carried on meeting and riding together for the following week. They swam in the lake and the sea and made each other happy when they were together

The Spelthorpe Lake

10

Union

It was Saturday the twentieth of August 1938. With hazy sunshine the weather was perfect. Before the King and Queen who sat beside Earl Simon and Countess Helen and the packed church of St Michael and all the Angels, the Reverend Paddy Collins took the right hands of Michael and Victoria and pressed them together. He held them firmly as he bellowed out the words:

"Those whom God hath joined together, let no man put asunder"

Then he spoke to the whole assembly:

"Forasmuch as Michael and Victoria have consented together in holy wedlock, and have witnessed the same before God and this company, and thereto have given and pledged their troth either to other, and have declared the same by giving and receiving of a ring, and by joining of hands; I pronounce that they be man and wife together, In the Name of the Father, and of the Son, and of the Holy Ghost. Amen."

A brief prayer and blessing followed. As the bride, groom,

parents, best man and bridesmaid retired to the vestry to complete the legalities, Joanna and Jennifer performed on the violin and piano. They played Elgar's *'Chanson de Matin'*. That had followed Vaughan Williams' *'Prelude on Rhosymedre'* for the bride's arrival. The musicians looked spectacular. The king was enchanted once again.

When the parties emerged the church bells rang in triumph as the procession walked down the central aisle and into the churchyard for the customary photographs.

The planning paid off and the day went like clockwork. The King and Queen had arrived on time at the airfield in the Airspeed Envoy in the distinctive red and blue colours of the Guards Brigade. An hour later, Bertie dedicated the playing field by unveiling the plaque and saluting the support of the estate for the education and development of the children of the rural community. The reception and wedding breakfast went off with an appropriate level of humour but without the embarrassment that can occur on such occasions. At 6.30pm the king was scheduled to leave. He spoke briefly and commented on the palpable sense of community and affection that existed on the estate and said that he had one last thing to do before returning to Balmoral. At the front of the Hall, Ash, Michael and Gabriel stood in line. The king presented them with their British Empire Medals for their splendid service to the greater Norfolk community earlier in the year. Michael and Victoria thanked the guests, then dashed to the Rolls under a shower of rose petals. Victoria threw her bouquet into the crowd. It was Jennifer who caught it.

Simon drove the royal party with the bride and groom up to the airfield. Michael and Victoria had changed for the journey and their suitcases had been sent up to the aircraft in advance. They took off just after 7 pm and landed at 9 pm in Aberdeen. By 10.30 pm they were back at Balmoral.

Back at the Hall, music and dancing, with refreshments took place around a marquee on the extensive front lawn. Simon had invited all the estate's residents to join the celebration, and a significant number turned up including William Roy. He was the only one who Jennifer danced with. Her mother looked across realising that there was clearly something between them that had predated the event. Lisette and Helen had noticed too.

Lisette remembered the remark made by the school headmaster who was a reception guest with his wife. She shared it with the other two. "It looks like the Spelthorpe water might be working again. We did see who caught the bouquet."

Julia simply smiled and said, "She's a big girl now, but she's no fool. We will have to wait and see!"

On the following day it was church at usual. Simon had asked for Julian and Ash to meet back at the Hall for an hour.

After the service Jennifer walked over the road with her sister, her husband and baby James who had slept soundly in his carry cot throughout the entire service. It was obvious to Jeremy that his wife and sister-in-law wanted a girl chat, so he took James out in the pram with Boudicca for a walk along the quayside. Jennifer wanted to tell her sister about William. She had been out with him every day for over a week now, and she told her sister how they had met when she fell from her horse.

Joanna said, "We saw you two together last night at the party and it was obvious to us all that you knew each other well. You spent all your time with him."

Jennifer responded, "Well, that's it, Sis. I'm in a bit of a quandary, and I don't know what to do. Nothing like this has ever happened before. I'm sure that I've fallen in love with him, and I know he feels the same about me. It's not just because he told me".

"You seem sure. If you are then do it. Marry him. You are nearly twenty-three and he is the same age. If you don't seize the moment, it may never happen again. Have you done it?" asked Joanna. "You know what I mean. It happened to me with Jeremy. You remember back then, and I was only eighteen. It was very quick, but it has worked out so well. Just don't throw your medicine studies away, but I know you won't do that. Do you think you could live with him?

She continued without waiting for a response. "Have you done it? You know what I mean?"

Jennifer shook her head.

"I can tell that you are thinking about it so before you go, I will give you what you need. Jeremy and I are not using them now because we are trying for number two but please keep that quiet."

"Thank you, Joanna. I just wanted to check with you. I know we both think the same way," said Jennifer. They talked for another half hour, but just before she left, Joanna went upstairs then came down and handed her sister a little package.

The three senior members of the Spelthorpe company met in the library at the Hall. As it was after midday Simon poured out three glasses of Jameson's Irish whiskey. Simon said, "Julian, I know you and Julia are off for a few days on the North York Moors tomorrow, and I know Ash will have it all in hand but there's a couple of things I wanted to settle before you go off. The two 3,000-gallon fuel tanks I ordered are coming next week. With war on the horizon, I wanted to make sure we never go short, and fuel is plentiful right now. We can put these out of the way at the back of the maintenance yard as we agreed. The other issue is with young William Roy. We need to settle his position and salary level. Have you any ideas on that? He's been here well over the month."

Julian replied. "For the tanks, all the groundwork and the bund is done. All we have to do is to crane them onto the cradles. We have a crane coming tomorrow. Ash is aware. I think this is wise. It's our choice. I know the others won't have thought of it. I think Paddy would say that it's the 'Parable of the Wise and Foolish Virgins'. Being wise has always paid off for us. As a farm we should be alright if they ration it, but what we get for the farm will probably have a dye in it so we will need a supply without the dye to make things run smoothly and that's our choice and as you say there is no restriction now. As for young William, the lad knows his stuff, and he knocks spots off the two mechanics we have. They are alright, but William believes in solutions not problems and gets things sorted. The airfield mechanic is a different issue, and Peregrine is in charge up there, and I would not wish to undermine him. They work together well and help each other out."

Ash joined in. "I agree on that. Everyone I speak to has been left with a good impression. He is very personable, too. Aircraft are a bit different and a specialism which at this stage William does not have, but we have introduced far more agricultural machinery. We now have four tractors plus the one in the forestry. We have a dozen trucks, too. I don't like to say it, but we can't take any more horses on although if we are low on fuel they will be a godsend, and they can do things in the forest that are still beyond a tractor. We have got to the stage where the farm needs a chief engineer. William is qualified for that, and he has shown that if we can't get spares, he will machine them. I suggest we appoint him as our chief engineer with a salary on the same level as Boynton i.e. at captain level. That would seem about right to me."

The conversation continued. Ash's proposal was confirmed. Julian would see William and appoint him on his return on the following Friday. Ash went on to mention another issue regarding chainsaws. He foresaw a huge demand for timber if war was to come. He had one chainsaw. It was a two-man device, but it had saved an enormous amount of time. As this was of German manufacture and with nothing else available, he proposed the purchase of another with sufficient spares to last a few years. It would give Spelthorpe an advantage. This was agreed. Simon concluded the meeting and thanked Ash for his head-hunting vision. The veterinary practice that he had proposed had been a huge success. Then there was Aggie for the school, the new head shepherd and now William. Ash had a unique gift for looking far ahead, and this was paying off for Spelthorpe time and time again.

Ash walked home and took a swim in the lake with Lisette, Lucy and the dogs.

Later, in the evening Jennifer and William went for another walk. They grew yet closer. Jennifer told him to come straight from work on the following day. She said she would have a meal for him, and he could clean up at the annexe as her parents were away on a four-day break.

At Balmoral, Michael and Victoria had settled in. They took breakfast with Bertie, Elizabeth and the girls or 'us four' – as Bertie used to call them. Bertie was happy in a family setting away from London. The estate was always closed to visitors at this time of year. Bertie said right from the start to both. "You can both cut out the "sir" while you are here. You are husband and wife, not at school, and we have valued your friendship over the years, so we are all on first-name terms from now on in private."

Victoria added, "Michael's flying instructor calls him Biggles."

"I've been told about your flying exploits," said the King. "As one of my commissioned officers, if you fly like Biggles then I will be absolutely delighted. We need a few more recruits like you."

Later in the morning they went to church as expected and in the afternoon the king with Lillibet and Margaret took them for a horse ride in the estate, set in the heart of the Cairngorms. It was so different to Norfolk with its grouse moors and fast flowing rivers. The queen stayed behind. She was less keen on the actual riding but passionate about racing and she owned several first-class racers. She was an expert fisherwoman and on the following day, she introduced them to the art of fly fishing. They caught two salmon, which they feasted on in the evening.

William got to the annexe just after 6pm, having told Elsie that he would not be eating at home. Jennifer had been cooking, and there was a casserole on a low heat in the oven. She came to the door and beckoned him in. He looked a bit grubby from work but had brought a change of clothes. Jennifer was just in a dressing gown. She took him upstairs to the guest room and showed him the shower that was en suite. While he was showering, she closed the curtains and switched on a bedside lamp. She heard the shower stop, so she walked into the en suite with a towel. As he emerged from the shower, she held the towel out and wrapped him in it and started to rub him dry, then she reached up and pulled him down towards her. They kissed passionately and as she did this, she allowed her dressing gown to slip to the floor. They stood there naked and gazed at one another, then she took him by the hand and led him to the bed. They lay side by side and kissed. William whispered "I love you, Jennifer. I want you so much. You are the best thing that has happened to me."

She held him firmly against her. "I love you too and I want you to make love to me. I've never done anything like this before, but I want you with me always. I'm certain of that."

William replied. "I've never done this either, but I'm sure we will work it out. Things have been good so far. After what you have said everything is clear to me. I'm asking you now if you will marry me."

She responded, "Yes, I will because I want that too. You make me happy, but we must be sensible. I do want your babies one day, but not till I am a doctor, and that's not too long. I know this is not what happens in romantic stories, but you will find what we need in the side cabinet in the top drawer." William and Jennifer made love and lay together for an hour.

"I think I've made you hungry." she said and with that, they put on dressing gowns and went downstairs. It was a good casserole with freshly baked bread and a bottle of red wine. They talked. She told him about her sister and the arrangement her parents had made while she was still at school but engaged to Jeremy. She felt it would be no different for her.

William said, "I know we are both over twenty-one, but I will still ask your father when they get back because that is the right thing to do, and it's important to me that we start on the right foot, especially as he is my day-to-day boss."

They finished the meal, then Jennifer took him by the hand. "I think it's time that my future husband made love to his wife again." With that they went back upstairs. William proved very willing. They awoke together as the first light penetrated the curtains. Jennifer made breakfast and after William had established that Jennifer was free for the day he rang Ash and asked if he could take a day's leave as he needed to sort something. He said that everything was in order with his work situation, and he would explain later. Ash agreed.

William dashed out and returned a twenty minutes later with his Morris Eight convertible. "Where are we going?" asked Jennifer.

"I'm taking you to Norwich," he said, "and I'm going to get you an engagement ring." They set off and went to the jeweller near the cathedral. They selected a diamond ring with a full bezel setting. It was totally practical because Jennifer would be able to wear it without it snagging on anything or catching a patient. After a slight size adjustment, they were able to take the ring away. Jennifer insisted on wearing it.

They had lunch in Cromer, then drove back to Spelthorpe where they called on Ash and Lisette. Ash quickly understood the nature of the call from the morning, and it came as no real surprise given what Lisette and the ladies had noticed at the wedding party. Congratulations were extended. Lisette came out with it straight away. "We are delighted for you both. We have known you and your sister since childhood and one thing is certain. You are both excellent judges of character and once you have made up your minds nothing stands in your way! There is something that stands out at Spelthorpe. Here it's always a case of no sooner said than done. I understand why you think you should wait a year before you finally tie the knot although Michael and Victoria have done it, and they will be apart for periods so realistically, what is there to stop you? The only constraint is the obvious one, so the patter of tiny feet will no doubt have to wait until Jennifer qualifies, but I'm sure you have full control over all that. In the meantime, I think Ash has something to say to you William."

"Julian will confirm this to you on Friday after they get back. We had a meeting yesterday to review your situation. You have impressed us all with both your dedication and technical ability. This estate needs a chief engineer. You have got the job. Julian will go over the details with you but until then that is just for the two of you to know". Jennifer beamed with pleasure knowing that they both had a future and a future at the place she loved. William thanked Ash and shook his hand firmly.

Ash added, "You can forget about the day off. What you did today benefits us all so as far as I am concerned it was a day for Spelthorpe. When you are in the role, how you manage your hours will be up to you. It's a salaried post so the only constraint is to get the job done and I know you will do that. You will start from the first of September."

William and Jennifer called on his father and Elsie to give them the news. William's sister Emma was also at home. They were a little surprised at the suddenness but could now understand why William had been going out every evening and seemed so happy. They all expressed their genuine delight. Jennifer had a chat with Elsie and Emma whilst William went outside with his father. William explained what he and Jennifer had planned, and all Robert could say was. "She's a lovely Sheila! Crikey! You've only been here a month and you're going to marry the boss's daughter. You've done a right ripper there, mate." William held back on the news about the job, but he thought he'd put the icing on the cake when it was official.

They returned to the annexe, had supper and spent their second night together. William went to work on the following day. Jennifer called on her sister to pass on the good news. When she emerged, Paddy was in the churchyard opposite with his faithful wolfhound, Gelert. She had always been close to Paddy and was bubbling with so much happiness that she couldn't resist the temptation to give him the news and to put him on notice that another wedding was on the cards.

Paddy hugged her and suggested that they both come and see him. "Alleluia!" he cried. "Three weddings in a year. That will be a hat trick." And he confirmed Lisette's view that if they had made the decision, they should get on with it.

Michael and Victoria left Balmoral on the Thursday morning. They had been given a time to treasure and thanked Bertie and Elizabeth for their kindness. Lilibet was a little sad to see them go because they had gone out riding with her throughout the visit. Bertie said that he would look forward to seeing them in three months' time when he was scheduled to be shooting at Spelthorpe again. They had told him of the loss of Trooper and

Rafe, and that had saddened him because he had been impressed by their performance on previous visits. The duty chauffeur took them to Aberdeen where Simon was waiting with the Dragon Rapide. By 3 pm they were home. Simon stopped at the Hall where Helen was waiting at the door. There was a brand-new Morris Twelve on the front lawn.

"Who does that belong to?" asked Victoria.

The reply came back from Simon, "It belongs to you both. It's your present from us all. You will have to run it in for the first 500 miles so not too fast and vary the speed. You will be needing this between the agricultural college and Cranwell and to come home together when they let you out. You can drive it straight away because it's on the estate insurance."

They went inside and spent an hour telling them about Balmoral and passing on the best wishes from the king and queen. Then they drove the new car down to the cottage. Ash and Lisette were out but Lucy was there, so they dumped their bags, and all took a run down to the lake with the dogs where they swam au naturel. Half an hour later they got back to the cottage. The parents were back from a shopping trip. They all had plenty to talk about, not least the news that Jennifer had got her man.

On Thursday morning William left the annexe for work. They kissed and Jennifer thought it best that she should allow her parents to settle back in before presenting her future husband who in any event was scheduled to call to see her father on the following morning. William duly turned up at the annexe at 9 am on Friday morning. He was wearing his overalls as he had been fixing one of the balers as the hay harvest was in full swing. Julian invited him into the large kitchen. They shook hands. Julian said, "I think you know what this is about as I spoke briefly to Ash Cromwell this morning, but this is the formal part. We are offering you the post of chief engineer for the estate.

We have been impressed by your performance, and we know we have got the right man for the job. I'll have a contract for you to sign this afternoon as the job is salaried. That will be officially dated for 1st September as you will be paid monthly and not weekly as hitherto. It's a significant raise on what you have been getting, but it is a significant role and an expanding one at that, so if you have any issues, I will be here. As far as the estate is concerned you can assume your new role with immediate effect, and I will let them all know. I always work on a policy of total transparency. When we all know where we are at, things go better. If you have any ideas to make things better, I want to hear them. How is that?"

William responded. "I thank you for your faith in me and I swear I will not let you down. I only have one thing to ask, but it's not about work."

"Stop now," said Julian. "I know what you are going to ask me and the fact that you intended to show that respect means a lot." He went to the kitchen door and called out for Julia and Jennifer who were waiting outside. They came in together. Both were smiling, and Jennifer rushed over and wrapped her arms around William. She was wearing her engagement ring.

Julian continued, "Jennifer explained it all to us last night. We are absolutely delighted because you make each other happy, and you are old enough to make those decisions. I must confess we found it a little odd at first because people often get together where there is a common work interest that links them but with Jennifer as a trainee doctor and you as a mechanic, it didn't seem to be there, although we know that you are both keen on riding and the countryside."

William answered, "We do connect. Jennifer fixes people and I fix engines! There are similarities."

Julian came back, "You make a good point there. Julia and I have been down this road before with her elder sister Joanna, so given all the circumstances we propose the same solution until you are both able to get a place of your own. We suggest you live here as man and wife and occupy the large guest room at the end of the upstairs corridor. It has a nice view of the lake. Whilst it is up to you, we see no point in delaying things any longer than absolutely necessary, so we suggest you aim at the fifteenth of October, so if that suits you, we suggest you see Paddy as soon as you can. And finally, Julia and I welcome you as a son. If Jennifer wants it, we want it too. Julia loves the ring. It's beautiful but totally practical. Can we expect you back here to move in after work?"

William held an arm firmly around Jennifer as she continued to hug him. He responded. "You are both very kind and we thank you for that. We will gladly take up your offer and you are right. The sooner we are wed, the better, so we will aim at the fifteenth October as you suggest. Hopefully everyone can come, but we have a bit of time for that. I should get back here for about 6pm, unless we have a major breakdown."

Julian told them to wait, and he returned with a bottle of sparkling wine. He said that he didn't usually go along with drinking at work, but every rule has an exception. He poured out four glasses and they toasted health and happiness together. Julia explained that Joanna and Jeremy would be coming round for dinner that evening to meet William.

William hugged his prospective mother-in-law then took his leave. Jennifer said she would see him up in the hay meadows as it was a day when the whole estate turned out to get the job done and the Saturday would be the same.

Over the next few days, the younger members of the Spelthorpe Company made the most of their time before they headed on to pastures new. The news of Jennifer and William's engagement was very welcome. In the evenings they participated in parties, riding and swimming events around the estate in the lake and the sea. Hunter's visit to Boudicca had been successful with puppies due at the end of September, but unfortunately, that was it, with no wedding or sharing of a kennel. William and Jennifer had met up with Earl Simon and Helen to pass on the news. The estate would lay on a wedding reception for them. Paddy expressed his usual cheer and confided in Jennifer that she had picked a good one. The wedding was lined up for October the fifteenth, so yet again an opportunity was provided for the ladies to go dress shopping. Lucy and Joanna would be the bridesmaids. Jeremy had agreed to act as best man. He got on well with William who had been accepted in his elevated role.

Lisette took Lucy into Norwich, where she fitted her out with a few essentials for her new role at the foreign office. At Spelthorpe as August came to an end there was a feeling that they were about to enter a new era, and the winds of change were afoot.

11

The winds of change

Monday the fifth of September was the day of the watershed. On the Friday before her scheduled start Lucy had gone down to London to settle into her temporary accommodation for her foreign office induction. In two weeks' time, she would be off to Paris and realised that it might be two or three months before she would come home. Paid leave was allocated in four one-week blocks. Flying home would be expensive, and the journey by train and ferry would take a whole day.

On Sunday morning Michael and Victoria drove up to Nottingham in the Morris. Victoria had a room allocated at the college for the duration of her one-year diploma. The hours would match school terms with weekends free and breaks at Christmas and Easter. Michael had found out that his first eight weeks would be similar with weekends off and as a married man he was allocated a larger room in a separate block where wives could visit and stay. Both realised that they would have to play it by ear for the first few weeks.

Officer cadet Michael Cromwell BEM found that his first

few weeks had very little to do with flying, and he had to bite his lip as Stooper had told him. He had to remember that his new colleagues lacked his experience. There were thirty cadets on his course. The first two weeks were spent in uniform fitting, square bashing and familiarisation with military pettiness and the pointless activity to which all recruits across all three services were subjected. He managed to get away on Friday afternoons and drove across to pick up Victoria. He took her back to Cranwell but a RAF college at weekends is not a place for the newly wedded, so they found a nice little hotel in Oakham near Rutland Water that suited them, so if time was short, they went there and if longer, they would go back to Spelthorpe.

They both managed to get back for William and Jennifer's wedding. Lucy had managed to get a day on each side of the weekend away from Paris. The journey was a lot quicker because Simon took the Dragon Rapide down to Le Bourget airport just north of Paris and flew her back on the Monday. It was great to come home. The wedding was a joyous occasion with a reception for sixty guests in the Hall. Jennifer had gone back to Cambridge and was working towards her finals in May, after which, and armed with her degree, she would be free to work anywhere including general practice. She did manage to get back every weekend other than when she had short attachments to major hospital departments.

Michael's first eight weeks went quite quickly and towards the end there was some very rudimentary training in navigation and flying principles. At the end was a short examination. He came out top of the class with little effort. He then moved on to the Elementary Flying Training School. On the first day all were asked to write down their flying experience (if any) and out of the twenty-six that had moved on, there was only him and two others that had flown. The other two were flying club members with Gipsy Moth experience but that was all. At midday, Michael was called in for an interview with the squadron leader who oversaw the course. He asked him about his flying experience and after he produced his logbook the squadron leader took him out to the edge of the airfield. He was kitted up and they walked over to a Harvard parked on the side. The squadron leader asked him to take it up with him as a passenger. Michael went through all the ground checks, then the controls and visual inspections of the cockpit. The squadron leader got in and was impressed that Michael checked him too. Then Michael got in and they took off.

Michael headed east climbing to 3,000 feet over Skegness. The squadron leader then said, "Right young man. I want you to show me what you can do, and I will only take over if there is a safety issue."

"Anything, sir?" asked Michael.

"Yes, anything. Off you go!" said the squadron leader.

Michael thought, "*Well, here is my chance,*" so he was off. He looked at the fuel gauge and saw there was sufficient for two hours. He did three successive loops, then a couple of rolls, then an Immelmann turn, then he put the plane in a spin at 5,000 feet and pulled out at 2,000 feet. After that he took the plane down and flew along the coast doing some mock strafing attacks along the edge of the Wash just above the waves then over to Hunstanton, having pulled up to 1,000 feet over a built-up area. He tore along the coast to Spelthorpe and turned low over the castle keep, then up the valley at low-level, but at speed. Then he pulled up high at the end of the valley, doing a lap of the airfield and having seen it was safe, he took the plane down and landed, taxiing over to the hangar where he switched off. "I thought you might like a cup of tea, sir," he said.

Both alighted and Stooper walked over. "Hello, Biggles," he said. "I see you've brought the boss along. No introductions needed. We know each other well."

"Hello Stooper." said the squadron leader. "How did you end up here?"

"It's a long story." said Stooper and with that he led him inside where Michael put the kettle on and made the tea. It was apparent they knew each other well and they talked while Michael wandered outside and had a chat with the air mechanic. After half an hour, the squadron leader came out, and they took off with the instruction to go straight back to Cranwell. Fifteen minutes later, they were back on the ground.

"I have to admit that was most impressive Mr. Cromwell," said the squadron leader. "You never told me that Stooper had given you hours of tactical flying," he said.

"You never asked me, sir." replied Michael.

"I might as well stick your wings on you now and send you to an operational training unit on Hurricanes. To put you back with your colleagues would destroy their confidence and the same at the Service Flying Training School, but there is a course there with six weeks to go so in two weeks' time, I will leapfrog you onto that for the final month. The problem is you must take a few paper exams which you should walk, so I'm giving you the books for a week of private study after which you will take the exams and move to the next level. How does that suit, Biggles?" said the squadron leader as he grinned.

So that was it. Michael went back to Spelthorpe where he swotted up. He picked up Victoria early that weekend and they came back home. The following week he sailed through the theory and was inserted into the Service Flying Training School with just four weeks to go on the course. There was lots of flying, and a lot of it was tedious stuff about flying in formation, but he bit his lip and carried on with success in the final examinations. Michael passed out and was given his wings on Friday, the sixteenth of December with the rank of Pilot Officer, but in view of his final grade before gaining his wings, that was immediately upgraded to Flying Officer on the second of January 1939 when he was posted to an operational training unit based at RAF Duxford just south of Cambridge.

Friday, the sixteenth of December was a good day. Victoria, Ash and Lisette turned up for the passing out parade. It was the last day at Victoria's college and because of her husband's passing out, they allowed her to go a day early. Michael had collected her on the Thursday evening, and she spent the night in his 'married officer' room. Michael had got off quite lightly because of his experience. In fact, his training had taken just fourteen weeks which probably made him one of the quickest cadets ever to get his wings. On the following day Pilot Officer Michael Cromwell BEM was up early and flew with Victoria in the Dragon Rapide to Le Bourget, Paris where Lucy was waiting. She had managed to get a full two weeks off.

At Spelthorpe, as autumn drifted into winter, there had been changes. William had suggested to Julian that there was money to be made from selling and servicing agricultural machinery. If Spelthorpe took on a dealership from a major manufacturer then all the farms in the district would end up as clients. Contact was made with a major manufacturer, and a sign-up was provisionally agreed. He also introduced a preventative maintenance regime. Doing nothing until things went wrong was costly and inconvenient, particularly when key work could not be undertaken. With this new regime the number of breakdowns was significantly reduced.

Aggie had made major inroads at the school. For the first time they had a proper curriculum with age-related targets. Surplus books and materials from her old school were donated. She enlisted the retired members of the local community to come in to help the children read and do basic arithmetic. This benefited the elderly who at last felt they were doing something useful, and it benefited the children too. The maintenance department was used to carry out repairs. The education authority was charged the standard rate, but the work was done more quickly, and to a higher standard and when the money came into the estate, this was diverted into a special fund that paid for extra books and materials. People would bring well-trained dogs into the school, and the children would read to them. She introduced French to widen the children's horizons, and Lisette came in two days every week to help with that. Arithmetic was applied so it related to work on the farm because that is where a lot of the children ended up working. Aggie's influence was palpable, and it started to snowball with new initiatives. As Aggie always maintained, she was lighting fires, not filling buckets, and when parents could see the difference in their kids, she got their full support.

The weather up to the eighteenth of December had been good. With a few exceptions it had been generally good for the last forty years and that had helped productivity on the farm. November had broken temperature records. All that suddenly changed, and the next few days became a prelude to the appalling winters that were to follow. Christmas at Spelthorpe was a white Christmas, and whilst that matched the views on the Christmas cards, it meant extra work to ensure that livestock had access to water and that hay was made available, but, as ever, all joined in. A day of hard work in the ice and snow made the warmth of log-fired homes, good food and company even more appreciated. In all it was a good Christmas, despite the cold and possibly it was the best ever, because although part of a generation had been away, they were pleased to be back within the greater family. Those that remained had carried on with a determination to make things better for all. The warmth was in the air and not just in the brandy and around the log fires.

Things got milder into the new year, and this made the return to work easier although it eventually turned into a see saw winter with greater reliance on the railway to come home or for Michael and Victoria to meet up, as vehicles remained garaged. The same applied to William and Jennifer, but at least the steam trains always seemed to get through. Similarly, it reduced flying opportunities. By the end of March things were getting a lot better but on the national picture, the storm clouds remained. Everyone remained aware that back at the end of September in the previous year, Prime Minister Chamberlain had returned from visiting Hitler in Munich, waving his famous scrap of paper, but that was all it was, because although people wanted peace, most could see that it would be war. The government contingency plans for air raids and evacuation from the cities underlined that view. In March, Hitler broke the bargain as Czechoslovakia was occupied. As Winston Churchill was to say, they had all fed the crocodile on the basis that it would eat them last.

Michael settled in easily at Duxford. The routine became less regular as he moved into operational duties. As a married officer, he was allocated married quarters. Victoria made it there on most weekends and the Cambridgeshire countryside presented them with pleasant opportunities. He swiftly made the change to the Hawker Hurricane. Compared to what he had flown before, here was a real beast. With a top speed of 340 mph, it was 130 mph faster than the Harvard. Importantly, it had eight machine guns with sufficient ammunition for fifteen seconds of fire to be used in short bursts and that meant 160 rounds into the enemy for every second. They were only rifle rounds, but if concentrated they should do the trick. He remembered Stooper's advice to get in close and really close at that in order to be effective. The plane was responsive. It could turn well, and he made the most of any opportunity to put it through its paces although for most of the time they seemed to be obsessed with flying in tight formations of three, called 'Vic' formations from the word 'victory'. Each squadron would have four 'Vic' formations of three aircraft. Three aircraft were a section, two sections made a flight, and two flights made a squadron of twelve aircraft. There were formations and drills that would choreograph an attack on enemy bombers. Everybody seemed to think that this was total bunk. Some were aware of the German system of flights of four fighters with two sets of buddies to look after each other. This seemed to make a lot more sense. Germany was the only country with recent combat experience – in Spain. The RAF seemed stuck in the ways of the 20s and 30s with flying displays to thrill the public, but that was about to change.

Michael remembered what Stooper had told him, so he bit his lip and went with the flow because it had been hinted that the best pilots would be moving onto the newer Spitfire that was almost fifty mph faster, and if he was going to take on the enemy he wanted all the edge he could get. It took a while to get used to being called 'sir' all the time by the ground crew, but he remembered the advice he was given and befriended them. Some had worked on farms previously, so they had something in common. He spent time with them, going over every aspect of his aeroplane, and he learnt that they could alter the firing angles of the guns. He wanted his to converge at a hundred yards which was a lot closer than the others. They could mix the ammunition belts with amour-piercing, tracer that would leave a smoke trail and standard ammunition. Gun training was poor with very little tuition on the need to give a degree of 'lead' when aiming and firing at a crossing target. It appeared to Michael that all they wanted to do was to get pilots in the air in beautiful formations then spray the enemy at a distance and hope for the best. They did have a couple of shotguns on the base and a clay trap. It was a start in teaching the importance of allowing for a degree of 'lead' when shooting at crossing targets. However, with targets at the same speed and slowing at that, it was an absolute doddle compared to the skills that Michael had picked up from wood pigeon shooting over many years. When given the opportunity to perform, he made sure he did it, and this was noticed by the others. He came across as a totally natural pilot, polite, modest but with a killer instinct. Time would tell.

His instinct paid off because, in April, he was one of a few who were assigned to a new Spitfire squadron. This was truly a pilot's aeroplane. He remembered his archery where the longbow was an extension of one's own body, and the Spitfire gave him that same feeling. It was good, and over the weeks, he got the best out of it. There were some good things that the RAF had like the radar system that was coming into its own. The enemy could be spotted a hundred miles out and that meant squadrons could be directed from ground control to intercept. They knew where they were coming from, how high they were and as time went by, they were able to estimate numbers.

At Easter, Michael managed a week's leave, so he went back home and spent it with Victoria and the rest of the family. Lucy was stuck in Paris, but her letters indicated she was doing well. It was a good chance to get to know William, and they all spent time riding along the sands. Boudicca had produced five good puppies – three dogs and two bitches. Ash had taken one of the dogs and called it Hardy after the naval hero. Joanna kept one bitch for herself calling it Foxie and the other bitch she retained for Jennifer and William, and that was called Nellie or Nell after Lord Nelson who was raised only a few miles away. Another dog went to the Hall as a companion for Zulu and Helen. In line with her custom, she called it Mbwa, which means dog in Swahili. Boynton took the last dog for Aggie, as he was mindful of the fact that Black and Tan were approaching middle age. She would be able to take it to school with her. She simply called it Hund which is dog in German. Boynton, as a student of the German language would frequently be heard to say, " Wo ist mein Hund?"

As a precaution, Simon had asked Boynton to cut down on the number of birds to be raised. The last season had gone well, but the possibility of war meant that a lot of the commercial customers had decided not to reserve a slot for the next season. They would still have enough for family shoots and a few commercial days on a first come first served basis.

Victoria's course was going well, and she did not find it too onerous, given her farming background. It filled in a lot of theoretical gaps, and she found the areas relating to fertiliser use, crop rotation, stock rearing, cost management, animal disease, cure and prevention quite useful. At the end of the course, she would gain a Diploma in Agriculture that should give her a degree of credibility amongst those who thought qualifications were more important than real practical experience. In June Victoria finished her final exams and came home having been awarded her diploma with distinction. Simon and Helen were absolutely delighted that their daughter was preparing herself to take on the estate in the long term. Simon asked Julian if he would take her under his wing so that she could get to grips on the finances and work across the different disciplines within the estate.

At the same time Jennifer qualified. She returned to Spelthorpe with her degree and a certificate to practise, but she was without a job. She looked in the medical journals to see if there was anything available in the local area. There were cottage hospitals but that did not appeal. News travelled fast in Spelthorpe. About two weeks later there was a knock at the door of the annexe. It was John Bowen the village general practitioner wanting to talk to Jennifer. He had known her since she was a baby. John had finally realised that he was slowing down and was feeling the strain, but he wanted to carry on. Dr Bowen's reputation for diagnosis was legendary. He came straight out with it. The money was not what motivated him. To him, medicine was a calling, and he thought he had a solution. He offered Jennifer a position as a junior partner on a sixty: forty basis for the first year and at fifty: fifty thereafter if things worked out. There would be no requirement to buy herself in. He took the view that her contribution would be to allow him to continue, and he would pass on the benefit of his experience as the months went by. To Jennifer this sounded like manna from heaven but there was a lot to take in. John said that it would be unrealistic to expect an answer straight away and asked that she telephone him if she wanted to take up the offer. He explained that as he saw it, he would deal with the majority of callers at his surgery and that Jennifer would take on most of the home visits, but to start with they would work side by side for part of the time. Jennifer told him that she was very attracted to the idea because looking after local people was what she wanted to do most of all.

Jennifer spoke to her father and Major de Lisle, who ran the Spelthorpe Veterinary practice as she felt they were in the best position to advise her. Two days later she called at John Bowen's surgery and told him that subject to contract, she would be delighted to take on the role. Two weeks later the name Jennifer Roy MD appeared on the brass plate outside the surgery.

Duxford was less than fifteen minutes flying time from Spelthorpe so with Michael's squadron leader's permission he was allowed to bring the others from his section and the colleagues from the rest of the squadron up to take tea at the airfield that could easily take half a dozen Spitfires at a time. He flew up with his squadron leader who was impressed with the set-up. Stooper entertained him. Aware that there was a need for a greater amount of basic flying training facilities, the squadron leader asked if the airfield could be made available for Tiger Moth training, with the RAF paying for the use of the facilities and the services that Stooper and his deputy could provide as civilian instructors. Stooper showed him around. He saw the training rooms and the accommodation that could take up to ten at a time. The squadron leader said that he would let the group captain at Cranwell know so that he could visit and consider.

Michael and his team would usually use the airfield as a tea stop. Whenever Victoria heard the distinctive throb of the Merlin engines overhead, she would race up to the airfield for a quick hug from the man she loved. Now that Victoria was home, Michael could usually get away for one or two days on most weeks and there was up to four weeks leave annually. He arranged for two weeks leave in mid-September. It was a good time when the water was at its warmest and the kids were back at school. Lucy had managed to do the same, so they would all be back together again.

12

Pied Piper

Aggie and Elsie turned up at the King's Lynn town hall at 11am on the morning of Saturday the second of September. There were about 150 children, all with bags and cases, gas masks and labels tied onto their coats. There were a host of women's voluntary service ladies and busybodies all under the direction of a very bossy large lady in her early sixties with a big clipboard who made the children tremble every time she passed making the floorboards vibrate. She lacked a sergeant major's uniform because they wouldn't find one to fit her. This was Operation Pied Piper – a mass evacuation of the children of the main cities that immediately followed the news that Poland was being bombed and invaded by the Nazi blitzkriegers. There was paranoia that London would be next, even though there had been no declaration of war, but massive contingency plans swung into effect and train load after train load of children departed the capital bound for rural England and Wales. Norfolk was on the top of the list, although there were reservations in some areas with memories of the Zeppelin Raids on Great Yarmouth,

King's Lynn and Sheringham in the last war. Consequently, it was the rural villages that came to the fore with a massive appeal for fosterers.

"You! Who are you?" bellowed out the bombastic hippopotamus as she approached Aggie and Elsie.

"We are not you," replied Aggie as she fixed the woman with her well-polished headmistress stare. "Good manners cost nothing, and people are more likely to listen to you if you treat them with respect and lower your voice unless it is absolutely necessary to raise it. Now, I am the headmistress of Spelthorpe School, and this lady is one of my teaching assistants so write that down and please get on with your job without terrifying these children. The Germans will do that without your help. They have been through enough already. They do not need you making it any worse for them! An occasional smile will go a mile. Remember that!"

The woman blushed and apologised. The children were lined up, and what followed was more like a slave market. Some children were very smart and tidy with larger suitcases. Others less so. Volunteer fosterers haggled and shouted to take the tidy children and the pretty girls. Others wanted one sibling but not the other. Over the next hour those selected were led away for registration, and what was left was whittled down to just three. There was a sister and younger brother aged seven and five, and a girl of eight. They were grubby with holed clothing and stood there in the clothes they wore with just a label and a gas mask and no cases. The boy had a small teddy bear and the older girl a doll.

"We will take those three," said Aggie as she and Elsie walked forward smiling. They got down and put a welcoming arm around each in turn. They took their hands "Don't worry," she continued. "We are going to take you to the best place in the world. It was good that you waited." With the registration procedure complete they drove back to Spelthorpe. They had agreed that Aggie would take the brother and sister. They had a spare room at the cottage they could share. Elsie would take the girl as she felt that now that William was living in the annexe with his wife Jennifer, Emma would take the girl under her wing.

The journey back was amazing. The children had never been in a car before, and it was obvious they had never seen a cow or a sheep. It was question after question. Elsie sat in the back with the boy and girl, and the older girl took the front seat. On arrival at the cottage the first thing was to get some food inside them. They had a bacon and egg sandwich each and an apple whilst Aggie filled the bath. A phone call to the Hall resulted in Helen and Victoria coming up with a wardrobe of clothing from a storeroom where it had remained after Victoria and her brothers had grown out of it. There were toothbrushes and some toys. Within a couple of hours, a total transformation had taken place. Underneath that city grime, three good looking kids had emerged, and had they appeared like that back at the town hall, they would have been the first to taken in the bidding. Boynton returned from his pheasants and introduced the children to Black, Tan and the young Hund. The dogs were all over them and they loved it. They were like real teddy bears so he took them all out for a walk to show them the woods and the deer while the ladies took tea together.

That evening, after a good meal all three slept soundly in their beds.

The following day was very warm and balmy, although in parts of the country, there had been heavy thunderstorm rain on the previous day. In most parts of England there was the occasional chime from church bells advertising the morning service. It was quiet, and the only sound in residential areas was the pushing of lawnmowers. Many were fixed on the radio, listening to the BBC Home Service. An announcement was expected just after 11am. Paddy had brought a radio into the church and halted the Sunday service.

At 11-15am the announcement came from Prime Minister Chamberlain in the cabinet office at Downing Street. He spoke of an ultimatum to Germany demanding a withdrawal from Poland. The broadcast ended with the words: "I have to tell you now that no such undertaking has been received and that consequently this country is at war with Germany."

In London a few minutes later the air raid sirens sounded. Some people donned metal helmets. They watched and waited. It was a false alarm.

In Spelthorpe there was a stunned silence. Paddy quoted the 23rd Psalm. "Yea, though I walk through the valley of the shadow of death, I will fear no evil: for thou art with me; thy rod and thy staff they comfort me."

He changed the last hymn to 'O God, our help in ages past.'

The rest of the day passed peacefully. Very early on Monday morning Michael returned to his squadron. Two hours later, the children from the village started to make their way to the school and they were joined by the three evacuees.

13

Into the Abyss

September – October 1939

Despite the declaration of war, for Michael, nothing had happened over the last two weeks apart from training flights. Two new sergeant pilots had joined the squadron. They had been posted because their flying ability was above average. They had been welcomed as fellow pilots despite not being commissioned officers. Michael had supported them and shared some of the tips that Stooper had passed on to him. In the meantime, he had worked on his relationship with the ground crews and at his request they had adjusted the guns on his '*Spit*' to converge at a hundred yards which was a lot closer than the standard, but he asked them to keep it quiet, which they did. Some aircraft had been fitted with cameras to film when the guns fired, and Michael had one of these on his plane.

On Friday, the fifteenth of September, Michael managed to take his two weeks' leave. It was good to be back and to see his sister after several months. Lucy returned on the following day having travelled from Paris by train and ferry. Things had carried on as near normal as possible although there were a mass of new rules and regulations to get through but with very little guidance other than what had been hastily prepared. Phone lines were jammed with overuse, so it was largely left to common sense. Rules on blackouts had been introduced two days before war was declared and a new force of 'Little Hitlers' was being created to enforce matters. This remained critical in built-up areas but less so in the countryside.

The first week of the war had brought about the British pet massacre. Mainly in the cities the population had panicked about food supplies and as a result some 750,000 dogs and cats – about one-quarter of the total had been destroyed. The government had produced a leaflet to encourage this and even went so far as to advertise a captive bolt humane killer. Joanna, as the small animal specialist at the veterinary surgery steadfastly refused to put down any healthy pets. She was firmly backed by Jeremy and her father-in-law. Those who asked, were told that the only thing on ration at that stage was petrol, not food. In any event there was always a supply of pet meat at Spelthorpe from fallen cattle and sheep. Fish at that stage was plentiful, and there were always a supply of pigeons and rabbits. Simon's vision with respect to the secret fuel tanks had paid off, but for now farms remained a priority for fuel, and they still had the horses.

The three families met on the beach on the afternoon of Sunday the twenty fourth of September. Lisette, Helen and Julia had prepared a buffet picnic. There were games, swimming and bareback riding on two of the ponies. It was just like the old days they had enjoyed over the years. Nothing had changed other than the construction of concrete pillboxes at one-mile intervals to allow defensive enfilade machine gun fire. There were another two up at the airfield where the RAF had expressed an interest in its use as a basic flight training facility.

The war dominated the conversation. News that Russia had invaded the eastern side of Poland confirmed that they were every bit as bad as the Nazis, but there was little condemnation of that. Michael complained that the RAF were bombing Germany with propaganda leaflets and couldn't understand why they should be supplying Germans with free toilet paper. Simon confirmed that this had been raised when he was last in London when colleagues had asked why our air force was not dropping bombs on Germany especially after what they were doing to the Poles and the torpedoing of the British Liner *Athenia* off Ireland on the day war was declared. The War Secretary had responded. "We can't bomb Germany. That's private property. You'll be asking me to bomb the Ruhr next." The French had invaded the Saarland on the German frontier only to retreat a few days later. The Germans couldn't believe their luck as they cleansed Poland. The German's didn't call it the Phoney War. They called it the '*Sitzkrieg*' because their enemy was just sitting on its backside.

About mid- afternoon Lisette asked Simon. "When are you going to take me up in your Gipsy Moth? I've been up in the Dragon but that's not open to the air. I've always wanted a go at that."

Simon said, "I don't know what the rules are, but I'll take you up for fifteen minutes now if you want. It will be just a quick run along the coast and back."

"I'd like that very much," said Lisette. "We will fly by and wave at you all!" Michael confirmed that if they kept it below 1,000 feet the radar would not pick them up and so Simon and Lisette walked back to the cottage where they jumped in the truck and drove up to the airfield.

Simon took off, flying inland and over the church at Burnham Thorpe where Nelson's father had been the rector, then they headed east and out over the Wash just south of Hunstanton. He turned and headed back along the coast about two miles out at 800 feet towards the beach party. As they got closer, they heard the noise of a much larger faster plane coming from behind them. Simon looked back and saw that it had twin engines and bore the dark cross markings of Germany. Instinctively he started to zig-zag and turned inward to land. It was then they heard the stutter of a machine gun and felt the impact of bullets on the airframe. They were barely a mile from the beach party. They saw everyone running into the dunes. Then, more bullets struck. Simon lost control, and the aircraft plummeted towards the sands on the edge of the sea. There was a huge crash as the aircraft hit the exposed sand. Michael saw the impact and recognised the other aeroplane as a German Junkers Ju 88 long range fighter-bomber. It veered off out to sea. He ran forward along with Ash and was followed by Victoria, Lucy and Helen. In less than a minute, they got to the crash site. There was nothing they could do. Both were dead, killed by the impact and there were bullet wounds. Ash cradled Lissette in his arms. He got her out of the plane and laid her on the sand. Helen was covered in blood, holding onto Simon. Victoria gently eased her back while Ash and Michael got his body out of the plane. They carried him and laid him next to Lisette. Julian got there along with Jeremy and Rufus. They had brought beach blankets from the picnic and covered the bodies.

Ash stood there speechless. Helen was by his side. She held onto him, and he held her. Both were crying as the last twenty-five years of love and challenges, triumph and struggle flashed through their minds.

Helen just said one word, "Why?"

Ash was unable to answer. He stood holding Helen, then said, "It's war but that wasn't war, that was murder. Even in war there are some rules!"

It was then that Ash's military background kicked in. He asked Julian and Rufus to put all the calls in: to the police, the coroner, the military authorities and so on, and to get Paddy to go to the Hall and to put a call in to Boynton. Then he asked Victoria to take her mother back to the Hall with her brothers along with Jennifer and to stay with Helen until relieved. He asked Jeremy and Joanna to deal with all the dogs and horses. Julia would look after baby James. Ash said he would stay there with Michael and Lucy to await the arrivals.

Ash waited with the twins who held each other. They said little because of the shock. Boynton turned up half an hour later. He came with a couple of stretchers that they kept in case of accidents on a shoot. Ash asked the twins to go back to the cottage and to return with a bucket of warm water, a sponge and some soap with towels and sheets. They came back ten minutes later. Boynton and Ash tended to the bodies placing them on the stretchers and cleaning up around the faces. They carried them up to the gap in the dunes where they waited. About an hour later the authorities started to arrive. First was Detective Chief Inspector John Skingle who knew them well from the robbery incident. He had the police photographer with him. Ash identified the bodies to the chief inspector. John Skingle was personally affected as he used to take tea with Ash and Lisette years back when he was the village constable. Then came the coroner and the RAF crash investigators who took charge of the scene and wreckage.

While Ash and Boynton dealt with those issues, Michael and Lucy walked a short distance away under one of the pines. They talked and then swore an oath together that they would avenge the two deaths. Then Michael said, "Sis'. We will not display anger. We will calculate and think how we can do this best. If we act rashly, we will get nowhere and make mistakes, but we will avenge. Revenge is a dish best served cold." They held each other firmly then walked back.

The undertakers came. Ash made them wait while the twins said goodbye to their mother, and he instructed them to stop at the Hall so Helen, Victoria and the boys could do the same with their father. Apart from the wreckage that would be removed on the following day, the beach returned to its natural state. John Skingle said he would come back in a couple of days to take a statement from Ash.

By now it was 7pm and starting to get dark. Ash went back to the cottage with Boynton, John Skingle and the twins. They took coffee laced with a large tot of brandy. Ash's mind was racing, and everywhere he looked, there was Lisette and the things she had done and created. It just would not sink in, and in his mind, he expected her to walk through the door in her usual cheerful way. She was the one who, for years, had kept everything going, not just at the cottage but within the enlarged family, but that would never happen in the same way again. His mind raced with all that had to be done, and there was so much and that made him tired. Boynton and John Skingle left.

Just after 8pm Victoria came back in. She had all the dogs with her. Victoria clung to Michael. The dogs had been fed at the Hall. Jennifer had supplied Victoria with some sleeping tablets.

She said to Ash. "Can you go back to the Hall? Mummy is asking for you. She wants you there with her. We three will be alright here, so don't worry." Ash headed off to the Hall after he had cleaned himself up and got rid of the blood-stained clothes. The twins and Victoria took a pill each and retired. Lucy took all the dogs with her to her room. They knew what had happened because they had seen it, and she just wanted to be with them. Michael and Victoria despite the tablets could not sleep. They talked as they clung to one another and became as physically as close as they could for the entire night until the pills eventually kicked in.

Ash got to the Hall at 9pm. He was met by Amrik and his wife, Jasmir. Both displayed red eyes and were trembling still. They said they would do anything that was needed. They had been looking after the boys who were sleeping in the same room with Zulu and the puppy. Ash thanked them. He said that he wanted to make things as normal as they could be. If Jasmir could open the shop as normal that would be good. He told them that there would be people coming and going for the next few days and if Amrik could arrange it that tea and coffee was always available and simple food, that would keep everyone going. Amrik said that the mistress was up in her room, and he should go up.

Ash went up and knocked on the bedroom door gently. Helen came to the door. She took his arm and led him inside. She just clung to him. He clung to her. Words had no meaning. The way they held each other expressed how they felt. Simon, the man she loved had gone and with him Lisette, her best friend, and they would never come back. Ash's feelings were the same. To Helen, Ash became Simon and to Ash, Helen became Lisette. Helen was a very attractive woman. Ash had always recognised that, but his loyalty to Simon and his love of Lisette meant it stayed that way. Helen had always admired Ash for his strength and loyalty. He attracted her. They kissed, and then they kissed again. They cuddled each other and soon found themselves making love. They repeated this throughout the night until they slept. Being so close was the only way they could come to terms with their internal agony. It was not wrong. It was not disloyal because if it had been the other way around, they would have wanted Simon and Lisette to be the same. It was not that they needed to get to know each other because they knew each other intimately through the years of togetherness that had existed within the family. As god parents to each other's children, they were fulfilling that role. They talked it over when they woke and realised there was no guilt, only loyalty and the quicker normality was restored, the better because that was the Spelthorpe way. Thereafter, they became inseparable.

On the following morning Ash telephoned the cottage at 7am and asked the three of them to come up to the Hall for breakfast. They left the dogs on guard and turned up half an hour later. The boys were soundly asleep because it turned out that Dr Jennifer had made sure that the sleeping tablets had been taken. They ate well because all were sensible enough to realise how important that was. Ash said that for the remaining week of their leave they should base themselves at the cottage looking after things and taking as much time to do the things they always liked to do even though it would be hard. They could eat at the Hall. Michael said that he would let the squadron know but would go back if required and likewise Lucy with the foreign office. It was then that Victoria asked. "This may shock you, but this is something the three of us have discussed. We would like you to know how we feel about things and the future"

"Go on," said Helen. "We know how direct you can be, but we must be open as a family".

"It's simply this," said Victoria. "Daddy and Lisette are no longer with us, and we loved them but there is nothing we can do. You are our parents and god parents and although we are not babies anymore, we have always been one big family, really, and we want it to stay that way, so we would like it to be that the two of you stay together. Put it another way, it means that we would like you to be married."

Helen responded, "We are both mixed up, but we were thinking the same way, and we were wondering how we might break it to you, but you have made it easy for us. The rest of the world doesn't think as quickly as we all do, so please can you keep that quiet for a while?"

Ash added, "People will see us as close in the days ahead, and they will think we are just supporting each other, but you know what they are like out there. They all want something to talk about, and if things happened too quickly, rumours would circulate. That could harm this place, and none of us want that. We love you all, and this is the best way to preserve it. We both thank you for that".

The phone never stopped that morning. Flowers were left on the front steps. The king called to express his sympathy on behalf of Elizabeth and the princesses and said that he would be attending the funeral of his good friends. Helen told Ash about Simon's will that he had changed three months earlier. She had a copy. As it would affect the running of the estate, Ash summoned a meeting with Helen, Julian, Boynton and Victoria.

The will was unequivocal. Victoria would inherit the estate on her reaching the age of twenty-five, but in the meantime, Helen, Ash and Julian would act as trustees. She would also inherit the title, but that would involve intricate arrangements and the king's consent because she was not male. In the meantime, control would rest with Helen as she would have a veto on all issues. Helen had made it clear that she wanted Ash to step into Simon's shoes acting for her on a day-to-day basis at a strategic level. Julian's position would remain unchanged. Boynton would be elevated to take on Ash's role of coast, harbour and forest manager. As heir in waiting, Victoria would attend all meetings at strategic level. The decision was accepted by all. Julian recognised that for much of the time, through strength of character and vision Ash had been driving things forward for the last few years, so he saw this as a natural evolution. Boynton thanked them all for the confidence in him that they had demonstrated. Above all, they were pleased that stability had been established so quickly after the previous day's tragedy.

Over the next two weeks things were inevitably chaotic, but chaos did not reign. There was firm leadership. The press pestered. It made national headlines, but that would pass. Lucy returned to work but was reassigned to the French desk in London pending the funeral and a review in the light of the war.

Over the past year she had become respected for her ability and diligence. Michael returned to his squadron. He was champing at the bit to take on the Luftwaffe. All the dogs moved up to the Hall in the week but at weekends the whole family with Helen would spend time at the cottage. The boys had returned to school on the Tuesday. For the sake of appearances, Ash was allocated a room at the Hall but he and Helen slept together every night. They had become man and wife in all but name. Ash continued with his role as the chair of the Norfolk farmers' group. That entailed meetings with the central government given the increased demands for food production. He continued his presiding role with the Norfolk St John's Ambulance, with whom he had been involved for the last thirty years.

The double funeral conducted by Reverend Paddy Collins took place at the Spelthorpe church on Wednesday, the eighteenth of October. Ash and Helen both spoke. Much was made of Simon's vision and benevolence and Lisette's diplomacy, kindness, and the way she had kept local people together. Michael and Lucy spoke of a wonderful mother who swam in the lake with them, spoke French with them daily and allowed them an adventurous childhood. Both Simon and Lisette had made an enormous contribution to the local community. The church was packed. Lisette's collie, Odi, and Simon's Labrador, Zulu, were present as they were buried side by side in the churchyard. There was sufficient depth to accommodate one more in each grave when the time came. A tulip tree was planted quite close to the graves. It was planted by the king and had been chosen because the leaves looked like a dove of peace.

The king spent half an hour with Ash and Helen in private at the wake held in the Hall. As a friend to both, they confided in him their personal plans and Simon's wishes in respect of the title passing to Victoria. Bertie felt that they had come up with the optimum solution and they could count on his full support.

Michael and Lucy returned to their respective roles. For the immediate future, Lucy was proving a real asset at the French desk, and the increased visits from the French ministries to London required her skills. In the week she worked quite long hours and on occasions that meant she would have to stay at Chequers and other country houses used by the government. However, it also meant that for most weekends she could return to Spelthorpe on the train.

Both Ash and Helen went to the graves several times each week to talk to Simon and Lisette and to reassure them that all was well.

14

Retribution

Michael had returned to Duxford after the funeral. Across the base the staff were aware of the recent events, not least because it had made the national papers, and they went out of their way to support Michael. He'd had an interview with the group captain asking if he wished to take a break from his current role.

Michael said, "I joined the air force to fly and without wishing to seem arrogant, I think I've come a long way on that, but now I want to kill Germans, not all of them, but those who come here to kill our women and children who have never done them any harm, and I can't do that if I take a break. But I will do it calmly and carefully, because the longer I survive the more I can kill. It's as simple as that but thank you, sir, for your consideration. The best therapy for me now is to get up there and to get on with it."

"I couldn't have put it better myself. I'll see what I can do." replied his boss.

Two days later, his squadron leader held a briefing.

"We need some volunteers. I'm sending a flight over to north Norfolk to be based at Horsham St Faith near Norwich. I want two for one section and three for another. We are getting incursions from Junkers 88'-s probing our defences and eyeing up ports like King's Lynn. They are probably after our coastal convoys. The sections will work opposite one another with four days on and four days off. They will be quite long days from first light till dusk. One flight will cover it, and the other flight will be here in reserve. Gentlemen?"

They all put their hands up. The squadron leader looked straight at Michael and said, "Not you, because you will be leading it as acting flight lieutenant." He then selected five more and indicated they would all fly over early on the following day for familiarisation, then one section would fly back for four days' leave to be ready to take over in four days' time.

Scramble

Michael managed to get permission for him to fly up to Spelthorpe to take his leave there. It was only five minutes flying time from

Horsham St Faith. The squadron leader was familiar with the airfield where Stooper and his deputy were now undertaking basic flight training with six cadets at a time. The RAF had flown up two more Tiger Moths and a flight lieutenant trainer from Cranwell to oversee the operation. They were accommodated in the rooms on site and Amrik's staff were doing the catering. The RAF had topped up the tanks with fuel and there was ample camouflage netting for the aircraft.

Two days after their arrival at Horsham St Faith, in midmorning there was a phone call to the room on the airfield where Michael and his two colleagues were based. He had another flying officer and one of the sergeants in the team. They scrambled and took off. Several planes had been spotted at a hundred miles off on the radar and they were vectored towards Kings Lynn. Within minutes they were over the Wash at 10,000 feet. Michael ordered them to test fire their guns. They worked. The sergeant was first to spot them still on the same vector. They were about 8,000 feet. There were five Junkers 88's in an unusual formation, with three in a line and two flankers. Michael took the team around to meet them head-on. He looked around and above for escorts even though it was unlikely given the range from Germany. Nothing was seen, probably because the enemy thought was that these versatile aircraft could handle themselves. Previous forays had met no opposition.

Michael directed, "Hold here. I'm going to take out the line. They won't expect this. Come down to take the flankers when I call or if I mess things up!"

Michael had worked out his plan of attack and it would not be what they might expect. Attacks on bombers were usually from the rear. He dived down and approached the leading aircraft head-on. As he closed, he let out a three-second burst directly into the cockpit of the Junkers. He demolished the entire cockpit with a mixture of armour-piercing ammunition, ball and tracer, then at the last fraction pulled up above and flew straight over the top of the second aircraft. Then he repeated the same frontal attack on the third that couldn't shoot forwards for fear of hitting the Junkers in front. Both aircraft broke up and plummeted down into the Wash.

Michael said to himself, "That's for Mum, and that's for Simon." Then he pulled up high on maximum power to loop, rolling at the top, to go down on the Junkers in the centre. He called through the intercom, "Take out the flankers!" as they had started to turn away. Then he dived down almost vertically and let out a four-second burst with plenty of 'lead' ahead of the Junkers. It didn't see him coming and flew straight into the stream of bullets that Michael had let out. He dived past the tail then turned upwards to rake the underside from a hundred yards. The aircraft burst into flames.

"*And that's for me,*' thought Michael as he swerved to the side and watched as the aircraft exploded. He then climbed high to watch as his two colleagues took out the other two aircraft. They used a lot of ammunition, but they got there in the end, and he was able to confirm their two kills. The Junkers both crashed in the sea with no parachutes.

Mission accomplished; they returned to the airfield. Michael spoke over the intercom:

"Five aircraft, five kills. That's twenty of those bastards that won't fly again. Good kill, chaps. Well done!"

His remarks over the air had been heard back at base and as they landed and taxied back there was a reception committee clapping and cheering as they alighted from their planes. The flying officer in the other plane walked up and said, "That's the gutsiest piece of flying I've ever seen, and that's going in my report".

In the afternoon the squadron leader flew across from Duxford to give his congratulations. The film from the camera had been developed. He couldn't believe his eyes as he saw the devastating effect of Michael's gunfire. Michael confessed that he had picked up the ideas from Stooper. He had studied the design and had worked out the best way to tackle a Junkers 88. He also told his boss that he had got his guns altered to converge at a hundred yards,

The squadron leader commented, "We are going to need to re-write the tactics book after this". The squadron leader continued, "Have you any other bright ideas?"

"Seeing as you mentioned it, sir," replied Michael. "We need to stop this 'Vic' formation of threes. Better we have three flights of four with the guys paired up to watch each other."

The squadron leader continued, "You've done well and shown splendid leadership in combat. I will be recommending that your acting promotion be made permanent. I can't wait to see the group captain watch that film."

After that debacle, the Germans stayed away, and there were no more exploratory missions across the North Sea. The Phoney War resumed. It was quiet again at Horsham St Faith apart from the occasional call to escort Wellington bombers for part of the way when they went across to supply Germany with yet more toilet paper. This only served to strengthen German defences.

Two days later, Michael took his leave. He landed at Spelthorpe in the Spitfire and told Stooper how his advice had paid off. The sight of the Spitfire raised considerable interest with the cadets, and Michael spent a bit of time with them. He told them to listen to whatever the Stooper came out with, because it had worked for him. The whole estate, even Paddy, were delighted that he had avenged the deaths of Lisette and Simon, and would continue to do so, but he was now home to relax with Victoria and the others and to make the most of every day. So, that was precisely what he did.

At the end of his days off he was asked to fly back to Duxford, where his promotion was confirmed. Michael took charge of half the squadron. That was well received by the others. Most of the other pilots got their guns modified and listened to his tactical views. After seeing the film, the group captain had recommended him for the Distinguished Flying Cross. A month later that was confirmed. It was announced in the London Gazette. The king had spotted it, and he telephoned Helen to say, "Well done!"

At Spelthorpe there remained a determination to carry on. The blackout rules meant an end to the November the fifth festivities, but Helen was determined they should continue, so instead they held them on the Sunday afternoon. There was the usual historic fancy dress parade to the castle keep and a smaller fire on arrival. It came as no surprise to see that all the Guys were Adolf Hitlers. They burnt well. Generous servings of roast pork rolls with lashings of cider followed, with ginger beer for the children. As the light dimmed, they fired off a dozen rockets and dished out sparklers for the children. The villagers walked home in the dark pleased that at least in their village, their Countess was not going to allow the 'Bohemian corporal' to rule the roost. Her courage after the tragic event was recognised.

15

Moving on

December 1939

Mid-morning on Saturday the sixteenth of December 1939 found Boynton and Constable Dave Carter walking down Vallance Road in London's Bethnal Green. There was not much green about the place. It was very grey with only a few delivery vehicles in the street, and some of those were horse-drawn. It was cold and overcast with smoke from the chimneys of the Victorian terraces. Some of the kids were playing football in the road, and a couple of women were scrubbing their front steps. Girls had chalked up the footpath and were playing hopscotch.

In the light of the Phoney War most of the evacuated children had returned home but there had been no contact with the three Spelthorpe evacuees. When Aggie had enquired, all the authorities had was a couple of addresses. There had been no contact from the parents. Emily Solomons – the eight-year-old who was staying with Robert and Elsie had told them that her mother worked in a posh hotel in the evenings. There was no father. Aggie and Boynton, who were looking after Harry Baker and his sister, Beverley, knew very little. The children had said they were always being sent up to the Blind Beggar pub to get their father, and their mother was at home, but she was always ill. There was never any money in the house and sometimes the neighbours fed them.

Since arriving at Spelthorpe the children had thrived with good food and regular schooling. Most important of all, they felt that at long last they were loved, and any bad behavioural traits had been corrected. They had told their fosterers that they wanted to stay and never go back to London. Dave Carter had shown an interest as he had three abandoned children on his patch. His sergeant had authorised him to go to London with one of the foster parents to investigate. The police had issued them both with railway warrants to cover the travel cost.

As they neared the first address, they saw two young boys beating and kicking another one. Constable Carter grabbed hold of the two bullies and told them to stop.

One of the boys said, "Who do you think you are? Are you the Old Bill?" Constable Carter enlightened them at which the boy said, "Our mum says we shouldn't talk to you lot. She hates coppers."

The Constable said, "Who are you then? Do you live here?" The boy said, "I'm Reg, and this is my twin brother, Ron."

The other twin joined in the conversation. "We are the best fighters around here. We scare them all. What do you want here anyway?"

"We are looking for Emily Solomons and her mum. Are they here?" asked the constable.

"We know that Emily, but she ain't been here for ages. They took them all away round here because of the bombs. Our mum wouldn't let us go and they all came back a couple of weeks ago cos there were no bombs but not Emily, but her Mum's dead. Went under a bus. Our mum said she was a prosie. She'd drop her drawers for a sixpence!" said Reg.

Boynton asked, "I thought she worked in a posh hotel up West."

"Her? No," said Reg. "She was always down them docks. Our mum said she went there every night hawking her mutton, but she never said what that was about."

"Thanks, boys," said the constable. "And don't you go round beating people up because if you carry on, you'll end up inside and you know what that means."

"Means nothing to us, copper. There are loads around here who have done time. They like us!" said Ron.

With that, Boynton and PC Carter walked on.

The constable said, "I always talk to the kids. If they are under ten, they will tell you everything. It's amazing the amount of stuff I've cleared up just by talking to kids. Those two will end up in trouble – big time. You can spot 'wrong uns' from five years old. It's in their genes, and I'm very rarely wrong on that."

They checked the other address and knocked on some doors. People remembered the kids. The father was always drunk and shouting. The mother went into hospital a couple of months back and never came out. They said it was TB, and they never saw the father after that. He just took off.

The next stop was the desk sergeant at Bethnal Green police station. He was able to confirm everything that they had learnt. He filled in the details. The Solomons woman was well known as a prostitute. She had been arrested a dozen times but every time she said she had to work to keep her girl because there was nobody else, so in the end, they just didn't bother arresting her anymore. She came to her end down by the docks in the blackout. A bus went over her. She just ran out in front of it, and that was it. The driver never saw her until it was too late. That was the trouble with the blackout. There were accidents all over the place. The police went to the house, but there was no sign of the girl and no relatives. The other parents were also well-known because of the rows. The mother had died, and the husband just disappeared after that. He had loads of convictions for drunkenness.

The sergeant said, "It looks like these kids are in the best place with you. I'll make a note, but if you are happy to keep them, we won't tell. Best thing would be if we found the father floating in the Thames. There's a lot who end up in there. Some people should just not be allowed to breed. They say they love their kids, but to them, it's no different to having a dog or a cat and not looking after it."

They thanked the sergeant and headed back to civilisation. Boynton was happy with the result because they had bonded with the children, and he knew that the Roys felt the same about Emily. He would make a record and keep it safe, but he shared the sergeant's view. The best thing was to lay low and carry on. The last thing they wanted was all the welfare experts sniffing around, but they probably had enough on their plate anyway. With what Boynton and Carter knew, they would always be able to get birth certificates for the children in the future if ever they needed them.

While Boynton and Carter were in London, Michael and Victoria were having a relaxed day at the cottage. It was Michael's turn for a long weekend off. He didn't have to go back until Tuesday. It was eight in the morning and just getting light outside. The other good news was that he had managed to get Christmas Eve and Christmas Day off but was expected back at Duxford early on Boxing Day with his half of the squadron. He would have to spend a week there but would return home early in the new year if it was quiet.

Ash and Helen were also sleeping at the cottage with George and Lucy. Edward had remained at the Hall.

Victoria had spent most of the last week in the office with Julian. It was busy and even more so without Lisette who used to fill in. Victoria thought they needed a junior to train up. Michael suggested Rob and Elsie's daughter, Emma. She was quite bright and presentable and at fifteen, that would be a good time to start. Victoria said she would put it to Julian.

Then, Victoria suddenly said, "I have to tell you something and it's important. You are going to be a Daddy!"

Michael was taken aback. He kissed her and said, "That's marvellous, but how come? I've always been wearing a raincoat."

"But not on one night in September when raincoats were the last thing on our mind. It's a farewell gift from Daddy and Lisette. Well, that's the way I see it. Jennifer knows because she tested me, but she won't say a word. I suppose we will have to tell the future grandparents, and they can tell the great grandparents," said Victoria.

Michael kissed her again and held her close, "I want to be a dad, but I do wish we didn't have this bloody war on. I don't suppose it has really started yet, but we will get through it. I'm certain of that."

They got up and took all the dogs out for twenty minutes. On the return Ash and Helen were making breakfast, or rather Helen was making it, and Ash had his arms wrapped around her. Helen had taken to being at the cottage at the weekends. Its informality made them even closer, and she enjoyed preparing food rather than just eating it as they did at the Hall. Michael fed the dogs, cats and chickens and came in with a dozen eggs. They had so many eggs at the moment that on some days, they would do a large omelette for the dogs and mix it with some biscuit for a change. He thought that a spot of flight shooting for pigeons might not go amiss in the afternoon as that would top up the dog food for the week ahead. They would invite Lucy and George to come too. The wind was up and that would bring the birds down low and fast, and Michael liked that.

With Lucy and George still abed they sat around the table with eggs and bacon followed by marmalade and toast.

Victoria came straight out with it "Mummy, I thought I had better tell you both that in six months' time, we will be calling you Grandma and Grandad." She went on to say that it wasn't exactly planned, but planned from on high, and on that basis, they were both very pleased. Ash and Helen had not been expecting an announcement so early, but they too, were clearly very happy.

Helen went on to say that they had an announcement, too. They had decided that they would be tying the knot in just over a month's time. Their inability to show their true feelings outside of the family environment was becoming a strain. It was time to move on. They had discussed matters with Paddy, and he welcomed the opportunity to join them together. They had thought about a registry office wedding, but that would be a betrayal of the place they loved. On reflection they wanted it low key with just close friends and relatives and certainly nothing too lavish. There would be no honeymoon, just two or three of nights up in Edinburgh in a nice hotel, taking the fast train to mark the occasion. A proper honeymoon could wait until the worries of war were out of the way. Anyway, at Spelthorpe, the countryside was so idyllic that everyday could be seen as a honeymoon, so it didn't matter. The most important thing was to be with those they loved and to legitimise their position.

Michael and Victoria expressed their deep satisfaction. What they had suggested a few months back, was shortly going to come to fruition.

In the afternoon, they first went up to the shooting ground past the airfield. The cadets had been given the weekend off, and everything was locked up. Michael gave George a bit of tuition on the clay pigeons, and he quite enjoyed it. Then, for the last two hours before sunset they set themselves up under well-established flight lines on the edge of the woodland. The two girls took one spot, and Michael took another with George, who managed to get five on his own. The girls added another fifteen to that and with Michael's contribution the total bag was thirty-six. They had taken Nimrod and Kipling with Shackleton who was serving his apprenticeship. Once back at the cottage Michael made sure they all participated in taking off the breast fillets. The three Siamese cats pestered until they got one each. George had enjoyed the experience. He was coming up to sixteen in a couple of months. Victoria said she would get the forms from Constable Carter so he could have a firearms certificate like the rest of them.

The following week was taken up with festive preparations. Helen had decided that she would like to invite the whole extended family up for a Christmas lunch and party and that would include the Johnsons, the de Lisles, the Boyntons, the Roys and Ash's parents. She would also invite Paddy and Ruth. Above all, she wanted a convivial gathering without the need to dress up for the occasion. There would be twenty-six in all, but Amrik, Jasmir, the two cooks and two footmen would be able to deal with that. Although Christmas was not special for Amrik and Jasmir they always attended church to show solidarity. On a reciprocal basis their special days for the Guru Nanak birthday and Diwali were always accommodated. As far as Ash, Rufus and Boynton were concerned this was entirely proper. All had served in the trenches alongside brave Sikhs. In those days, their customs were respected in so far as it was possible to do so. It was also the custom at Spelthorpe that the senior managers would get up early on Christmas Day to quickly see to the stock and the milking and this year they were joined by Helen, Michael, Victoria and Lucy to allow the farm staff the day off. The same applied to the stable grooms. Joanna and Jennifer would take care of all the horses. For Christmas Ash and Helen had moved back to the Hall, but Lucy, Victoria and George stayed at the cottage with the dogs, but they all moved up to the Hall on

Christmas Eve. George was fast adapting to the cottage rustic lifestyle, and he thoroughly enjoyed it.

Michael had returned to Duxford on the Tuesday before Christmas and dedicated time to applying more imaginative thinking to his flight of six Spitfires. The squadron leader had backed his experiment. He paired his pilots up, and they practised dog fighting. They studied the design of all the enemy aircraft to work out where they were the most vulnerable and the best way to attack. Many of the older pilots saw the wisdom on this approach. Much time was spent in developing the skills of the newer pilots to boost their survival chances. He scrapped the notion of precise formation flying. This was something their German opposition would later call 'Idioten reigen' (a round dance of idiots) because tight 'Vic' formations meant easy pickings. Michael's view was to concentrate on all -around visibility to anticipate any enemy ambush. The shotgun and clay trap got a lot of use as he introduced them to the need for 'lead' when firing at a crossing target. It had been quiet, with no calls on the squadron time, so this extra training was more useful than sitting around. He encouraged a greater degree of involvement with the ground crews, so all saw themselves as part of one team.

Back at Spelthorpe, Ash was up at the empty pheasant pens with Boynton. For this season, they had only bred and released half the number of pheasants and partridges – a total of 5,000 – but it had still enabled them to run six commercial days and two guest days because much had changed after Simon's death, although they had still hosted the king and queen a few weeks earlier. Helen and Ash were scheduled for a day at Sandringham, along with Boynton and Aggie. Aggie had impressed the queen on the last visit, and Elizabeth wanted to talk more with her. Boynton took Ash up to one of the large secure pens where there were a dozen large black birds.

"Are they Turkeys?" asked Ash.

"No, not at all," said Boynton. "They are Norfolk wild black pheasants! Well, that's what I shall call them. They tell me there's food rationing around the corner and wild birds do not feature. There's a couple going down to the Hall for our Christmas dinner. My keepers have one between them because they normally eat together for Christmas Day, and we'll try and breed a few more for next year. I've got so much grain that we didn't use on the pheasants, and it's got to go somewhere."

"I think we will call that our little secret," said Ash. "And while we are at it, there's a lot of scope for breeding some more pigs. If we have fewer pheasants in the woods, we might as well put a few more pigs in. With all the acorns and what they grub out, they don't cost us much to feed. They are virtually wild anyway, and if they are in the woods the nit-pickers from the ministry won't see them to count them anyway. For the books we will have to show the paddocks in full production, and that will mean a bit more fencing to keep the deer out. I asked the forestry team to work on that a few weeks back."

They walked and talked. Boynton told Ash about the Bethnal Green visit and how well Harry and Beverley had settled in. A bond had been established, and the kids had asked if they could call them Mum and Dad because that was what they wanted. He confided that he and Aggie would like to adopt them, but for now they would carry on as there was no likelihood of the father turning up, and the longer he stayed away, the better. From conversations with Robert, the shepherd, it appeared that the situation was the same with Emily. They had told her that her mother had been killed in a road accident. Their daughter Emma had already adopted her as a little sister.

Victoria spoke to Julian about taking Emma on as an office junior. He concurred there was a need, and even more so as they had to navigate the mass of rules and regulations that were flowing down from Westminster. They had created a system of files: red, what they must do, orange, what they should do, and green, where they could pay lip service. Julian agreed that if she and her parents were happy, they would take her on but suggested she speak to Aggie first as to the girl's suitability for the role.

Aggie described Emma as competent, kind and methodical in her work. She had left at fifteen because there was no facility at the school beyond that age. That was a shame because the girl was sound in both literacy and numeracy and could have gone a lot further. She had been casually employed on the harvest and in the dairy, but in her spare time she had joined the local branch of the St John's Ambulance. Aggie's view was that she should be offered an apprenticeship as a trainee bookkeeper and accountant with release to a college to gain bookkeeping qualifications. Aggie got back to Victoria to say that the college in Hunstanton was providing that facility with either a three-month course or day release over one year. She could get there easily on the train. It would be a start.

Victoria called on Emma and her parents. Emma knew the annexe well because her brother, William, was living there with his wife Jennifer, and she would call on them. Emma was a pretty girl with blonde hair. One couldn't help but like her because of her kind and helpful nature. When Victoria offered her an apprenticeship, she just couldn't believe her luck, and neither could her parents. They agreed for her to start on Monday, the first of January 1940 and that she would attend at college on one day every week. To the Roys, that was the best Christmas present of all.

Christmas Day went splendidly. After church in the morning, the Christmas lunch commenced at 1 pm. There was a choice of Boynton's black Norfolk pheasant or venison. At 3pm they listened to the King's message on the radio. He spoke of the spirit of the Empire and the help from across the Empire in the dark times ahead. With the uncertainty, the only answer was to connect hands with the hand of God to get through whatever was to come.

Understandably, it came across as a sombre message. Helen was keen to lighten the mood. As they relaxed with after-dinner drinks, she handed out little presents to all. The gentlemen received Parker pens, the ladies – toiletries, and the young children toys appropriate to their age. Boynton piped up that it should be known that the gentlemen of Spelthorpe were now officially literate, and the ladies would remain eternally fragrant. Helen then announced on behalf of Ash and herself that they would be joined together in marriage on Saturday, the twentieth of January. It would be quiet affair with all currently present invited to the reception. Julian had agreed to give Helen away and Boynton would be the best man so providing a link to the original Spelthorpe Company. There would be no bridesmaids, but Jennifer and Joanna would be providing the music along with Ruth on the organ for the hymns. There was clapping and rejoicing that what many had seen as a natural way forward would now become official and permanent. Joanna and Jennifer took to the piano and violin. Their initial musical sublimity evolved into a good old-fashioned singsong, and this was followed by musical chairs, blind man's buff and charades.

There was a determination to seize the day and that happened across the board. Whilst Edward remained a little aloof it was good that George was much more confident and personable. The drink flowed sufficiently freely for inhibitions to be lowered and that is what both Helen and Ash wanted. Helen noticed that George was paying a lot of attention to Emma, and she was enjoying the attention. As the evening wore on, they were spotted under the mistletoe, but it was Christmas!

On the following day, Michael returned to Duxford. The

two flights from the squadron were sent to Horsham St Faiths, where they alternated for the next three months. There were more training sessions, and Michael managed to get back to Spelthorpe sometimes taking his flight down to the airfield for an extended tea break whilst they were on duty. It made a pleasant change from the monotony of the base, and they took it in turns to monitor the radio. Ash, Helen and Victoria came up to introduce themselves.

Back at Horsham one morning early in January when they were taking breakfast and reading the papers, one of Michael's flying officers suddenly exclaimed, "Look at this, Michael. The king has just given your old man a knighthood."

There it was in black and white in the list of New Year's honours: *'Mr Ash Cromwell MC BEM – Knight Commander of the most excellent Order of the British Empire for services to agriculture, medical support and the people of Norfolk.'* Michael was taken by surprise because nobody had mentioned it, but he was aware of the huge amount of time that his father had given to those causes over the last twenty years.

And so, it came to pass on Saturday, the twentieth of January 1940, that Countess Helen of Spelthorpe and Sir Ash Cromwell MC BEM were joined together in holy matrimony. It represented the icing on the cake of a deep and loving relationship that tied them together.

16

Dynamo

January – June 1940 England and France

In January, food rationing was introduced. On such a large-scale operation there was always room for a few items to slip through the net. If they were of genuine community benefit, then benevolent blind eyes were turned, but it was made clear that any activity that fuelled the black market would not be tolerated. There was no need for this in any event as most of the workers were in the habit of growing much of their own food and keeping chickens, and these could be fed from wheat gleaned from the fields after harvest and scraps.

In March, six Land Army girls arrived on the estate. They were allocated to the dairy, the forestry and field work. Victoria, who was starting to show her condition, introduced them to the estate, along with Aggie. They were accommodated in two of the empty estate houses. Victoria had called on Aggie to go into her headmistress mode. Aggie had a way with words and could instil a degree of severity when it was called for, so she read them the riot act on day one. It was always best to do that and then slacken off rather than to work it the other way round. As it turned out these girls were well-intentioned and fitted in well.

The Phoney War continued other than around Narvik in Norway, where in April the Royal Navy had some success. The German navy lost half of its strength in destroyers, but this was out of range for land based British fighter aircraft, so Michael was not involved. Land operations culminated in a withdrawal.

At Spelthorpe, Ash had gone through the list of reserved occupations to ensure that those needed the most were not conscripted. Some had age restrictions, but those in restricted groups below the age of twenty-five could still be called up. Trades like agricultural machinery fitters had full protection and most stockmen, shepherds and foresters were over the age limit. Some of the younger men were called to serve. The estate took on boys who had left school at fifteen but could not be called for three more years. There were a few volunteers for military service. This was difficult when there was a need for an increase in agricultural production.

France's greatest military commander, Napoleon, once said, "The side that stays in its fortifications is beaten." That advice was ignored. The French had built a line of eighty-seven miles of defensive forts called the Maginot Line on its border with Germany. It was here that the guns would stop the Hun – but only if he came that way! Everything suddenly changed at 5.30 am on Friday, the tenth of May as the full weight of German blitzkrieg fell on Holland, Belgium and France. Paratroops paralysed communications in Holland, and in five days there was total surrender. Stuka dive bombers, with their screaming Jericho Trumpets, bombed with deadly accuracy and spread panic amongst the civilian population.

The German army poured into Belgium, which had hoped that neutrality would provide protection. It did not. The Maginot Line construction had stopped at Belgium because the French had not wanted to offend the Belgians. The bulk and best French divisions along with the token British Expeditionary Force, moved into the north of Belgium ignoring the heavily forested and hilly Ardennes as they were considered impassable, but that is where the German panzers broke through en masse and headed across to the coast below Boulogne to cut off the French and British.

France was in total panic, despite having more tanks than the invaders. Her top generals were in their late sixties and seventies and remained in their command bunker outside Paris with no radio links to the front. It was like a submarine without a periscope.

One French general broke down in tears. Another said to a British commander, " Je crève de fatigue et contre les panzers je ne peut rien faire" (I'm worn out and can do nothing against the panzers). A British general nicknamed 'Tiny' (He was six feet four inches tall) picked him up and shook him.

The following day, the same French general was killed in a road crash. Another French general allowed himself to be captured by a German catering unit. French soldiers surrendered in their thousands. Outdated British bombers were instructed to bomb the wrong places, only to be shot out of the sky by German Messerschmitt fighters. Chaos reigned supreme. Where the British wanted to stand and fight, the French retreated.

General Gort who commanded the British force, but was nominally under the command of the French, swiftly realised the only option was to get out and to fight a rearguard action whilst evacuation took place around the port of Dunkirk. That rear guard action was bloody. Terror ruled.

At Wormhoudt in France about eighty British captured soldiers were murdered in a barn by the German SS and this was repeated elsewhere. In Le Paradis, members of the Norfolk regiment were lined up and shot. The roads were packed with civilians fleeing the onslaught. The Lufwaffe mercilessly machine-gunned the elderly, women and children as they attempted to get away with the few possessions they could carry. Corpses and broken-down vehicles littered the roadside ditches.

On the twenty sixth of May a signal came out from the Admiralty: "Operation Dynamo is to commence."

Naval vessels headed to the port of Dunkirk. As part of that order, steps were initiated to commandeer small seaworthy vessels owned by members of the public and to get them to Ramsgate Harbour in Kent. The plan was for the big ships to take men from the harbour whilst the 'little ships' would act as taxis between the beaches and larger vessels further out.

On that same day, Michael's squadron was moved down to Manston in Kent so they could patrol over Dunkirk – its beaches and port. Manston was only ten minutes flying time from Dunkirk. The problem was that in France, they lacked any radar location of the enemy, so it became very much, a hit-and-miss affair. The main objective was to take out the Stukas that were playing havoc with the troops on the ground and the ships just offshore. The cloud cover was quite low but patchy. Initially, they were deployed one flight at a time. Michael had split the team into three pairs. He had paired up with the sergeant pilot. For the first couple of days, the Stukas came in unescorted, but Michael was taking no chances. Despite the terror they inflicted on the ground, the Stukas were slow and vulnerable, particularly when climbing up after a dive when the pilots and gunners were affected by the g-force on their bodies as they pulled up sharply. Michael called for his flight to go in a pair at a time, so one pair would dive in and attack whilst the others kept an eye out for enemy fighters. Tempting it might be but to go in as a whole flight it would be reckless if they were suddenly bounced by Messerschmitts. On a sweep along the coast four Stukas were spotted. Michael and the sergeant were the first to engage taking the first two as they pulled up. Michael closed to less than a hundred metres, and his two second burst destroyed the Stukka. His sergeant did the same. They climbed away as Michael called on the next pair to engage the others, and this was the way they worked. The first day was a turkey shoot. The team took out seven, of which Michael took two. The cameras demonstrated the effectiveness of their tactics. It was good that the other flight members had got themselves blooded.

On the second day nothing appeared, but on the third as they arrived Hurricanes from another squadron were engaging Stukas far below them. They watched from on high and spotted four pairs of Messerschmitts diving on the Hurricanes. There was nothing else visible. Michael gave the order to engage. The Messerschmitts just didn't know what hit them as they were so focussed on the Hurricanes. Michael took out one with a one second burst that destroyed the cockpit and as he flew over, he poured a three second burst in front of a crossing Messerschmitt. It flew straight into the stream and broke up. The rest of the flight took out another three, by which time the enemy had worked out what had happened and the remaining three fled. As the Hurricanes broke off, they passed and waved in appreciation, but Michael saw them lose one, but not from the enemy. He broke the basic rule by following at Stuka down to see it crash on the edge of the sea. The Hurricane was hit by a mass of ground fire coming up from soldiers on the beach. In a state of anger and fear, they just shot at anything in the air.

For the next week whilst they remained at Manston, the cloud cover remained quite low and dense. This limited fighter operations, but Michael got another Stuka and another Messerschmitt 109, bringing his personal total kill score to nine. The rest of the flight bagged two more Stukas, a Heinkel bomber and two Messerschmitt 110s (twin-engine fighters). The tally from Michael's flight of six Spitfires was nineteen enemy aircraft destroyed and for no losses. That was quite exceptional. Once a pilot achieved five or more kills, he became an 'ace', but Michael was not concerned with personal glory. For him the war was about killing the enemy but doing it in a way that ensured his survival and importantly the survival of those he was entrusted to lead. Reckless 'tally-ho' cries over the intercom and charging in were not for him because those who played that game did not always look in their rear-view mirrors. They paid the price for that folly. His doctrine was one of, "Go in, make your kill, then get out and reassess," and he made sure that those with him applied the same rule.

Whilst this was going on, the appeal message for 'little ships' had reached Spelthorpe via the harbour master on the late afternoon of Monday the twenty-seventh of May. On getting wind of it, Ash drove up to find Boynton and met him halfway because Boynton was looking for him for the same reason. There was no question of it. They went back to Boynton's barn to get what they needed from under the secret trap door. Boynton selected the Browning automatic rifle; four Mills bombs and two Mauser 'Broomhandle' pistols with the one silencer as well as forty rounds for the Browning and two spare clips for the Mausers. There was also an oiled, waterproof satchel.

Aggie emerged from the cottage, curious as to what they were up to. When she saw the weaponry, she went pale and shook because she too had overheard the telephone conversation.

"You are going to France, aren't you? I don't want you to go. You've both done enough already and this place has lost too many. Have you told Helen?"

"Not yet," said Ash, "but we have to go. We have a good boat that is doing nothing. We must get those guys back or we won't have an army or anything to defend this place. We have no choice. This is just a bit of insurance to make sure we keep the advantage!"

"Don't worry, love. We will come back, and that's a promise. We have both done far worse than this in the past," said Boynton.

"I'll be down at the harbour with Helen, so don't you go without seeing us first." said Aggie.

An hour later, Helen and Aggie appeared at the dock. They had bought extra clothing and some food and drink. They were both in tears.

Helen said, "We know we can't stop you because that's the men you are, and that's why we married you but just promise us that you will stay safe."

"We will be back. Don't worry!" said Ash. They stepped onto the jetty. They hugged and kissed their wives then jumped back onboard the six berth cabin cruiser and took off. They didn't look back. They had a job to do.

The boat was powerful. They drove it through the night, and ten hours later, at 4am, they docked at Ramsgate. They ate some of the sandwiches and noticed that Helen had packed half a dozen amphetamine tablets that had obviously come from Jennifer. There was a short note saying when to take them. At 6am on Tuesday morning they registered and were checked out in respect of their boat-handling ability. They were given basic charts, ration packs, and fuel. Fresh water was topped up. After a few hours' wait they set off in a flotilla to Dunkirk with a naval escort. It was not a direct crossing because of part of the French coast had been mined, and Calais was in German hands. Fortunately, there was low cloud, and that prevented aerial attack, and the sea was calm. As they neared the coast at Bray Dunes, plumes of smoke hung over the port to the west and in the hinterland, and they could hear the rumbling of shell fire. The beach was not unlike the one at Spelthorpe, but there were no pines, just dunes with marram grass and behind that a road running parallel to the seafront with houses, shops and hotels, many of which bore shell and bomb damage. The tide receded up to half a mile across sandy, muddy flats. Thousands of soldiers were sheltering in the dunes, and long lines stretched down to the edge of the sea. There were lines of trucks acting as piers running out to sea and soldiers clambered along these to get to the 'little ships' that were taxiing them out to the naval vessels and larger ships which had to wait in deeper water. There were some wrecks of ships that had been bombed. On arrival Ash and Boynton got to work straight away. They took the wounded as a priority. Discipline was usually good over the next few days from the men who were desperate to get home. There was only one issue when some French soldiers who had been waiting in the queue and were getting onto the cabin cruiser. A British soldier started pulling them off and was shouting. "Don't let these fucking Frogs on. These bastards ran away."

Boynton drew his Mauser and said, "This is our boat, and we say who gets on it. Not you! If you try and pull anyone off, I'll give you an extra eye socket with this. Now you help our French friend get onboard or you can stay behind. The choice is yours!" The soldier realised his mistake and helped the Frenchman on board.

And so, it went on – day after day, night after night, with sleep in snatches. They ferried the soldiers out to the sides of destroyers and other ships with up to thirty at a time. Once at the side of the bigger vessels they climbed up scramble nets to get on board. When there was a gap in the cloud, the Stukas came down, bombing and strafing the beaches and boats. Everybody scattered. The boats attempted to zig zag if it was possible, but in the main, they were sitting ducks. Soldiers shot at any aircraft they saw even though most of them were out of range and unlikely to be affected by a single bullet. Boynton spotted one on a low strafing run aimed at the vessel they were loading. As it came over, Boynton took aim with the Browning and emptied an entire magazine of 20 rounds into the aircraft belly in a couple of seconds. He must have hit something vital because the aircraft dropped and smashed into the sea 200 yards ahead. A massive cheer went up. A soldier asked, "How the hell did you manage that?"

"Just like taking a high pheasant! Nothing to it," said Boynton.

.

17

Escape and evasion

June 1940 France

On the third of June, the perimeter was closing, but miraculously thousands had been taken off the beaches and from the harbour mole – in fact, more than seven times the 45,000 originally anticipated. There had been a cost with ships sunk and the beaches were littered with the bodies of the dead.

Ash and Boynton had just emptied their boat onto a destroyer that was taking off when the shelling started. A shell exploded to the front, taking off a large chunk on the bow above and below the water line. Going forward would flood the vessel in seconds so Ash put it into reverse on full power and they went backwards until the vessel hit the beach. They jumped off. Boynton had grabbed the watertight satchel and Ash had the chart which also mapped about twenty miles inland. There were a few remaining soldiers on the beach, mainly wounded, and an officer was with them. The officer had seen what had happened to the boat and said, "Looks like you're going to end up in a prison camp with the rest of us. I don't know what they are doing with civilians, but one thing is certain. We've missed the boat."

Ash replied, "There's no way we are going to spend the rest of the war in prison. We thought we'd go back through their lines and make our way west. They won't be expecting us to go back, so we might have a fighting chance." The officer replied, "You might have a fighting chance if you can get through the first couple of miles into open countryside. There won't be many out there because they've cleansed that bit in a fashion. They will just be aiming for the main roads and towns. I wish you luck because you are going to need it, and you will need to move fast."

Ash and Boynton waited until it was dark, then headed inland. They hugged the hedgerows and ditches. The Germans were in large groups and noisy as they celebrated their victory. They had raided houses for alcohol, and many were drunk, and their officers didn't seem to mind too much. The pair made good progress. Every ten minutes they stopped and listened and smelt the air for cigarette smoke. By 2 am they were ten miles inland. They discreetly looked in scattered houses and gardens for anything they might need. They found food and clothing that would give them the appearance of farming folk. In another in the back garden there were bicycles. As the landscape was flat these were common. They picked the best, and rode south, deeper into the countryside. In the three hours before dawn they managed another thirty miles. Ash had a good knowledge of the area from trips years back when they had visited Lisette's parents. They knew they had to get down to the Somme and then head west after crossing the river. As it got light, they stopped and looked and listened more often. They hadn't seen or heard anyone since they took the bicycles. They had taken the amphetamine pills.

After another fifteen miles they went through a small village called Beaumetz-les-Loges. As they emerged, Boynton noticed a grey lorry parked off the road in woodland. At a hundred yards off they turned into the wood and Boynton said, "Wait here while I check it out."

Boynton took out the Mauser and silencer and crept forward. As he got closer, he saw dark crosses on either side of the lorry. There was a tarpaulin over the back. There were two figures in the cab asleep – both wearing German uniforms. He skirted all around. They were alone, probably on a delivery run, and had stopped for the night. There was an empty bottle of brandy on the floor of the cab. In the back were boxes with marked with red crosses, some jerrycans and other boxes full of papers. Boynton fired quickly and quietly, with two head shots. He pulled the bodies out and stripped off the uniforms. He ran back to Ash who came forward. "We have transport," he said. They went back and dragged the bodies into the undergrowth. On checking the lorry, there was half a tank of fuel. The papers in the back were maps of the area between the Somme and the Seine. There were about 500 of them. They changed their clothes. One tunic was a bit baggy but otherwise alright. They kept their old clothes and got in the cab. The helmets fitted, and there were two Schmeisser MP 40 machine pistols. Boynton put those in a hold-all he found along with spare magazines. That made up for the loss of the Browning at Dunkirk.

Boynton drove. The signposts indicated that the village was just off the main road from Arras to Doullens which had served as a headquarters in the last war. Ash knew that Doullens led on to Abbeville, and they needed to go further south to cross the Somme where it was quieter. They carried on down south and saw signs to Serre and Albert. It spurred them on at a pace. Boynton had prepared what to say if they were stopped. He would say they had urgent maps for the German forward command at Amiens. They got through Albert. They saw a couple of Germans on foot. They waved and carried on. Two miles south of Albert they saw a woman walking by the road.

They stopped. The woman looked fearful until Ash spoke to her in fluent French and told her they were escaping British soldiers, and they had stolen the truck. After that, she told them as much as she could. There were hardly any Germans there. Most had moved on. They saw a few coming up with supplies on horse and cart. As far as she was aware the Germans had stopped at Amiens but there was no one at the bridge ahead over the Somme at Sailly- Laurette. If they carried on, they should reach the French lines about twenty miles further on, but everybody was on the run.

They carried on across the bridge on a minor road and through Breteuil. It was apparent that the Germans were sticking to the main routes but sooner or later they would cross the front line. Ash fixed up a white flag on a stick just in case, but they stopped at vantage points and every mile or so to look for signs of a French line. After another twenty miles they saw a civilian convoy ahead of them heading towards Rouen. They scattered when they heard the noise of aircraft overhead. It was amazing. They now knew they were ahead of the German front line. Although they hadn't seen Germans anywhere behind them, being in a German truck was not the wisest thing if they encountered retreating French soldiers, so they slowed as they got closer to Rouen. They passed several cars in the ditch but many of these appeared to have been shot up. There were unburied bodies too. They passed another. It looked sound. Ash checked it – no petrol. When they put petrol in from a jerrycan from the truck it fired up on the third attempt. They filled the tank with fuel and put two jerrycans in the boot along with a couple of the first aid boxes and the holdall with Boynton's booty. Then they changed back into their civilian clothes and ditched the uniforms in the back of the truck. Boynton couldn't resist taking the pin out of a Mills bomb, having wedged it between four full jerrycans. When the Germans found it, any movement of the jerrycans or the truck would give them a nasty surprise.

Ten miles further on they came across a retreating French convoy. They were heading for Rouen. Ash spoke to the officer and told them of their escape from Dunkirk. He was pleased to hear that so many Frenchmen had got away too and hoped they would be coming back to fight on. They mentioned the German truck and the booby trap, and that brought a smile to his lips. He invited them to join the convoy, but they declined because of the Stuka threat. He wished them well and told them to head to Saint- Nazaire as he had heard that a big ship was coming to take refugees away.

An hour later they crossed the Seine at Rouen. The town was in a state of panic although most had already left and were heading south. After another hour they stopped halfway to Caen in Normandy. They put the rest of the petrol from the first Jerrycan in the car, just in case the cans got confiscated by the French. At least they had a full tank. They found a bar that was still open and managed to get a sandwiches and coffee which they got by bartering two gallons of fuel. They parked up off the road and tried to sleep for an hour, but the amphetamines would not let them, so they carried on. Ash was a lot happier now they were in Normandy, which he always considered as home territory. He took his turn at driving. An hour later, they got to Caen, and from there it was only a twenty-minute drive up to the Ranville home of Lisette's parents. It was 10pm.

Lisette's parents lived in a comfortable house on the west side of the village close to the coast road and the bridge over the Orne River. They had a large south facing garden that was full of vegetables. When Ash suddenly appeared at the door, they were shocked, to say the least. Ash had managed to speak to them when Lisette and Simon were killed. Because of the war, communication had been difficult, but they had received Ash's letters, and they knew that he had married Helen. Ash brought them up to date with all the events including Michael's shooting down of the three Junkers fighter bombers which he had not mentioned in his letters. He also told them that shortly they would be great grandparents as Victoria was due in a month's time and that Lucy was now working with cabinet ministers at the foreign office. He told them of their experience at Dunkirk and their escape but left out some of the gory details.

Ash outlined his plan to get them out and back to England, but they would have none of it. Having lived there for the best part of twenty years, this was their home, and they were determined to remain even if that meant being under enemy occupation. For all intents and purposes, they were French. They used the language all the time including with each other and they had so many friends in the area who said they were staying too. Ash mentioned the liner due in at Saint-Nazaire but added that it would not be the way to go home. It smacked of all eggs in one basket. Ash and Boynton had seen the brutality of the Luftwaffe at Dunkirk.

Lisette's father was of the view that the quickest option would be by boat from Dives-sur- Mer. There were a lot of boats there. The owners had fled south and would not be back. It was only eight miles away along the coast and he knew the two gendarmes who looked after the port area. He said he would take them there in the morning. After a meal, they both slept soundly for a full eight hours.

On the following morning, they handed over all the rest of the fuel and the first aid boxes. The first-aid boxes went in Lisette's parents' loft, but the jerrycans were emptied into old wine containers and discarded on the way to Dives. They met up with the two gendarmes who had been plotting to get away themselves so they could join up with the Free French in England. They believed that if they remained, they would be compelled to work with the Nazis and betray their own people. That was not for them. The only problem was that they needed a sailor and navigator but with Ash, that problem was solved. They found a sailing vessel that would comfortably take up to six. With a wooden hull there was less of a threat from magnetic mines. It had a diesel inboard motor with half a tank of fuel. They turned it over. The weather for the next twenty-four hours indicated a force four breeze from the southwest. That was perfect to sail across and looking at the vessel, with that wind they should make eight to ten knots. The only thing was the sail. It was white and that was not good. They looked around the sheds and found a gallon of creosote. It would smell a bit, but that would do the trick. They agreed that they should leave at 10.30 pm. That should get them two-thirds of the way across the Channel by early morning. Ash said they should bring their identity documentation with them as that would speed things up with the British authorities. Ash thought it probably best that they stay at the port to make sure of everything, so he said farewell to Lisette's father and thanked him. Her father pressed an envelope into his hand, adding that he had lost contact with London because of the war, but he had a letter that he had written overnight addressed to the Head of the Foreign Office offering his full support if there was anything he could do in the years ahead.

Ash took the sail to the large shed and doused it with the creosote then hung it up. They now had a dark brown sail that was less likely to reflect the light. The gendarmes turned up at 9 pm, and one who was married had brought his young wife with him. She was coming too. She was about the same age as Lucy and had an uncanny resemblance, but Ash felt his mind was playing tricks because of his urgent desire to get home. They left the port at 10.30 pm on Wednesday the fifth of June. It was in total darkness because of the blackout. Ash eased the boat out using the inboard motor until they were clear, then at half a mile offshore, they hoisted the mainsail and jib sail. The wind bit and they took off at a pace. Ash had set a bearing for Poole harbour but knew that with the wind and current drift, they were more likely to make Portsmouth.

Dawn broke early, about 4.30 am, by which time they were well over halfway across. The wind held. No other ships or craft were seen, nor any aircraft and that was good news. At 7 am, they could make out the lighthouse at St Catherine's point on the Isle of Wight. Ash veered the course to take them around the eastern side of the island and into Portsmouth.

As they passed five miles off Sandown, they became aware of a large boat heading straight towards them at speed. When they saw the white ensign flying from the mast of the motor torpedo boat they cheered and waved. The MTB came alongside demanding identity. Ash shouted back. "I am Sir Ash Cromwell returning to England having escaped from Dunkirk where the cabin cruiser we were using was sunk by enemy action". He carried on but the naval lieutenant in command was clearly in a hurry and he beckoned them all on board as quickly as possible.

"I can't tow you in. We'd be a sitting duck," said the lieutenant.

Ash replied, "It's of no matter to us. We pinched this boat from Normandy. Suggest you put a shot or two below the waterline, or I can go back on board and open the sea cocks if I can find them". "Don't bother we will deal." said the Lieutenant and with that they pulled away. At 50 yards the man on the Vickers heavy machine gun put a burst of .50-inch rounds that blew big holes in the yacht just below the waterline. They took off at speed. Ash and Boynton went below with the officer where they outlined the full story. He was amazed at how they got away.

Boynton said, "Just goes to prove there's still a lot of life in us old dogs from the last fight, but we want to get home now because we have got two wives who are back in Norfolk crying their eyes out."

At Portsmouth, they had a debrief with the police and army intelligence. They bade farewell to the gendarmes and the lady who remained at Portsmouth for further interviews. An invite to Spelthorpe was extended and a telephone number passed on. Ash put in a call to Spelthorpe and spoke to Amrik, just to say that they were both alive and well and would telephone later with an expected arrival time at King's Lynn station where they expected to be met. The police issued them both with travel warrants to get back home and took them to the train station. All this time Boynton managed to keep his satchel and holdall away from prying eyes.

Two hours later they were in London. They called at the foreign office to deliver the letter. The official at the desk was very stand-offish until Ash lifted him by the lapels and whispered in his ear, "I am Sir Ash Cromwell and with my friend here for the last week we were on the beaches at Dunkirk rescuing soldiers. We were shelled and bombed and left on the beach, but we got through enemy lines and killed some Germans on the way, then we stole a boat to get back here, so unless you want me to get really, really angry, I suggest you take us up to meet your boss straight away!"

The man trembled and took them straight up the stairs to the under-secretary's office. The under-secretary was helpful and appreciative on reading the letter and was impressed at the speed of its delivery. He knew Lisette's father and Lucy and mentioned that she was very highly regarded.

They left and crossed London on the tube, then boarded the train for Norfolk after telephoning Spelthorpe with their arrival time. Two bouquets of flowers were purchased. They went to the buffet car where they had a snack and two large whiskies.

They experienced a rapturous welcome on arrival at King's

Lynn from Helen and Aggie. On returning to the Hall, Helen said to Ash, "You have been a very naughty boy, and I am going to teach you a lesson!" And with that she dragged him up the stairs and took him straight to bed. That lesson was replicated in the Boynton cottage.

On the seventeenth of June the requisitioned liner RMS *Lancastria* overloaded with troops and British nationals, was bombed by German Junkers 88 bombers just off Saint- Nazaire in Brittany. There were up to 7,000 deaths – the greatest British maritime disaster ever. News was suppressed on the orders of Prime Minister Churchill, but it leaked out a month later.

18

Survival

Now that Ash was back in England, he was called upon to deal with an issue that had festered over the last month.

On the same day that Hitler's blitzkrieg was unleashed on Western Europe, Winston Churchill became Britain's prime minister. Even though he didn't get it right all the time, at last, there was leadership with the backbone that had been sadly lacking for many years. In mid-May a call had gone out for what was initially called the Local Defence Volunteers. With so much else going on, things were quite messy to start. Volunteer organisations sometimes act as magnets for well-intentioned idiots. In the weeks that followed, and with the subsequent name change to Home Guard, there was a clear need for discipline and leadership at local levels. Ash was asked if he would sort things out locally in north Norfolk.

Ash was commissioned as a lieutenant colonel, and he initiated a north Norfolk coast battalion with companies at Spelthorpe, Hunstanton, Sheringham and Cromer. Ash wisely selected the company commanders who were commissioned as captains. Boynton was put in charge of Spelthorpe. It drew in men from the surrounding villages. Given his expertise he also oversaw what was euphemistically described as weapon training for the battalion. Major Rufus de Lisle served as Ash's deputy, and various others with managerial or military experience served as Lieutenants and non-commissioned officers (NCOs). It came as no surprise that, despite national shortages following the losses at Dunkirk, the Spelthorpe Company always seemed well supplied in weaponry, and they were the only company in the land with two German MP 40 machine pistols.

In addition, Boynton and a selected few were chosen to engage in the construction of secret underground bunkers concealed in the forest from where attacks on the enemy could be undertaken in the event of German occupation. The bonus was that this resulted in extra weaponry and explosives being made available for it to be stockpiled in the secret locations.

On June the eighteenth at 9pm, people listened to Churchill's 'finest hour' speech. Close to the end the reality of the situation struck home.

"The Battle of France is over. The Battle of Britain is about to begin."

People prepared for invasion and total war. Submarine attacks in the Atlantic pressed for greater food production, and this, coupled with the preparations to repel any invasion meant leisure time was seriously restricted, but the longer summer daylight made things easier. Julian did a splendid job in holding things together on the farm. He had some good people around him. Ash and Helen made a point of regular rounds to thank all the workers for their efforts. As far as was possible, Sunday remained a day for leisure.

Following his return from Manston, Michael had a brief period of respite. To the south of Duxford, the RAF's 11 Group was charged with defending London, Essex, Suffolk, Kent,

Surrey, Sussex and Hampshire and they would always bear the brunt of any German air attacks. Duxford formed part of 12 Group that covered the Midlands up to Lincolnshire, with Norfolk and the northern part of Suffolk. They would be the first reserve for 11 Group. Michael returned to Horsham St Faith in Norfolk as this was best placed to intercept any enemy forays from the east. Work continued with the tactics that Michael had initiated over Dunkirk and the squadron leader believed this to be the way ahead. The other flight had been pleased to take it up, so the squadron was reorganised into three flights of four with two pairs in each, with a flight lieutenant leading each flight.

Mid-morning on Monday the twenty-fourth of June saw Michael jump in his Spitfire and take off for the five-minute flight to Spelthorpe following a call that the baby was on the way. The squadron leader was sympathetic to Michael dashing up to Spelthorpe for the birth of his first child subject to any exigencies of duty. Officially, this went down as a training visit to the cadets who were training there. On arrival Stooper gave him a lift down to the Hall and during the journey Michael updated him on the success at Dunkirk and that he was now an 'ace', thanks largely to Stooper's robust training regime.

When they reached the Hall, Michael dashed across the front lawn still in his flying kit as if on a 'scramble', but the object of the interception on this occasion was Victoria's room at the top of the stairs. He burst in as Victoria was in the final stage of delivery. She was attended by Jennifer and the midwife. Victoria reached out, and he took her hand as she made a final push and a few seconds later the baby arrived. The midwife took the baby who instantly started a gentle cry. All was well. The midwife announced. "You have a little girl Mr. and Mrs. Cromwell." And she handed the baby wrapped in a towel to Victoria.

After a couple of minutes of private time Michael strode out onto the landing and called Helen and Ash up from where they were waiting in the foyer, "You have a little granddaughter". There were smiles and tears all round at the arrival of Lisette Helen Cromwell. Michael stayed for an hour. He held the baby and Victoria. He thanked the midwife and gave Jennifer a hug. He took tea, then announced. "Sorry but I have to get back to the war. I'll be back for two days leave on Thursday, I hope!"

Ash gave Michael a lift back to the airfield. Michael spent twenty minutes with the six cadets telling them about Dunkirk, then he jumped in his Spitfire and flew back to Horsham St Faith, but not before doing a loop and a victory roll over the Hall to announce to all on the estate that they had a new member. Five minutes later, he returned.

That afternoon, Michael took off with his flight of four to a report on the radar of 'bandits' approaching King's Lynn. It looked like another attack on shipping that was happening all around the coast. Fighter escort was usually absent because of the range, particularly for the more dangerous Messerschmitt 109s, but it paid to never take things for granted. They climbed high and spotted eight Junkers 88s way down below being engaged by Hurricanes that had come across from Lincolnshire, but then they spotted a similar number of Messerschmitt twin-engine 110's diving down on the Hurricanes. The 110s were relatively slow and lacked manoevreability compared to the Spitfires, but they were well armed. Michael and his wingman dived down on the 110s and took out two of them with total surprise, but then, as the others scattered and attempted to engage Michael and his sergeant wingman, the other pair came down with more surprise and took out two more. Michael turned and put a three second burst ahead of another 110 that flew into it and disintegrated. The rest fled with the other pair hot on their tails, and they managed another kill. The total score for the Flight was six. Down below the Hurricanes had taken out four of the Junkers but had lost one plane. The pilot managed to get out and parachuted down, landing on the beach, so at least he stayed dry. It was a good afternoon. Michael's score had risen to eleven, and all the other pilots got at least one each with the other sergeant on the flight getting two, so on return to Horsham, it was drinks all round.

And that was the pattern for the rest of June and the best part of July. There were a few coastal attacks, but with little success for the enemy. By the end of July, Michael's personal tally had risen to fourteen. The squadron's success was getting noticed.

Michael got back to Spelthorpe as much as he could to spend time with Victoria and the baby at the cottage. Lucy would come back at the weekends so swimming in the lake and the sea resumed on Sundays. Joanna, Jeremy Jennifer and William joined in the fun. William needed a break because he was working from dawn to dusk on the farm and doing a lot more than purely his engineering duties. Joanna's baby James, at eighteen months, was now walking. With the number of participants, there was always somebody to hold the babies whilst the young mothers could fully engage. The dogs and the horses loved the extra attention. The biggest surprise of all was young George, who now turned up with his girlfriend Emma, who had been working extremely hard in the farm office while Victoria had two weeks off after the birth. George had seemingly emerged from his shell in more ways than one, and that pleased Helen. Victoria was back at work in the office. She took baby Lisette with her, and if she had to get out on the farm there was always Emma or Julia who would step in temporarily, and on some days, Helen would take Lisette for the day.

As August came things got serious. The Luftwaffe made moves to destroy airfields and radar all along the southeast coast. Michael and his flight joined the rest of the squadron back at Duxworth, but the squadron played to their new tactics. They often found themselves coming in to reinforce 11 Group. Things were not easy if the bombers had a fighter escort, but there were rich pickings when the fighters left the bombers because of their limited range. There were few days off. The German bomber crews complained that their fighters were not with them, so Göring ordered the fighters to fly with the bombers, which gave the RAF a huge advantage. With German fighter losses mounting they soon abandoned this practice and went back to their old ways. Michael continued to get his team to hold back until the fighters were spotted. This saved lives. Michael saw so many inexperienced pilots who were lost because they courageously went straight in without thinking. Some criticised Michael for holding back, but the statistics showed that his team survived, and over time they, shot down far more of the enemy.

On some days every plane was up, but somehow, they got through it. There was a lot of politicking going on at high level about massing fighters together in what they called the 'Big Wing', but in practical terms this often took too long to organise in the skies. Michael was no fan of the 'Big Wing', although when it did work, the effect on enemy morale was devastating because the Germans kept being told that the RAF was finished.

Finally in September, the Germans started targeting London rather than airfields. This was in revenge, because the RAF had managed to bomb Berlin – something that Hitler thought was impossible. That saved the airfields, but ordinary citizens paid the price in what became known as the Blitz. Increasingly the Germans bombed at night, and this was easy navigation for them because the water on the Thames Estuary shone in the moonlight and showed the way to London. The fight went on, and German losses mounted.

On one occasion, Michael had to ditch in the Thames Estuary after his engine failed due to enemy gunfire. It was inevitable given the number of aircraft in the skies. He got out and, within an hour, was picked up by a RAF rescue launch from Sheerness.

Two days later, he was back in the air in a replacement Spitfire, but he insisted on the guns being modified to converge at a hundred yards before he took her up. Spitfires and Hurricanes were flying off the production line at up to a hundred every week, but that was not matched by trained pilots to fly them.

By October there was a realisation that the invasion was not going to happen, and the majority of attacks were at night on cities. Michael and his flight went back to Horsham St Faith. They liked it there. Michael's personal tally had risen to twenty-seven and of those fifteen were Messerschmitt 109s. His sergeant wingman was now on twelve. He and the others were tired. They were never alone because pilots from Poland and from all over the Empire had joined in the struggle. Over the last three months the squadron had lost just one pilot, but the majority had survived, and that was what it was about – survival, survival to fight the enemy day after day and survival for the very nation. Together, they had done it.

19

Pastures new

November 1940 – June 1942

In November 1940, Michael was called up before the group captain. His outstanding leadership in combat and fighter tactics had been recognised. He had been awarded the Distinguished Service Order, and with effect from the second of December he was promoted to squadron leader. Michael was also told that on his recommendation, his wingman, Sergeant Richard Chandler, was to be awarded the Distinguished Flying Cross. He was also to be commissioned with immediate promotion to flight lieutenant following a short commissioning course instructing him how to behave as an officer and gentleman. The urgency of war had changed the way things were done.

The RAF had identified a need for tactical fighter pilot training because there was far more to it than just jumping in a plane and learning by trial and error. That had cost too many lives. From the first of January, they were both to be posted to Cranwell in Lincolnshire to teach and instruct pilots who had recently gained their wings the combat skills they would require. The first two months would be taken up with course preparation, and the first four-week course would commence early in March.

Michael asked, "When will I be permitted to return to operational duties?"

The group captain replied, "You will be operational throughout because I will expect your aircraft to always be combat-ready, and if Fritz turns up on the radar, I will expect you to deal with the bastards, but I know what you mean. This will be a commitment of at least one year. I understand you are owed about four weeks' leave, so December will take care of that." Michael thanked the group captain for his good faith and confidence and the opportunity to get back to his wife and baby. They shook hands. The group captain wished him and his family well.

Michael was delighted to get back home with a full month off, although most of the others remained busy. It was not his way to sit around, and it was good to get back to the old ways of farm work. He spent some time ploughing with the horses and showed the Land Army girls how it was done. Two of them had struck up relationships with the air cadets under instruction. The war had resulted in much separation, but this was matched by a commensurate increase in yearning and passion. Aggie who took the lead in overseeing the welfare of the girls, took a liberal view on this. They had warmed to her and respected her advice. She spoke of 'Durability, Reliability and Excellence', which put together formed the trade name of a certain product that would prevent membership of what her husband called the Spelthorpe Pudding Club. She ensured that a supply was made available to the young ladies. The same applied to young George who finished Michaelmas term on the thirteenth of December. He had spent all his weekends in the company of Emma. He was approaching his seventeenth birthday. Emma was sixteen.

Michael made a point of spending time with him as since Ash and Helen's marriage, he regarded him as a younger brother. George's relationship reminded him of the ardour he and Victoria felt at the same age. He would take him flight shooting for wood pigeons on most afternoons in the week. George was uncertain as to the future and understandably so. He had considered the army. Michael advised against the infantry because if peace was to eventually come, to emerge from the military with no skills other than killing people would leave him high and dry. A commission in the Royal Engineers would stand him in far better stead and might serve him well for an eventual return to the land. Lucy had managed two weeks' leave and she often joined them. The dogs were always delighted to come along too.

With less of a requirement for game keeping much of Captain Boynton's time and that of his two underkeepers had been taken up with his new Home Guard responsibilities and preparation of the secret resistance shelters. They looked after the deer herd. Boynton had his new managerial role, but Ash would step down from his strategic role on occasion to make that run smoothly. There was one less boat in the boathouse, but the government had paid compensation for the loss at Dunkirk. Generally, Ash was happy with the way the Home Guard was working. He had some first-rate captains across the four companies. He restricted the number of ranks because he didn't want things top-heavy. They were not the regular army, merely a volunteer force but they should still be professional. He made it clear from the outset that any bullying by NCO's would not be tolerated, particularly as the volunteers often had to work together when not in uniform. He remembered the 'canaries' from the 'Bull Ring' at Étaples. At Spelthorpe the three sergeants were Jeremy, Robert, the shepherd and his son, William. Each had two corporals for the three platoons of twenty men. The whole company would meet in the memorial hall every third week. There would always be a one-duty platoon on any week. Shooting skills came naturally to many of the men from a rural background. Accordingly, the regular army on joint exercise avoided shooting competitions that often took place in other parts of the country, for fear of embarrassment. There were occasional exercises, patrols and night watches but the men had adapted well and now that the immediate threat of invasion was out of the way, things became less onerous.

Christmas Day followed the same pattern as the previous year, with a convivial lunch and evening party at the Hall although for much of the time, Helen and Ash preferred the cottage. With Michael's new role there was an extra degree of relief for Victoria, Ash and Helen. He had served his country well and they were proud of him.

On the first of January, Michael and Richard Chandler took up their role at Cranwell. Manuals had to be written, and a good relationship with the ground crews was established. Michael and Richard took rooms in the officers' mess but for most weekends Michael went home, and he invited Richard to go with him. Richard was initially accommodated in a guest room at the Hall.

Sometimes they would fly down and park their Spitfires or a two-seat Harvard trainer in the hangar at Spelthorpe. That way, they could be back at Cranwell in fifteen minutes. They were always contactable by telephone, so there was rarely an issue. They would engage with the air cadets and their course instructors.

Michael and Richard got on well. Richard was two years older. He never knew his father who was killed in the massive Allied offensive of 1918. He had originally enlisted in the RAF in 1934 and worked his way up from air mechanic. In 1938, he was selected for pilot training. Richard was a good mixer. Aggie fixed him up on a blind date with a new schoolteacher that she had taken on. Linda Evans had qualified as a teacher in 1938 and took the first job that came along in London. Whilst she liked the teaching, she hated London and yearned for the countryside, so when the Women's Land Army came into being she jumped at the opportunity and came to Spelthorpe. Aggie found out about her past and offered her a trial at the village school as another teacher was about to retire. The trial went well, so Aggie took her on. Richard and Linda met in the village pub and hit it off straight away. Thereafter Richard was always keen to come down to Spelthorpe on his days off.

The first course at Cranwell was favourably received. Clearly there had to be some classroom work, but Michael and Richard concentrated on making them think about threats to their survival and how best to make a kill in any situation. Sometimes not engaging was as important as engaging. Seizing the moment and going in hard remained critical, and this was matched by constant challenges in the air and in the classroom. The trainees would fly with Michael and Richard coming at them from all angles and using the cloud and the sun as cover. The trainees had to evade and attempt to turn the tables. They achieved a lot in the four short weeks with each course, and the feedback from above and below was excellent. Unlike some of the other trainers, Michael and Richard had the combat experience that underlined their credibility. In the spring, newer Spitfires arrived. As well as retaining four machine guns, these were fitted with a pair of 20mm cannon that could destroy an opponent with far fewer hits. Climb rate was better, and increased armour around the pilot was reassuring.

Opportunity to test the new weaponry came earlier than expected. In late June, Michael and Richard were up with two students who were approaching the end of their course. Radar had detected an enemy force heading for the Humber Estuary. Michael radioed up and asked to join the party. Permission was granted. A squadron of Hurricanes had been allocated to intercept. The enemy consisted of 12 Junkers 88s, and there were no fighter escorts. The Junkers scattered as the Hurricanes piled in, and four Junkers headed south directly towards Michael's flight. Michael opted for a frontal attack. The effect of the cannon was devastating with large chunks of the enemy aircraft breaking away as the cannon shells exploded on impact. It proved a point and boosted the confidence of the trainees. They got one each. Michael had fulfilled the group captain's expectations.

In August, whilst Michael had two weeks leave Victoria gave birth to a son. He was pleased to witness the arrival of Simon Ash Cromwell and on this occasion, he did not have to dash back to the war.

Richard was on leave at the same time. His relationship with Linda had deepened considerably over the last five months. As she was no longer with the Land Army she had moved out of their accommodation and had been allocated one of the unused holiday chalets where she could prepare lessons and mark schoolwork in peace. They both enjoyed Richard's leave in this perfect escape from the war and had adopted the Spelthorpe habit of swimming in the lake. Friends they had made on the estate would sometimes join them. Linda had befriended the dogs at the Hall and cottage and would often walk with them and feed them. This was helpful to Ash and Helen as they juggled with conflicting demands on their time. In turn at least two of the dogs would keep her company and stay the night.

In December 1941 Churchill received his best Christmas present ever, courtesy of the Japanese with their attack on Pearl Harbor in Hawaii. The writing was now on the wall because despite disastrous setbacks like the fall of Malaya, Singapore and Hong Kong, President Roosevelt's 'Arsenal of Democracy' was now fully unleashed on Germany as the agreement with America was that Nazi Germany would be the priority of the war effort. Early in the war Reichsmarschall Göring, as head of the Luftwaffe had said that all the Americans could produce were refrigerators and razor blades. He was going to have to eat those words as progressively, East Anglia was turned into the biggest bomber and fighter aircraft base on the planet.

At Spelthorpe, with the pressure of war, the Christmas party of 1941 would be the last for a few years. Celebrations, thereafter, would be spontaneous when opportunity arose.

In February 1942, Joanna and Jeremy were blessed with the arrival of their second child, a girl named Juliet in the family tradition of ensuring that all first names began with the letter 'J'. Not to be outdone, her sister, Jennifer and husband, William, had their first child, a baby boy named Jack. The annexe took on additional role as nursery for the Spelthorpe grandchildren. Helen and Julia were delighted to manage it between them. This allowed the three mothers to stay at work with minimal interruption. In May Richard and Linda tied the knot. It was a minimalist wartime wedding. Michael was the best man, and a buffet reception for close friends and family was held at the village pub where they had first met. As a wedding present, the estate would allow them to remain rent free in the chalet for the duration of the war, but on a reciprocal basis they helped out on the estate whenever there was a demand, and they were available. Edward had gained a scholarship to Cambridge University to study mathematics. Some universities had slimmed down because of conscription, but there was always a place for excellence. The other change was that they were taking many more women. Helen just hoped that Edward might find one! George had one more year at school and had taken Michael's advice and was seeking a commission in the Royal Engineers. If successful the training would take place in Chatham, Kent and it would be much longer than the standard commission. His relationship with Emma remained strong.

The Hall was no longer available for large-scale receptions because partition work was underway. Ash, looking ahead as ever, saw that huge numbers of American servicemen would be heading to East Anglia. He had nothing against Americans but felt that any mass influx could have a detrimental effect on the close-knit Spelthorpe community and the huge efforts they were making in respect of food and timber production for the war effort. Aware as ever, that stupid decisions were made by people in high places with maps but no local knowledge or empathy, he thought it best to pre-empt matters by offering the bulk of the Hall up as a convalescent facility to the Royal Air Force. Bomber Command was increasingly striking at the industrial heart of Germany, but that involved casualties in the aircraft that got home. The RAF gladly took up the offer and saw Spelthorpe as a place of tranquility that would help the healing process. Ash did insist that it was for all aircrew and not just officers. With greater egalitarian thinking at higher levels, this was accepted. Amrik and his staff would be fully engaged with catering, maintenance and reception. The only areas out of bounds would be the staff accommodation, the library, a small dining room and three upstairs rooms of which one was occupied by Ash and Helen and the other two by Edward and George. These areas were partitioned off. Items of value were kept there or stored in the attic. This allowed more than two-thirds of the space to be taken up by the RAF and their medical staff, for which a modest payment would be made that would cover all costs incurred by the estate. There was sufficient space for fifty beds at any one time. The handover would take place in June. Spare capacity for family needs remained in the annexe which continued to serve as the farm office hub.

In the spring, preparations were in hand for Michael and

Richard to return to operational duties. Their two replacements were sent up to act as understudies for the duration of a full course. Both were invited for an interview together with the air commodore. His praise for the work they had undertaken was glowing because new pilots were now joining squadrons with the edge that so many of their predecessors had lacked. In recognition of their dedication and the needs of the service both were to be promoted. Michael would now be a wing commander and Richard a squadron leader. It was now practice for a squadron of twelve aircraft to be commanded by a wing commander, with a squadron leader in charge of a flight of six aircraft. They were both to be posted to a newly equipped squadron to operate from a base in Norfolk. After a month of familiarisation with the new aircraft they would move to run the squadron. The new aeroplane was called the Mosquito.

20

Sleeper

November 1942 – June 1943 England and France

L ate in 1942, Lucy received a note on her desk in London asking her to ring a telephone number. There were no details left as to the origin. She telephoned the number and after identifying herself she was simply asked if she would like to do something special and dangerous to help the war effort. Lucy responded positively but wanted to know more. She was asked to meet with a lady wearing a blue headscarf on the bridge across the lake in St Jame's Park during her lunch break on the following day.

The woman she met was middle-aged. They spoke entirely in French. It was explained that the work would mean her going to occupied France and working alone. It would not be pleasant, and she would be living on her nerves. It would be risky and if found with anything incriminating and captured, there would be little hope, but the work was vital, and she would get the best training. Lucy was given a week to think about it, and if she wished to be considered she should come back to the bridge at the same time the following week. She should not mention anything to her employers.

The following week, Lucy appeared at the bridge. She was told to go to an address in Baker Street when she finished work. Lucy went to Baker Street and was admitted. It looked like a standard commercial office but once inside she was ushered through a locked door into a labyrinth of corridors and offices. She met a man who introduced himself as a Colonel Buckmaster who headed the French section at the Special Operations Executive (SOE). This was a secret organisation initiated by Churchill in 1940 with the order to 'set Europe ablaze.' The colonel had a file in front of him that appeared to hold a mass of information about her and her family. Her linguistic ability, and at a colloquial level, was what they wanted. She would be landed in France at a location familiar to her, where for six months she would absorb herself in the local community. In other words, she would act as a 'sleeper', and when activated, she would be required to gather information about the area, to encode it and forward that information to a contact who would identify himself or herself to her. She would assume the identity of a genuine French national who had lived in the area briefly but was now in the United Kingdom, and she would meet that person to learn every single aspect of that person's life. Her accommodation and employment had been arranged.

Prior to her departure, she would undergo specialist training in Scotland in unarmed combat, precautionary measures and encryption but in her role, she would not be a radio operator. That carried too much risk of detection if operating from a fixed site. There was one addition. She would undertake a short course in watercolour painting , specifically of landscapes and wildlife. This would serve as an innocent cover for her walking in coastal and rural locations. Training would start in three weeks. She would leave her employment. They would be told that she had enlisted and had been commissioned in the First Aid Nursing Yeomanry. This would serve as a cover during her training period.

"My mother was a FANY," said Lucy.

"We know!" said the colonel.

Prior to leaving she was measured for uniform and introduced to a genial Jewish gentleman called Leo Marks, who explained that he dealt in codes. He told her that before she started, he wanted her to write a short poem with as many letters of the alphabet as possible. This would form the basis of a personal code unique to her because it had never been published, and theoretically, it would be difficult for any enemy cryptographer to break.

Lucy returned to her room at the foreign office accommodation. On the following day she went to a specialist art shop where she purchased an art pad and a set of Sennelier French-manufactured watercolours and brushes. Lucy had been quite good at art at school, so she didn't regard this as an extra burden and the expert help would be useful. She thought deeply about the poem, thinking about Spelthorpe, and family members and the tragedy she had encountered in her life and hopes for the future. She came up with a poem. It did not rhyme perfectly but it did have all the letters:

Quivering palms, Kilimanjaro zebras are but nothing
to a windswept lonely beach in November, indented with our
footprints, sometimes facing and sometimes side by side.
The tide invades and washes them away. Perhaps, one
day they will return, older, wiser, deeper and
higher up the beach, so the tide can't wash them away.

x

The following weekend Lucy went up to Spelthorpe. She made the most of her time but prior to leaving she spoke to her father. She told him that she had enlisted in the FANY. She was going away, but she couldn't say where, but he should not worry because she would be in good hands. Ash was upset but he understood, just as he understood about Michael and how Helen and Aggie had to understand about his and Boynton's little adventure some eighteen months earlier.

A week later Lucy found herself at a country house in Scotland. The instructors were mainly army NCOs. When it came to self-defence one instructor picked on Lucy and told her to attack him. "Are you sure?" she asked. "Anything? I don't want to hurt you." "Just get on with it, miss. You won't hurt me."

Lucy assumed a defensive stance.

"Well get on with it!" he bellowed.

"No, you attack me," she said.

With that he surged forward and made to slap her. She blocked the blow, punched him hard in the voice box and kicked him firmly between his legs. He collapsed in agony on the ground and had to be taken away on a stretcher. So, Boynton's little course came in useful, and nobody asked her to attack them again. When it came to the shooting she equalled or beat the instructors. The years of practice at Spelthorpe had honed those skills.

The following week she met up with the lady she was supposed to double. There was a close resemblance. She told Lucy that she had escaped in a yacht that her gendarme husband and a colleague had stolen, ably assisted by what she described as a couple of swarthy-looking British desperados.

With extra clothing, documentation and a good supply of current French currency and a twenty krugerrands, on a dark, cold night, Lucy landed on the Normandy coast by kayak from a British submarine. Once on the beach, her kayak was taken back to the submarine by the two British commandos who had accompanied her. Madame Lyla Dubois knew where she had to go. After walking for two hours on familiar territory, she arrived at a house in Ranville that she knew well. She tapped on a bedroom window. Her grandfather answered the door and invited her in.

After hugs and a hot coffee, Lucy told them that they must get used to calling her by her new name. The story was that Lyla's husband had deserted her and run away when France had been invaded, and they had taken her in out of pity. That was all they needed to know. She had work arranged on a nearby farm and as a waitress at the nearby Café Gondrée by the bridge over the Caen Canal.

And so, over the next six months she did nothing other than to settle in with her two jobs. She would walk a mile at first light to milk the cows, muck them out and feed them on a farm. She did this in for three days a week. At the café, she worked for three afternoons and evenings. It was frequented by French locals and German soldiers who were always trying to chat her up in appalling French. She would flirt with them in the best traditions of the FANY (Flirt and Never Yield). Occasionally, she pointed to her wedding ring if they took matters too far. She called them naughty boys.

On days off she would ride out on her bicycle going further and further to paint seascapes and flowers. German soldiers would look at her work admiringly, and some would ask why she did not paint the barbed wire and bunkers.

She would explain. "I only paint what is beautiful, so what is ugly I do not see!" As time went by the quality of her work improved. Where she saw bunkers, she painted trees, and the tree species varied with the type of bunker. Heavy barbed wire became gorse and, tank obstacles were rocks.

Lyla settled in well and attracted no suspicion. Early in 1943, a lady with a small terrier called at the café.

When Lyla approached her table, she asked. "Do you have any lobster?"

Lyla responded, "No we only have Normandy mussels because they took the boats away."

The lady spoke again, "I did so much like a good Lobster Thermidor, not that you serve it here."

Thus, the code words of Normandy mussels and Lobster Thermidor established the link. The lady left a crumpled-up cigarette paper in her saucer, which Lyla collected after she had taken the cup and saucer away. Before she left, she asked if Lyla worked there full-time, to which Lyla responded that she only did afternoons and evenings on Mondays, Wednesdays and Fridays.

Back at home Lyla unpicked the stitching on her coat and removed a map with coordinates of some twenty miles of coastline from Dives-sur-Mer up to Port-en-Bessin-Huppain. It was printed on silk. She decoded the numbers on the cigarette paper using her poem. There was a request for details of all new coastline installations to be passed on, and specifically those that were not obvious from the air. They wanted types of guns and their calibre and evidence of bogus or dummy installations. Lyla went through her paintings and encrypted a response on a cigarette paper which she screwed up in readiness, then she folded up the map and hid it in a dry outside location. Two days later the lady called at the café, and the tiny crinkled up ball was exchanged.

Over the next few months, this practice continued but never at the same time or day. Walking a dog always gave the lady a reason for being out and about, and any scraps and leftovers were always gladly received.

21

Wooden wonder

June 1942 – June 1943

Michael and Richard loved the new Mosquito. It was the fastest plane in the sky and nothing could catch it, but the aircraft's journey to the RAF had been a difficult one. Created by Geoffrey de Havilland, who Michael knew from his youth at Spelthorpe, the very concept of the plane was dismissed by the pompous buffoons at the Air Ministry back in 1938 because the bulk of the plane was made of wood. They saw it as 'a frail wood machine totally unsuitable for service conditions', but de Havilland went ahead and built it anyway. He had one man at the Ministry who backed it. Being made of wood it was light and that made it fast. Because it was wood, when the patterns were available, most of the parts could be made in any furniture factory. The Mosquito could get to Berlin and back with a 4,000-pound bomb load which was more than some of the so-called heavy bombers. Once it had demonstrated its worth, by 1943, it was in heavy demand because of its versatility. The version that appealed to Michael the most was the fighter bomber with four 20 mm cannons and four machine guns all in the nose, and with its twin Merlin engines it was faster than the Spitfire and had almost twice the devastating firepower.

1943 became the turning point in the war. The Germans were thoroughly beaten in North Africa, and they had suffered crippling losses, total humiliation and poor morale following Stalingrad. The war in the west had turned from defensive to offensive, with German cities and industry bombed by the RAF in 1,000 bomber raids at night and by the Americans during the day. Mosquitos fitted with a location radar marked the targets precisely for the main bomber force which previously had probably killed more cows than people. Mosquitos would drop tin foil 'window' to confuse the enemy's radar. They would carry out low-level, precise attacks on Gestapo headquarters and key industrial sites. They attacked shipping off the coasts of Norway and Denmark. If there was one aeroplane the Germans hated more than anything else, it was the Mosquito because it could strike into the heart of Nazi Germany and get away in broad daylight.

Reichsmarschall Göring complained, "It makes me furious when I see the Mosquito. I turn green and yellow with envy… They have the geniuses, and we have the nincompoops." The myth of German invincibility was being destroyed.

With his promotion Michael found himself increasingly desk bound. There was a mass of organisation required to keep the squadron in the air, which involved more than just flying. There were maintenance and supply issues to oversee, and operational planning. Each aeroplane had a pilot and a navigator, and they had to be looked after in terms of leave and support if there were issues. To fly with the squadron too often could undermine the role and confidence of the excellent squadron leaders who managed and flew with the two flights. However, he got in the air as much as he could and more often if one of the two squadron leaders was absent. He still needed to put his stamp on the way the squadron operated. What pleased Michael most of all was low-level attacks on enemy airfields. This needed careful planning, navigation and execution. The low-level approach put the raid out of German radar detection, but extra attention was needed because of power lines. Some aircraft would even return with tree vegetation attached when they flew extra low to avoid enemy radar detection.

The fast approach gave those on the ground no time to react. Good photographic intelligence and analysis indicated where aircraft might be concealed. Michael's maxim remained: "Go in fast and get out faster." Those who lingered or went round for another strike would often get shot down by ground fire or enemy fighters who had time to get up to hang around along the return route. With the speed advantage there was no point in throwing that away because they could always come back another day. To Michael there was nothing better than seeing his cannon fire destroy a whole line of German aircraft on the ground.

There were periods when nothing was planned or when the weather might stop operations for several days. This gave time for leave. If the weather was bad Michael and Richard would go home to Spelthorpe by car. In good weather, they would hop in a Mosquito and get back in a matter of minutes. Somebody would always remain at base. They took turns for that, but Michael made sure that they all got time to recharge their batteries and that applied to the ground crews, too.

Back at Spelthorpe there was no news of Lucy, just the very occasional phone caller who wouldn't give a name but stated that she was OK. They all kept their fingers crossed. It was obvious to them that she was in France, but they said nothing to anybody else. The farming activity was going well with Ash, Julian and Boynton at the helm despite abstractions from farm work for Home Guard activities. With the turn of the tide and the threat of invasion over, these occasions dwindled somewhat.

The convalescent home in the Hall was working well. They loved being in the countryside. The visiting regime was unrestricted for the greater part of the day. Michael and Richard would always make a point of going in to exchange flying stories. The patients wanted to know what was going on and were delighted to hear that at last the enemy that had sown the wind was now reaping the whirlwind. Many knew that they would not be going back, but with the visits they knew they were not forgotten and would always remain part of that band of brothers that had been forged in the air in the desperate times they had encountered together.

Victoria and Linda had resigned themselves to being RAF wives. They made the most of the time that their husbands were back and the four would often dine together while the dogs watched over baby Lisette and Simon. Lisette was still crawling but taking her first steps. Almost invariably, if they lost sight of her, she would be curled up in the basket with Shackleton and Hardy.

Ash's judgement in respect of the Americans had proved correct. They were brave men, and so many were lost over Germany because, in the early days they thought they could defend themselves without fighter escorts. That all changed with the advent of the long-range Mustang fighter fitted with a Merlin engine that could go all the way to Berlin and back to wreak havoc on the German fighters. The Americans were friendly enough and too friendly as far as some locals were concerned. They would complain about them being "oversexed, overpaid and over here". The lure of nylons and candy was just too much for some of the local ladies and girls. Boynton would say, "We now have the Norfolk Pudding Club".

There were a quite a few black soldiers, some of whom flew, but the segregation policy of the US Army disturbed the British 'treat as you find' attitude that welcomed these men in the same way as their white counterparts. They were served in the pubs but if seen walking with a white woman, deep-seated prejudices in some Americans emerged that sometimes resulted in violence. Ash was glad that Spelthorpe had managed to avoid all that.

22

Death's Head

June 1943 – June 1944 France

By the middle of 1943, Lucy had settled in firmly to her role as Madame Lyla Dubois. She continued with her reports, and everything seemed to be going well, but she remained cautious. On a June afternoon she had a long ride and ended up on a track leading to the edge of the cliffs between Arromanches and Longues-sur-Mer, where there was a big German battery that would have been easy to spot from the air. She was aware of a vehicle behind her but rode on until it overtook and stopped in front of her. It was a standard German four-seater Volkswagen Kübelwagen. The two men inside wore black uniforms with SS insignia on the lapels and Totenkopf or 'Death's Head' badges on their caps. The first one approached her. She dismounted.

He asked. "What are you doing?" Lyla made as not to understand. He repeated in clumsy French.

She replied, "I'm just riding my bicycle." She had picked up enough German to understand what he said next.

" I can see that, you dumb French slut." With that he grabbed her bag and emptied her paintings and art materials on the ground and said, "What is this? You are a spy, you whore."

Lyla answered. "I'm not a spy. I live here. I just ride my bike and paint things from nature. You can see that when you look in my painting book."

With that, he just slapped her around the face and said, "You are a French whore and a slut and we are going to teach you a lesson, bitch!"

The other German grabbed her from behind and held her firmly against the back of the vehicle. She started to struggle but he had a firm grip. As she kicked out, the first German slapped her hard again and then ripped the front of her dress apart exposing her breasts. Then her pulled her dress up and violently ripped her panties off, throwing them on the ground. Lyla trembled because she knew what was coming as he undid his trousers and underpants that slipped to his knees as he exposed himself to her. He forced her legs apart.

Suddenly she heard a shot, and the soldier behind her released his grip, and his arms fell away as he dropped to the ground. With her arms free, Lyla punched her attacker with full force into his voice box. Then, with all her strength, as her adrenaline kicked in, she brought up her knee into his testicles. He doubled over in pain as she punched hard into his solar plexus winding him. Then she side-stepped and went behind him grabbing him under the chin firmly and twisting his neck to the side in one violent movement. She felt the neck snap. He fell to the ground with his neck broken. She stood there motionless then suddenly burst into a flood of sobs and tears.

She heard a voice speaking in French. "Don't worry. You are safe now. Nobody will hurt you anymore."

She felt an arm around her, and she instinctively hung on to the figure next to her. He took out a handkerchief and wiped her tears away. She saw he had a uniform, but it was grey- green, like the ones she was used to, and it bore a red cross badge on the arm. From the insignia and the cut of the uniform she could see he was an officer. She buttoned up her dress front as best as she could and looked down at the other German who had held her. There was a bullet hole neatly between his eyes.

"I couldn't shoot the other one because I might have hit you, but I had a clear shot at this one. I hate these bastards. They are everything that is bad about Germany, but now they rule. They are a law unto themselves, but there will be hell to pay when they find them." He took her hand. "Are you feeling a bit better now? I am a doctor. They can't hurt you anymore."

She held his hand with both hands. She felt safe now, and he seemed kind. She looked up into his eyes. She could see that he wanted to look after her. She simply said, "Thank you."

Lyla's thought processes started to kick in. "If they find these two, they will think it is the resistance and then they will start shooting villagers. We can't allow that, but if they are missing, they will still come looking and when they find the one you shot, it will be obvious. How is it you have a gun if you are a doctor? What do I call you?"

"My name is Johann. I am a hauptmann in the army, but I am required to carry a gun for personal protection, so I have this Walther PPK. It's what the police have. I saw you ride down here. I had just been to the battery to visit a sick soldier then I saw the SS following you. We don't get them here very often. They have probably come out from Caen. I just had a feeling, so I followed, and when they stopped, I pulled into the verge a hundred metres back. I walked up slowly, but then I saw what they did, and I had to stop it".

Then Lyla had an idea. "The track goes right next to the cliff edge. If a vehicle went over, it would crash down into the sea. If they find one man with a broken neck that will explain it and better still if he stinks of alcohol. They will assume the other one has been washed out by the tide. All we have to do is to get rid of the other one where he won't be found, and I think I know where we can do that."

Johann went back to his vehicle and drove it up. He put the bicycle in the back. They wrapped the shot German in a blanket and put him in the boot. Then he got a tube from his medical bag and a bottle of brandy. He pushed the tube down into the man's stomach then poured in half the bottle. They put him in the back of the car and drove down to a bend, where going straight on would put a vehicle down and into the sea with a sheer drop of about thirty feet to the bottom. They put the SS man in the driver's seat kept the engine running and pushed the car over the edge. It flew down the slope and went flying over the top and they heard it crash into the sea. There was nobody about. Johann said. "I'll probably get the job of the autopsy when they find him. With all that alcohol and a broken neck there should not be a problem."

They walked back to Johann's vehicle. He collected all her paints and book and put them in the back and said, "If they see you in the car that will be alright because I can say I found you by the road when you fell off your bicycle and I'm giving you a lift. You'll have a bruise where he slapped you. Now, where are we going to get rid of the other one?"

Lyla explained that a mile towards Arromanches there was a farmyard that had been cleared out following the occupation. There was a deep well. She had discovered it two months ago on one of her rides. Before they left, Lyla did a good search around to make sure that nothing had been left at the scene and that there were no obvious signs of blood.

They found the farmyard at the end of a track off the main coast road. It was quiet. Lyla got out and had a good look around. She went to the well and pulled away three planks that covered it. She dropped a stone. It was deep. They got the body out and dropped it down. They searched around and found an abandoned wheelbarrow, which they filled with rubble and debris and put that on top. They put down several loads, then replaced the planks and drove back along the coast road. Johann told her that he was based in Caen and was responsible for all the medical care of those based in the batteries along the coast from Dives-sur-Mer to Grandcamp-Maisy.

He asked if she minded if they parked up by Ver-sur-Mer, where they had a view over the coastline. He clearly wanted to talk to her. Johann told her that he had qualified as a doctor at Heidelberg, which is one of the best medical schools in the world. He was twenty-six. Three years ago, after qualification they drafted him into the army because they wanted doctors. He didn't want to go, but there was no choice. It would be the army or a concentration camp. He explained that Germany was split in half. There were the obsessed and indoctrinated who always turned out at the rallies and bullied the rest, and the majority who did not want war but lived in fear. He hated the Nazis, and he hated the SS after what he saw them do to the Jews at Babi Yar near Kiev where the locals there were helping them. He felt utterly powerless, and the sooner that the British and Americans came, the better, but thousands would die in the process. He spoke of the bombing of Cologne a year earlier, where hundreds had died but most were just ordinary people.

When they found out he spoke fluent French, they thought it would be better if he served in France so they sent him to Caen about a year ago.

Lyla was surprised at how open he was and when she thought about it the huge risk that he had taken to protect her and it came as a shock that there were some good Germans after what had happened to her mother. She had now killed her first German with her bare hands. She was mixed up inside and needed time to come to terms with it all. She wanted to trust, but she couldn't because of her training. The words 'trust nobody' echoed inside her head. She stuck to her story of how her husband had left her in 1940 and told him where she had her lodgings and where she worked. Johann told her of his work. He said that he had a good reputation with the SS because he always treated them conscientiously when they caught a venereal disease, but he said that he only did that to protect others and the innocents they might pass it on to. When they had other complaints, he just let them go. With soldiers in the regular army, he treated them properly because they were usually well-disciplined and stuck to the rules.

They talked for an hour, then he drove her back to Ranville. He stopped outside, reached out, and held her hand. She took it and squeezed gently. She couldn't help it, but she felt attracted to him and he to her. He asked if he could see her again.

"I'd like that," she said, "but not here. If you are coming in a car, could I meet you by the smaller river bridge? If we could go along to Dives that would be better because they don't know me there and some can get nasty if they see a French girl with a German." They agreed to meet on the Saturday afternoon at 3pm. He would come in an unmarked car out of uniform.

Lucy thought at length about the situation she found herself in. She was attracted to him and had not been as candid with him as he with her, but she had to protect others. At the same time because of the killing of the SS men, each had the other's life in their hands, and there were few relationships underwritten in such a powerful way.

They met on the Saturday. They walked at Dives-sur-Mer and had a meal there. They walked hand in hand, and they talked. It became clear that Johann was a good man, and he was principled. He didn't force himself upon her. They watched the sun go down over the Cotentin peninsular, which they could just make out on the horizon. They gazed at one another, and then they kissed and again and again as all their pent-up feelings came out.

Over the next few weeks, they carried on meeting. Lyla continued to pass back information. There was more construction along the coast as the coastal defences were refined as part of Hitler's Atlantic Wall. The bombing increased around some of the batteries and strong points that were about a mile back from the beaches. There was more bombing inland, and occasionally twin-engine fighter bombers flew just above the rooftops heading inland in broad daylight. They were very fast. The area to the south of Dives-sur-Mer was flooded. All this was passed back to London.

Johann confirmed the autopsy report. The man was drunk, crashed and died of a broken neck from the crash. They assumed his companion had been washed out to sea.

On a Saturday in November, Johann asked Lyla to pack an overnight bag. He took her to Bayeux, which was about five miles inland. It was regarded as safe because the British rarely bombed cathedrals but when the Americans came over, everybody ducked. They were booked in to a small hotel that overlooked the magnificent Norman cathedral that had been completed in the reign of William the Conqueror. They walked around the cathedral just before it got dark and then went back to the hotel. They had a good-sized room with a bathroom. They both knew what was going to happen. They kissed and undressed one another. Johann was very gentle. They made love. Lyla let out a little cry to start with.

They lay together for an hour then Johann suddenly said, "You were never a married woman. That was your first time."

"How do you know?" asked Lyla.

"I'm a doctor," replied Johann. "There were signs. I love you, but right from the start, I knew there was far more to you than meets the eye. You watch everything, and you are careful: the way you cleared up the shooting scene, the way you dealt with the SS man, and when you came in here, you checked all around for hidden microphones. Despite what happened, you were able to think clearly. You are a total professional but that doesn't stop me from loving you."

"And I love you too," said Lyla. "You make me happy when we are together, and I want you. I just wish this war would end. You are right about me. I can tell you some but not all because there are people I need to protect, and if I don't tell you, it's not because I don't love you or trust you, but if you don't know, you can't tell."

"I think I understand," said Johann. "I feel the same about you. If we get through this, will you be my wife?"

Lyla was taken aback by his directness, but at the same time she felt happy that he had asked. She said nothing and it was clear to Johann that she was thinking deeply.

Then she gazed directly at him and said, "I will because when this is all over, that is what I want: you to be with me and to live in the most beautiful place. You will love it there." And she kissed him.

They took a bath together then they went downstairs where Johann had booked a meal for 7 pm. There were a few other diners. All were French speakers.

They went back upstairs and made love again. Then they talked about the invasion. They knew it would come but nobody knew where.

Lyla said, "I don't know but history provides an answer. Hitler is a lousy historian. He copied Napoleon when he invaded Russia and look what happened there. There were two occasions when England invaded France in the past. Edward III landed in 1346 before the victory at Crecy, and Henry V in 1415 before

Bayeux Cathedral

Agincourt, and on both occasions, they landed in Normandy. I only remember this because I used to do a lot of archery with a longbow and that was the weapon that gave them their victories.

Johann talked about the bombing. All around Calais was getting hit all the time and it was getting worse, far worse than Normandy, but time would tell. They slept as one, and after breakfast on the following day, they drove through the countryside. Johann had worked out in his own mind what Lyla was doing. He told her that he would help in any way he could. Lyla told him what she wanted – anything about new defences, airfields, stock piles, hidden batteries, and dummy installations and so on, but she said it was important that he did not make it obvious, and if anything was fed to him, that might be false to trap him, so far better to wait and check it out on a standard medical visit. Having a French girlfriend was not unusual – there were hundreds like it, but keeping a low profile was essential. He gave her a number to ring but only if urgent. He knew where she worked, and he could leave a message there.

1944 arrived. Lyla received a steady stream of good information, and that was fed back. The bombing continued night after night. The Germans were on edge and always looked pale and tired. When she rode her bicycle, the ones she knew and the ones in the café seemed much gloomier.

Johann and Layla met once or twice a week. They had a meeting point on the edge of some woodland about a mile from Ranville if it was to be short, but they normally went back to Bayeux at least once a month to be totally together.

23

Flak

June 1943- June 1944. England and France

Throughout the rest of 1943, the Mosquito squadron continued with its low-level precision attacks. There were skirmishes with enemy fighters, mainly with the very effective German Focke-Wulf fighters, which could almost match them in speed but not in firepower. The main danger was on the return run with deep penetration attacks where there was time for the enemy to get airborne along the anticipated return route. They lost one aircraft due to flak, but both crew members managed to bail out and were now languishing in a prison camp. In this time Michael and Richard managed to add to their personal scores. Richard added another three and Michael four, of which two had just taken off on an airfield that they flew over on the return trip. Ground fire had been limited because the gunners had wanted to avoid hitting their own aircraft. All were Focke-Wulfs.

In the new year, the squadron was moved south in the preparations for the invasion. This meant fewer opportunities to go home as the demands increased for attacks around Calais and Normandy. This was a mixture of precision attacks on airfields, coastal defences, and rail traffic. A new operational target was added, and this was the launch ramps for what was believed to be a pilotless flying bomb that the Germans were developing. Photos from the air had detected these sites, and these included an industrial complex at Peenemünde on the Baltic Coast, where these new weapons were being developed. In the previous year a force of over 500 RAF bombers, had flattened the place but development was still going on. Consequently, there was a huge demand for aerial photography. The Mosquito was perfect for the role, and two photographic Mosquitos were attached to the squadron.

On the first day of June 1944, an order was received for an urgent photo run along the Normandy coastline. Both flights were engaged, so Michael took on the job himself, especially as he knew the area so well. He dispensed with the need for a navigator. He took off in the evening just over an hour before sunset. There were advantages to this with the softer light and the shadows could help with the height estimation of objects. As directed, he ran the entire length of the coast from Cabourg to Grandcamp-Maisy. The first run was along the coast at 1,000 feet, and that was clear of any issues. The return run was about a mile inland, but when he was over Lion-sur-Mer, all hell opened up from below. His plane shuddered and he felt a pain in his right calf. All power was lost, but he could glide. It was too low for a parachute and in any case that would signal to all that he had got out, and they would be after him. If he ditched in the failing light, the plane would sink, and he might have a chance to get to the shore unseen. He glided down aiming for Le Home Merville, which was a quieter stretch of coast. He splash-landed about 400 yards out at low tide. He managed to get out quickly and left his parachute and life jacket behind and swam in by breaststroke so as not to make any splash. With the weight of the engines, the plane sank quite quickly. It was uncanny but he felt a strange force take hold of him propelling him to the beach.

Within a couple of minutes, he arrived at the beach and made it up to the dunes. As he passed a house, a voice called out and waved to him. Michael approached and spoke to the man in fluent French. He seemed very excited and was pleased to see him. The man took him to a shed in the garden and hid him under a pile of wood and boards. He told him to wait there as he would go back to the beach and walk with his dog to get rid of any footprints. About an hour later, he returned. He told Michael that two soldiers had come along the beach and had asked him if he had seen a plane crash. He told them that the plane crashed a long way offshore and that nobody got out. Then the plane sank. It was now dark. The man bandaged his leg. There was a nasty gash, and it appeared that there was metal inside. He gave him a drink and a sandwich. Michael told him that if he could get to Ranville he knew somebody who would help him. The man said if he was quick, he would take him in his car. It was quiet, but he would have to get back before the curfew. At night there was rarely anybody about, and the soldiers would stay in the town or in their gun batteries.

Ten minutes later, he dropped Michael off about a five-minute walk from Michael's grandparents. Michael thanked the man who told him that it was the least he could do for someone who was fighting to help France. He shook the man's hand and walked in total darkness, but he stopped and listened and smelt the air every hundred yards. His leg hurt him a lot, but he got there. He went into the garden and around the back where he tapped the window. His grandfather came to the door with a torch that he shone in Michael's face. He couldn't believe his eyes, but he quickly ushered him inside and into the lounge where his sister was sitting with his grandmother. They were both speechless.

Michael said, "Lucy. What are you doing here?" He hugged his sister. She looked him in the face and then at his uniform which was soaking wet.

She replied. "Here, I am Madame Lyla Dubois. I have lodged with these kind people for the last two years. You must remember that! Lucy only exists in England."

Michael grinned and joked, "Well, I thought I'd fly over for a pleasure flight, then some nasty people started shooting at me, so I flew down and parked my plane in the sea where it sank, so I thought I'd have a nice swim and come and see you all, and here I am!"

Lyla took off the bandage and looked at his calf. There was a six-inch gash, and she could see a piece of metal protruding. It was seeping rather than bleeding. Michael got out of his wet uniform and sat there in a dressing gown, but he had kept his dog tag on. Lyla said that she knew a doctor who could look at Michael's leg, but that would be on the following day. Michael told them that a man had helped him and driven him close to the house. He told them that when two Germans turned up on the beach, the man had told them that he saw the crash, and nobody got out before the plane sank, so nobody should be looking for him. It would take them ages to find the plane anyway. Lyla then switched on the radio because they always listened to the BBC's Radio Londres every night. It was illegal, but everybody did it, and the German's didn't have time to stop it. At the end of the short broadcast there were always odd, coded messages for the Résistance, which seemed meaningless to most. Suddenly, Lyla's ears pricked up and she sat with her mouth open in disbelief at the message: "Les sanglots longues des violons de l'automne".

"That's it," she said, "the invasion will be in less than two weeks."

"That makes sense," said Michael. "I had an urgent order to photograph this length of coastline. The only thing is that we don't know is if it is here or Calais. We have bombed Calais twice as much as here, but there is far more to bomb there in terms of defences. My bet is here. There was talk of Brittany and Cherbourg, but they would be more difficult for an army to break out. Calais is a lot closer to Germany. Whatever happens we will still get bombed a lot, but at least you have a cellar. You might have to stay down there if things start to happen."

On the following morning at 8 am, Lyla telephoned Johann on the emergency number he had given her. The phone was answered by a male voice, and she was put through. He said he was going on his rounds, and she asked if he could call at the house, which he agreed. He said he would be there in about an hour. Lyla spoke to her grandfather and Michael. She did not want to alarm her grandmother. She came out with it straight away after they agreed that what she said would remain with them.

"The doctor coming here shortly is a German. You can trust him absolutely. He hates the Nazis and has been helping me. Now, I am going to shock you! I am in love with him. A year ago, he rescued me when two SS soldiers tried to rape me. He shot one and I killed the other. We fell in love, and he has been supplying me with information that I have got back to London. Because of what we did, we have each other's lives in our hands, so that is why you can trust him. He is a very kind, caring man and a very good doctor, and he speaks perfect French. I don't think Grandma will want to know about this. I'm not her innocent little granddaughter, but when Mummy was killed, Michael and I swore that we would avenge her. I have learnt that not all Germans are bad, but we have both done something about what we swore we would do".

Both Michael and their grandfather were somewhat shocked by the revelation, but there was nothing they could do. Lyla had presented them with a 'fait accompli'. They would have to go along with it until they had come to terms with it. Their grandfather realised that he was not in charge. The war was in charge, and he had offered his services. It was as simple as that.

A few minutes later there was a knock at the door. It was Johann. Lucy let him in, and she explained to him in private the situation. She told him Michael was her brother, and her real name was Lucy, but they would stick to Lyla until they were safe. She also told him that the invasion was coming in less than fourteen days. He told her that all the top generals were going away early the following week because they thought that with the bad weather forecast, there would be no invasion. Lucy introduced him to Michael. They shook hands and he examined the leg. Johann intimated that it might take a little time to deal with it, but he had what he needed. He opted to knock Michael out with chloroform as he would have to probe the wound to remove the metal and any debris and necrose tissue to prevent infection. He would leave the wound open for a few days to make sure there was no infection, then he would suture it. He had some sulphur drugs. He mentioned that penicillin would be perfect, but as far as he was aware only the Allies had that at this time.

It took Johann about twenty-five minutes. He was conscientious in the extreme and left a solution that could be dripped into the wound every few hours. He got the shrapnel out and some threads of clothing. He said he would call back on Saturday in civilian clothes and would take Lyla to Dives-sur-Mer so they could talk things through.

That afternoon, Lyla went to work at the café, having encrypted the information that the generals were going away because of the weather and that RAF WCMC was safe. Her contact turned up and the information was passed in the usual way on the crumpled cigarette paper. Lyla engaged in the usual pleasantries and mentioned the bad weather on its way but said that every cloud has a silver lining. The contact nodded knowingly.

On the Saturday Johann checked Michael's wound. It was looking good. He would suture it on Monday morning, first thing. He drove Lucy to Dives-sur-Mer and they had coffee in a bar overlooking the seafront. It was raining, and the wind was rocking the few boats in the harbour. She told him how her father and a friend had been at Dunkirk helping the fleeing soldiers and then had to escape through German lines.

"They stole a boat here and got back to England," said Lyla. "I'm surprised there are any boats left," said Johann. Outside they got in the car where they held hands and talked. She asked him if he could sleep at Ranville every night for the next few days because if there was an invasion he would be cut off in Caen, and it would be bound to start at first light. He said that would be easy. He would just say that he had met a very sexy French lady, and he wanted to make the most of it for a few days while her husband was away. They would understand that. There were other doctors with no such luck who would cover for him as he had done for them in the past. He would bring a change of clothes and proof of his professional status and keep that at the house.

On Sunday evening Johann came to the house and stayed. He brought a few nice things to eat and drink with him. Michael and their grandfather warmed to him as he told them how he ended up in the army and some of his experiences, and how many of the German people shared his view but were too frightened to do anything. He slept alone in a spare room. Lyla thought it best not to push her luck too far.

On the Monday morning at 7 am he checked the wound and stitched it up using a local anaesthetic. Then he returned to Caen. Lyla went up to the farm as normal and did her work with the cows and in the afternoon worked at the café Gondrée until

8pm. Johann arrived at the house at 8.30 pm. They ate together. The weather had steadily improved throughout the day.

At 11pm, as usual Lyla switched on the radio, and they listened to the messages. They heard the next part of the poem. "Blessent mon cœur d'une langueur monotone." They looked at one another, and Lyla said, "Less than 48 hours. The only question is where."

24

Morning

June 6th, 1944. Normandy, France

"Good night then: sleep to gather strength for the morning. For the morning will come. Brightly will it shine on the brave and the true, kindly upon all who suffer for the cause, glorious upon the tombs of heroes. Thus will shine the dawn. Vive la France."
Radio broadcast to the French people by
Winston Churchill 21st October 1940.

They went to bed, but they couldn't sleep. Johann got up and sat on the sofa with Lyla. Michael sat in an armchair. They drank coffee with large shots of cognac from the bottle that Johann had brought up on Sunday. There was the noise of the aircraft overhead and more than they had ever heard before. They all went outside. They heard bombing in the distance a few miles away. It was a clear, moonlit night. Suddenly just after midnight, they heard explosions and small arms fire coming from the direction of the Gondrée café. It seemed to go on for several minutes, then stopped, then there was a huge bang with more firing.

"I know you want to go down there," said Michael, "but if you do, you will end up getting shot."

"I just hope Georges Gondrée and the family are OK. I've got quite attached to them," said Lyla.

They heard the noise of aircraft flying over then they saw hundreds of parachutes dropping down on the fields on the other side of Ranville.

"We must keep low. I'll assess it in the daylight," said Michael. "Those boys will be frightened, and they will shoot at anything that moves at the moment."

Then they heard a bugler in the distance. "They are gathering them up and will be organising themselves." said Michael.

They heard more bombing a lot closer and could see the flashes coming from the beach. At that, they all went inside and tried to snatch some sleep, although it was impossible, but they did manage to doze for a few minutes here and there.

Michael's grandmother produced his uniform which she had cleaned. She had stitched up the trousers where the shrapnel had struck. It was a good job. "You might need this later," she said. "At least they will know what side you are on." Michael's grandmother was a kind lady and had attempted to switch herself off from the war as a way of coping. Losing her only child Lisette, at the start had taken an enormous toll on her, but at least Lisette lived on through the grandchildren. In semi-retirement she taught part-time at the local school, but on the other days she continued as a loyal wife and homemaker.

Michael put on the uniform and took out his .45 calibre Colt automatic that he had cleaned up following his swim. He placed it in the holster. It was not the standard service weapon, but Michael favoured it because of its stopping power and the ease of changing the seven-shot magazine.

At first light there was a lot more noise coming from the direction of a German gun battery at Merville – about four miles to the northeast. Shortly afterwards they heard the noise of shells hitting the back of the beach at Lion-sur-mer. He went upstairs and from the window could see a huge armada of ships offshore. There was no doubt that the invasion had started.

At 7 am, Michael walked outside. The paratroopers were in their camouflage smocks with a mixture of Sten guns and rifles. They saw his uniform and acknowledged him. He spoke to a lieutenant explaining that he had crashed in the sea five days earlier on a photographic mission and had been in hiding with an SOE agent and a doctor. The lieutenant said that a perimeter had been established. Ranville was now the first village in France to be liberated, but now they had to secure their bridgehead and wait for reinforcements from the beaches and more glider landings. Michael pointed to the house. The lieutenant would ask his colonel to call if he had a moment but for now and until the reinforcements were there it was a case of staying out of the way. Michael returned. They had breakfast. Shortly after 10 am there was a knock at the door. Michael answered. It was an officer who introduced himself as Lt Colonel Pine Coffin – the same equivalent rank as Michael. He had the lieutenant with him. They came in and took coffee. Michael introduced Lucy as an SOE agent who had been undercover for the last two years. She had been feeding intelligence back to London over that time. Lucy said they could confirm that by speaking to Colonel Buckmaster who ran the French section of the SOE, and she gave him a phone number. She told him that her identity here was Madame Lyla Dubois. She introduced Johann as the doctor who had been working with her over that time, and he had fixed up the wing commander's leg injury. The Lieutenant made a careful note. Lucy said if they needed a doctor and a good one at that, Johann would help them out. Lucy told them that she had been working at the café by the bridge and asked if Georges Gondrée and his family were safe.

"I was there an hour ago and we have opened up a first aid post there. They were all safe, but Monsieur Gondrée is busy in his back garden digging up bottles of champagne that he buried four years ago when the Germans arrived. He has become very popular. As soon as as we are relieved and the perimeter is secure, I'll send someone up so you can come and help out," said the colonel.

About 1.30 pm, they heard the noise of bagpipes coming from the bridges. A lot more soldiers appeared outside and at 3 pm there was a knock at the door. They walked down to the café. Georges and the family were pleased to see that Lyla was safe. She told him her real name was Lucy. All he knew was that the Résistance had asked him to take her on, and now he knew why. Johann got to work straight away on the wounded. His English was quite good, but Lucy translated into French if there was an issue. The most important thing was to stabilise the casualties and identify those who needed urgent evacuation back to the ships. There were some bodies outside. They got these moved out of sight into the rear garden. One was of a young lieutenant who had led the charge to capture the bridge. There was a major there who told Lucy that it was even more sad because his wife was due to have baby who would never see the father. It was a staunch reminder of the sacrifice that these men were making and the agony back in England as the telegrams arrived. They could see the three gliders across the canal that had landed silently with the men to take and hold the bridge. They carried on working into the evening. Just before darkness fell, they looked to the sky over Ranville and saw a huge number of gliders descending to the other side of the village. It got busy. Another doctor arrived. He had penicillin and Johann made sure that Michael got a shot to deal with any infection in the leg wound. It was a precaution, but a wise one.

News of the vintage champagne got out, and the number of

The bridge over the Caen Canal (Pegasus Bridge)
with the Gondrée Café

soldiers with ailments increased, but when the champagne was administered for medical reasons, it was amazing that instant cures of the ailments took place. Nobody could blame the soldiers. They carried on treating the injured for the next three days. It got a little more relaxed but fierce fighting was taking place around Breville two miles northeast of Ranville. Some French civilians started to appear. They were overjoyed. They waved the French tricolour.

Some of the ladies were hugging and kissing the soldiers. None complained. Lucy spotted her contact walking over the bridge with her dog. She ran over. They talked for about fifteen minutes and there was no longer any need to be on their guard. It was she who sent the radio messages back by Morse code, but she changed location often to do this aided by a man who would deliver milk from his farm with a horse and cart. The radio hidden under the seat on the cart. They exchanged real contact details, and Lucy said she would visit when it was all over.

On the third day a truck turned up. The driver was under orders to get all three to the beach where a landing craft would get them onto a destroyer bound for England. They went back to the house, collected their things and made their brief farewells. They would see them again as soon as it was over. Seeing all the aircraft and vessels with huge numbers of men and materials there was now genuine room for optimism.

Morning had come.

25

Return to Eden

(June 1944 – August 1945)

Saturday, the tenth June at 6am found Ash and Helen swimming naked in the lake. Helen had thrown caution to the wind and had adopted the ways of the cottage, and she loved it. The six dogs were with them. Odi and Hunter had passed a year earlier and were now resting alongside Trooper and Rafe at the burial site in the wood at the back of the dunes. Their names had been added to the plaque. The water was calm, with just the slight morning mist above the surface. The only noise was that of the dawn chorus. A day earlier they had received a message from an anonymous caller to say that Michael and Lucy were safe and with British forces in Normandy, but they had no precise details in respect of their return to England. That was understandable given the current level of activity.

Helen said to Ash, "While you were out with Boynton last night, I got a call from Edward."

"You did well," said Ash. "He's not usually that communicative."

"He got his degree – a first, but I would not expect anything else. He told me that he was working at some top-secret place in

Buckinghamshire and he was with a lot of other mathematicians," said Helen.

"Are there any ladies there?" asked Ash.

"Strange you should say that," said Helen. "He said there are loads of women, and some are brilliant mathematicians like him, and all this time all I thought he was only interested in figures."

"I can understand that," said Ash. "I'm the same. All I can think about is 38-26-38. Can't keep my hands off. That's what I call a perfect equation!"

"And don't I know it. But I don't mind. I love you!" said Helen, and with that she wrapped herself around him until he carried her out of the lake to the bank. They shook themselves dry, then put on dressing gowns and walked back to the cottage. They had breakfast, then there was a call. Helen took it. It was Lucy. She said that she couldn't say much but they were all back in England – all three of them. They had just landed at Portsmouth.

Ash asked, "Lucy, Michael, but who is the third?"

"I asked her, but she wouldn't say. She said that she would explain it all when they got home. So, we will just have to wait and see. She said it might be a few days because they were going to debrief them." said Helen.

On the journey back from Normandy, Lucy and Michael had plenty of time to update Johann with the rest of their story. He did the same. Johann had been brought up in Alsace on the eastern side of France. It had been under German occupation between 1870 and 1918, so most people spoke both languages. He was an only son. When the war started, the family had moved to Cologne but in 1942, both parents had been killed in the first RAF 1,000 bomber raid. He blamed the Nazis for that because if they hadn't started things in the first place none of that would have happened. He had spoken of a plot to kill Hitler, but nothing had happened so far. A lot of his colleagues backed the idea. Lucy shed a tear because it reminded her of the loss of her mother. They had been well fed on the ship in the officers' mess and had a nice, roomy cabin allocated to the three of them.

The ship had docked at Portsmouth from where they were driven the five miles up to Southwick House, from where the landings had been coordinated. On arrival a major and a captain wanted to separate them. Michael noted that they were staff officers and lacked any medal ribbons on their uniforms. Michael refused extremely forcefully. He said, "We came together. We will not be treated like criminals particularly after the risks we have run which is a great deal more than many of you lot sitting on your backsides in a cosy office playing with maps. We will leave together. I understand there might be things you want to discuss with my sister on a need-to-know basis, but there is nothing private between us, and I will allow that only if essential. She will need some time off, too, because she has been living on the edge every day for the last two years." They could see that Michael was serious and when they saw the decoration ribbons on his tunic, they realised that their initial approach had been wrong. Thereafter, they were treated with absolute courtesy.

Lucy spent two hours with Colonel Buckmaster and Leo Marks. They told her that her contribution and the value of her information had a large impact on the planning, targeting and timing of the landings – not least the last message relating to the total absence of the German High Command. Johann spent the best part of the following day with intelligence specialists, with Lucy present to facilitate translation and help with the precise locations. Johann was surprised that they didn't seem to know about the small blood group tattoos that SS soldiers bore under the left arm near the armpit. They would need to know where the war criminals were likely to be found as uniforms would be changed if capture was imminent.

An air commodore spent time with Michael. His leg injury

would take at least three months to heal properly. Richard was temporarily the acting wing commander of the squadron that was now heavily engaged in the destruction of anything that could endanger the landings and eventual breakout, and there was now the issue of the V1 pilotless flying bombs that had started to spread terror in London. They had both spent two years in Mosquitos and the top command realised that a break was due their way. There was a vacancy coming up at Cranwell in September for a group captain to oversee all training of fighter and fighter-bomber pilots. In view of his past record in that area, coupled with his performance with Spitfires and Mosquitos, he was considered the ideal man for the job and the promotion was well deserved. It was his if he wanted it. Michael asked if he would still get a chance to fly whilst instructing and for time to consider. The air commodore said he would give him a week and that flying was integral to his credibility, so he would not be just flying a desk. At the end, the commodore told him that he would be getting a bar to his Distinguished Service Order. Richard's work was to be similarly recognised. Michael asked for one favour: that the three of them would get flown back to Spelthorpe.

"Take it as done!" said the commodore.

"I'll take the job. I tend to think quickly, but that's what us pilots have to do." said Michael.

"I thought you would say that," said the air commodore. "And by the way your promotion takes place from the first Monday in July." They shook hands and parted.

They spent another two days at Southwick. The rooms were comfortable. Officially Michael was in a room with Johann, but unofficially there was a separate arrangement. The food was good. It gave them time to recharge their batteries before the return to Spelthorpe.

On the last day, they had to resolve an issue with Johann

in respect of his status because technically he might have been classified as a prisoner of war despite the huge risks that he had taken for the Allied war effort. It was simply resolved by handing his custody arrangements to the future Group Captain Michael Cromwell. Papers were signed. At the same time an application for refugee status was made in respect of Johann.

On the evening of Monday, the twelfth of June, a RAF Avro Anson landed at Spelthorpe with three special passengers on board. They were met by Ash and Helen. As Lucy walked up to Ash and Helen, she hugged them both and then said. "I'd like you to meet my fiancé, Johann Muller. It's a long story but we will tell you as it is."

On the way down to the cottage, Johann was amazed at the beauty of the place. He said, "You told me it was nice, but I didn't realise I was coming to the Garden of Eden." Victoria was waiting at the cottage. She had Lisette and Simon with her Michael. After hugs and kisses and greeting the dogs, Michael couldn't wait to get his uniform off, and he was soon back in shorts and bare feet. Helen had prepared a special meal. It was a venison cooked like a Beef Bourguignon with masses of fresh vegetables from the garden and freshly baked bread rolls. You would not have thought there was a war on, but hardly any of the ingredients were on ration, particularly the venison. There were three bottles of the finest red wine that Helen had salvaged from the cellar at the Hall.

After they had enjoyed the food Lucy spoke. "I've waited until now because I didn't want to spoil your appetite but what I am about to tell you might shock you, and it will break the Official Secrets Act."

She told them everything from her recruitment to the SOE, her training and her identity taken from documents provided by the wife of the gendarme that Ash and Boynton had brought back from France after Dunkirk. She told them of lodging with her grandparents as Madame Lyla Dubois, her jobs, what she did and how the information got back. Then she told them of the attempted rape and how Johann had shot one SS offender and how she had killed the other one with her bare hands, the faked accident and the body down the well. She told them of how Johann the doctor hated the Nazis, his past, the loss of his parents and how they had fallen in love. She told of the huge amount of information they had gathered and passed back, and then briefly of Michael's rescue, the events of D Day, the work at the first aid post and the arrangement that was now in place for Johann and how they intended to marry as soon as was possible. Johann was highly qualified from one of the best medical schools in the world, and he had the certificates that should allow him to work in England.

They listened spellbound. It took an hour with just her talking but now they knew and would understand. Ash stood up. He got six glasses and a bottle of Calvados from Normandy that he had saved. He poured them out and simply said, "Johann, we welcome you to this family. You are a courageous and principled man, and I could not think of a better man to marry our daughter. You have our blessing. You two have been to hell and back and you deserve the best for your life together and I can't wait till you tell Boynton. His training served you well."

Helen added. "And I will second that absolutely. I welcome you as a son!"

They toasted the couple, savoured the Calvados and retired to bed.

On the following days they both had an opportunity to visit all around the estate. Boynton was impressed by Lucy's description of dispatching the SS man and was pleased that both he and Aggie now had another German speaker to practise on.

They were keen to meet Jennifer and William. Johann wanted to talk about medicine, and Lucy for special reasons of her own.

Two days later Jennifer confirmed that Lucy was pregnant. After that they made a visit to Paddy. He was delighted to see them. They told him the full story and Paddy agreed to marry them at the earliest opportunity which would be in a month's time. Lucy asked after Gelert, who was such a loving dog. Paddy told them that he had passed two years earlier and now had a spot with the other dogs in the corner of the churchyard. After much searching, he had found another puppy that he had to get from Scotland. Somehow, despite the rationing there had been yet another miracle of Spelthorpe because his car had curiously filled with petrol, and there was a four and a half gallon jerrycan on the back seat after Helen had learnt of the new puppy and the need to collect it. The puppy was a slate grey colour. Paddy and Ruth had decided to call it Methuselah – the oldest man in the bible, on the basis that it might live up to the name.

Michael went up to the airfield. The basic RAF flying training was still going on, but after D-Day, the writing was on the wall. The Luftwaffe was rapidly diminishing, and there would be less and less to bomb. Stooper was delighted with his star pupil's progress. He confided that both he and his deputy had been made a lucrative offer of jobs with Geoffrey de Havilland's expanding business. It was likely they would accept with a view to starting in the new year. The mechanic wanted to stay on. There was always work on the farm. Michael expressed the view that the market for private flight training would pick up again as soon as the war ended, and there would be plenty of pilots looking for work. They had a good set-up there coupled with the holiday side of things, and the commercial shooting would start again as soon as the war was over.

On the twenty-sixth of June, Johann received confirmation that his application for refugee status had been granted. Once news of his contribution to the war effort had got through, strings had been pulled to speed up the process.

Johann's English was coming on in leaps and bounds. He was quite good already, but Lucy refused to speak in French in order to give him total immersion. He had applied for registration to practise medicine in England and there would normally be a short interview prior to acceptance. There was no question as to his qualification, given the international prestige of the Heidelberg medical school. There were all sorts of things to fix, like a driving licence and test, but they were getting there. The wedding took place on Saturday, the twenty-second of July. It was a quiet affair but that was what they wanted. Helen arranged a buffet-style reception at the cottage because the Hall was still unavailable as its use as a convalescent home continued. Victoria had kept her dress, and it fitted Lucy perfectly. It looked good, so why waste money? The estate contributed a Morris Oxford motor car. The spontaneity of the event made it perfect, and everyone felt they could relax. All Lucy wanted was those she loved around her, including the dogs, and that is what she got. They were uncertain as to where they would live, but with the bulk of the Hall in use, nothing could really be resolved immediately. For the time being there was still plenty of room at the cottage for them all.

Richard and Linda had made it to the wedding. Richard had been given two weeks' leave. He was still owed much more leave because things had been nonstop on the run-up to D- Day. Strikes on V 1 launch sites were now the priority because the civilian deaths in London were fast reaching the same numbers as the Blitz of 1940. The other factor was that with these weapons, there were no aircrew losses for the Germans.

Despite this Richard and Linda seemed very happy. Richard broke the news. He had been promoted to wing commander and was joining Michael as his deputy at Cranwell in September. Two years on the front line was enough. Burnout was a factor. There was no point in training pilots if they never got the chance to engage in operations or advance in the service if movement was blocked. Both needed a break. The RAF hadn't bothered telling Michael because officially he was sick. In any event he would never object, given the way they had worked so well together in the past. Michael was delighted for Richard but also for Linda who had been under a huge strain and worry. All Richard had to do was to go back and hand over to his replacement before he took another two weeks' leave prior to going off with Michael in September by which time Michael would be fit to return. The new job would be mainly with weekends off. Flying back in a two-seat Harvard might even make it possible for the odd evening in mid-week.

George turned up with Emma at the wedding. He had been commissioned into the Royal Engineers and was now undergoing protracted training that would end in March of the following year. He was getting back from Chatham at least once a month. Emma would go down on the train once a month to spend a weekend with him at a hotel in nearby Rochester. She had gained several qualifications in accountancy and was still working hard in the estate office. George enjoyed what he was doing and was looking at long-term service which meant that Emma would be able to go with him once the war had ended. They planned on marriage when his training was complete.

Also in July, Lucy had told Colonel Buckmaster that she would not be returning as a baby was due in December, but she did agree to come back briefly on all-expenses-paid visits for two days in September and October to lecture staff on her experiences over the last two years. She was due a considerable sum in back pay as a commissioned officer. Buckmaster told her that a decision had been made to award her the George Medal for her courage. She would receive that at a private ceremony during her visit.

Hitler narrowly escaped death in a bomb plot. Hundreds were implicated and show trials followed where there was only one predetermined result. Even Field Marshall Rommel – a national hero, was given a choice of arrest or suicide to save his family. He opted for suicide. In August after a difficult campaign, the Normandy breakout took place. The Germans were on the run. Paris was liberated by French and American forces towards the end of the month, and a few days later, the British took Brussels.

Approval for Johann to practise medicine came through in August. He also passed his driving test, not that it was a challenge. The only difference was that the steering wheel and cars were now on the correct side. His registration proved opportune. Despite his struggling on, Dr John Bowen was no longer sufficiently fit to carry on. In September he retired. Jennifer was delighted to have such a skilled and knowledgeable working partner. Johann could not believe his luck.

When Lucy went to London to lecture and receive her George Medal, she received it from none other than Prime Minister Winston Churchill. It was he who initiated the SOE. When he heard about Lucy's contribution, he determined to present her with the medal himself. Two months later Lucy presented her husband, Johann with a daughter, Matilda, who thereafter, was known as Mattie.

1945 presented Ash with the challenge of restoring the estate to normality. At the start of the year, Boynton was rounding up hen pheasants to get egg production going again. He was happy to get back to his former role. Stooper and his deputy left for the de Havilland jobs. They were given a good sendoff, having made a lot of money for the estate over the years. Both received a farewell golden handshake in appreciation of their service. They promised to drop in when passing. The courses at the airfield had stopped. The RAF flight lieutenant returned to operational service. The RAF Tiger Moths went back with him. The Dragon Rapide, the Harvard, a new replacement Gipsy Moth and one Tiger Moth remained. Michael, Richard and the mechanic kept an eye on them. At weekends, they were flown. The Dragon Rapide and the Harvard were sometimes used to go back and forwards to Cranwell. With the end of the war in sight, the need to train so many pilots had fallen away, but the leisure sector was showing promise. Richard and Linda were preparing to move into the detached house formerly occupied by Stooper.

In April 1945, with the war about to end, Michael, Victoria and Lucy met in the churchyard. They had always been very close and felt this was the right place to come to terms with what they had been through over the last six years. Michael was troubled. In his career, he was one of the youngest to achieve such an elevated position, but he felt he had achieved that largely by killing, and he just did not want to kill any more. After the murder of his mother and Simon, he had felt that what he did was the right thing to do. Lucy felt the same. She had killed but closeup, and all the information she passed on had resulted in more efficient killing. Victoria was detached and had seen it from the outside but all that time she had agonised over the safety of those she loved, but with that detached view she saw it more clearly.

"You killed because you were up against a great evil and you risked all to help to bring that evil to an end, so you have nothing to be sorry about. What you did saved lives. The ones who should feel sorry are the ones who did nothing but profit from the advantage of what you and others have achieved."

They went to the graves of Simon and Lisette and spoke softly telling them what had happened to them. They had been there for about an hour when Paddy appeared. Paddy was the confessor they trusted absolutely, and they told him why they were there together. He reiterated what Victoria had said but told them that there is always an answer in the 'good book' as he called it. "Read the book of Ecclesiastes Chapter 3," he said, "and all will be revealed. I know it was written well over 2,000 years ago but the wisdom of the past is just as relevant today. I will be speaking to everyone on this as soon as it is over. You are not alone, and others need to come to terms with it all." Paddy hugged each in turn then left them in quiet contemplation.

A few days later, on the eighth of May the war in Europe came to an end. Michael had taken Paddy's guidance, and he spoke with Richard who had expressed a similar view. A week later, Michael and Richard resigned their commissions but agreed to serve on until the autumn to facilitate a smooth transfer. It was Spelthorpe where they wanted to be, and that was the future.

Linda finally allowed herself to get pregnant as her fears had subsided. From then on it was all out to take things forward. One of the land army girls had maintained a relationship for the last three years with one of the flying students. He was now a flight lieutenant flying Tempests and he too resigned his commission when offered a job at the recreated flying school. They married. The new wife and the air mechanic's wife were employed to run the hospitality and holiday chalet side of the airfield business. All the chalets were renovated and upgraded. Richard ran the flying school. Boynton and his keepers managed the shooting school. His secret underground store remained a secret, along with its collection of weaponry and explosives. Although Boynton had carried out the managerial role for the coast and woodlands in the war, his heart was not in it. He preferred to stick to game keeping and overall security for the estate. Michael stepped into his father's former role. Victoria was gradually taking on more from Julian. It was a natural and logical progression, but it was done in a way that preserved harmony on the estate. That was something that Ash and Helen wanted most of all. With the closure of the convalescent home, work was rapidly undertaken to restore the Hall back to its former glory. Ash and Helen moved back in on a permanent basis, and Johann and Lucy took a suite on the top corridor. Lucy worked for two days a week teaching French at her old school. They were delighted to see her back, and as a war heroine and former pupil, it was seen as another feather in the school's cap. She also helped out at the office if it got busy. The annexe served as the main farm office and nursery. Victoria and Michael remained at the cottage where the dogs resumed the regime that Trooper and Rafe had introduced. They seemed happier there than at the Hall.

It would all take time, but progress was being made. The war memorial in the churchyard bore two more names of Spelthorpe men who had given their all. One had been killed at El Alamein and the other in Normandy. The losses were less than in the first war, but the individual pain was no different. In due course others would return to the estate carrying the mental scars of what they had been through, but the process of demobbing would take far longer than expected particularly with the requirements that came about with the occupation of the defeated Germany, and others had to return from the Far East.

Once the dust had settled on the understandable hysteria of the eighth of May, the Reverend Paddy Collins preached a sermon in an effort to make sense of it all. He talked about the nature of evil. Without evil there would be no good. Evil was an inescapable factor of the nature of humanity, born from the fact that the Almighty gives us free choice. He quoted the popular saying, "Evil triumphs when good men do nothing," and saluted the courage and sacrifice of the two men added to the memorial. He went on to describe the centurion at the cross in Luke's gospel who said of Jesus: "Certainly this was a righteous man." The Romans were an occupying power, but they were not all bad, just as those they had fought were not all bad, but life had to go on. Bitterness, he said, is a natural emotion, but it will destroy us all unless we break the chain. He quoted the book of Ecclesiastes from chapter 3: "a time to kill, and a time to heal….a time to love, and a time to hate, a time of war and a time of peace." Despite the difficulty, the sins of the past must not be visited on the next generation and his gaze fixed on the booming number of babies, infants and pregnant ladies in the congregation. He concluded, "Now is the time to heal and a time of peace, Amen."

The beach at Spelthorpe looking across the inlet to Seal Island.

Later that day, the greater Spelthorpe family met on the beach. They shared food and drink. They swam in the sea with the dogs. They rode the horses bareback, and the young children paddled and played at the water's edge. There were no longer any threats from the sky, just the gulls. The castle keep had endured with the pines and the dunes. Michael watched as the dogs gathered in a semi-circle as if they were listening to somebody unseen. The hairs on Michael's neck stood up. He told the family members of swimming from the wrecked Mosquito when he felt himself being propelled to safety by an unknown force. The dogs came back from the water.

Paddy was further out pushing his shrimp net with Methuselah by his side. Paddy looked to one side. "Hello Minerva." he said.

"Hello Paddy," she said. "We did our best to keep them safe, but we didn't manage it all the time."

"Who does?" he said, "But we did what we could, and look. They are together, and they will heal."

Back on the edge of the dunes Lucy looked around, then said to the others. "This reminds me of my poem that saw me through it all:"

The tide invades and washes them away.
Perhaps, one day they will return,
older, wiser, deeper and,
higher up the beach,
so the tide can't wash them away

……………and they did!

Historic note

This is a work of fiction and all events directly relating to the characters of the Spelthorpe clan have been created. The same applies to the Spelthorpe Estate which has features that resemble the area around Wells-next-the-Sea, Norfolk but elements have been incorporated from other geographic locations in Suffolk, Kent and Somerset.

The background events have a factual base and every effort has been made to ensure these are historically accurate including measures described to deal with air and gas attack, the creation of the Home Guard, the evacuation of children, Dunkirk evacuation, the role of the Special Operations Executive and action close to Ranville in Normandy and the bridge over the Caen Canal (Pegasus Bridge). Most of this material stems from the author's extensive visits and research from the teaching of history as a school's battlefield guide. Inevitably, in the confusion of battle, and the aftermath, recollections vary, and sources will reflect this.

Specifically:

The attack of the Junkers 88's that resulted in the death of Earl Simon and Lisette is fictitious. However, in October 1939 an attack was made on the east coast of Scotland by twelve Junkers 88 fighter bombers. One of these was shot down by a Spitfire.

The Café Gondrée at Pegasus Bridge can be visited today, although the original bridge has been replaced. The original is at the museum grounds next to the site. The café was used as a first aid post and the owner did dig up a large number of bottles of champagne that he had secreted in his garden during occupation. The man who led the charge over the bridge was Lieutenant Den Brotheridge, aged 29 who had been a weights and measures inspector before joining the military. He is buried in the churchyard at Ranville. His wife gave birth to a daughter a few days later. Lieutenant Colonel Pine Coffin commanded 7th Parachute Battalion, who landed at Ranville in the early hours of the sixth of June.

The battery at Longues-sur-Mer to the west of Arromanches can be visited today. It is unusual because some of the actual guns are still present.

The use of poems as a basis for encryption by agents of the SOE is well documented, the most famous of which was the poem 'The love that I have' written by Leo Marks and used by agent Violette Szarbo (awarded a posthumous George Cross) who was executed at Ravensbrück Concentration Camp in January 1945. Leo Marks' book 'Between Silk and Cyanide' provides a detailed account.

The 1940 massacres at Wormhoudt by the SS (eighty executions) and Le Paradis (ninety-seven executions of Royal Norfolk soldiers) on the retreat to Dunkirk are well documented, and the sites can be visited today. News about Le Paradis only emerged after the war. In 1949 Fritz Knöchlein who initiated the Le Paradis massacre was hanged, but the man responsible for Wormhoudt evaded liability on grounds of insufficient evidence. The Schutzstaffel (SS) or protective squadrons initially started as a personal bodyguard for Hitler and combat arm of the Nazi Party. It increased from three regiments to thirty-eight divisions and as the war progressed, they included volunteers from the occupied territories who included French, Dutch, Danish, Ukrainian individuals. They were notorious for war crimes in the occupied territory of the east and in France. As Nazi fanatics their combat ability was renowned, but they were totally ruthless. They were not popular with elements of the German regular army on account of the way they conducted themselves.

The battle for France did not end at Dunkirk. Other British units fought further to the west. Some 8,000 men of the Highland Division surrendered to General Rommel at Saint Valery- en-Caux on the twelfth June 1940. The bombing and sinking of the *Lancastria* took place as described. It remains surprising that so few are aware of this, the greatest British maritime disaster.

German armoured units, or panzers, provided the spearhead of the invasion of France. Often, they were followed by other units that relied heavily on horses and carts for transportation.

The massacre of pets in September 1939 following the declaration of war took place as described.

Germany's second blitz of London started just a week after D Day using V1 flying bombs. Although this lasted less than two and a half months, the casualty rate was greater and the number of destroyed or damaged houses almost equalled that of the 1940-1 blitz of some twelve months, with not a single loss to German aircrew. In the first blitz German aircrew losses were over 7,000.

The number of French civilians killed by bombing in France exceeded those killed in the UK. Those killed by German bombers are insignificant compared to the majority of those deaths which came about as a result of Allied bombing particularly before and after D Day.

The issues relating to aerial fighting have been drawn from many sources. One very useful and comprehensive source is the late Air Vice Marshal J.E, Johnson's book 'The Story of Air Fighting', and he should know, because he was there. He was highly decorated and scored some 34 victories. Michael Cromwell's meteoric rise up the promotion ladder was not without precedent. Brendan 'Paddy' Finucane achieved the rank of wing commander aged 21. At the age of twenty-five Leonard Cheshire achieved the rank of group captain.

The events in German Southwest Africa (now Namibia) are accurately described. This was the first genocide of the twentieth century. The book 'The Kaiser's Holocaust – Germany's Forgotten Genocide' by David Olusoga and Casper Erichsen provides a detailed account.

About the author

Ashley Clark spent some thirty years with the Kent County Constabulary. In his early service at the age of twenty years he was possibly the youngest village constable in England when he looked after several villages around Betteshanger near Deal, Kent. The bulk of his service was spent as a detective. For his last twelve years, for much of the time he was based in France where he worked closely with French counterparts from the Police Nationale and the Gendarmerie. On retiring from the police, he worked as a schools' battlefield guide for some fifteen years taking both school and adult groups to the battlefields of France and Belgium. At the same time, he intermittently occupied himself on a Kent sheep farm and a large Exmoor shooting estate. He is widely travelled and lives in Whitstable, Kent where for the last 20 years has led the group that manages and maintains an award-winning nature reserve – believed to be the largest village green in England. In the warmer months he swims daily in the sea with his labradors.